Emma's Farewell

J. Olsen

Emma's Farewell

Acknowledgements

Particular thanks to Penny Cameron, who read a draft of this book
many years ago and pushed hard to get it finished and published.

Thanks also to Sue and Dalice Trost, who read drafts
and suggested changes and helped a great deal with editing,
and to Kylie Mason and Nicola O'Shea for considerable skill in
editing, providing advice and detailing themes in the novel.

Christine Croyden also made suggestions on an early draft.

Special thanks to Stephen Matthews at Ginninderra Press
for generously supporting his authors.

For those who fight domestic violence

First published 2016 by
GINNINDERRA PRESS
PO Box 3461 Port Adelaide 5015
www.ginninderrapress.com.au

1

David

At three a.m. he rose and walked downstairs, opened the fridge and lit his naked front, pulled out a bottle of Heineken, flipped the cap rattling onto the floor, and guzzled the bottle with one hand leaning against the fridge door. He stepped over the bottle cap and tipped the bottle upside down in the sink, climbed upstairs and lay on top of the sheets. He didn't switch off the light.

He got up again, dressed, hooked the carabiner to his belt, and attached the black baseball cap to the carabiner in case it rained. From the cupboard he pulled down a box of rolled oats, tipped them drumming into a plastic bucket.

Outside, on a dirt path away from the lit neighbourhood, he travelled past a tangle of wires, then under open sky with a clear vision of the moon. He followed a line of ribbon gum lit by white moonlight; shreds of hanging bark rattled and flashed as they turned in the silver light. Hands deep in his pockets, he walked uphill without a torch, slipped on a muddy spot, stepped over a large black rock embedded in the path.

Near the top of the path he ducked between two wooden railings and passed through an iron gate into the horse corral on the east flank of Mount Painter. Far down the hill and over the lake, yellow lights dotted the city.

The wind fell.

On wet grass he walked into the open field looking for bunched horses. Near a eucalypt grove he saw their dark forms and rattled the oats in the plastic bucket, banged the side of the bucket with an open hand. Three horses trotted to him. Others ran. He watched for the grey

Appaloosa, and when she came he pushed the others away and let her feed. With their necks drawn down and ears back, the horses bit at each other, kicked with hind feet and rushed at David, pushed their heads into the bucket. He waved them away. With the mare's nose in the bucket he slipped a rope hackamore over her ears and around her nose then tossed the empty bucket on the ground to distract the others.

He grabbed the base of her mane and swung up onto her back. She reared, then rushed forward. He put his head down along her neck as she pounded over the wide grassy slope. They ran together for twenty minutes in moonlight. The mare knew the fence lines and clumps of eucalypt, ditches and briar patches. She ran in a broad arc over the sloping hillside, panting, her sides heaving. She grew hot beneath him.

At the wood-pole corral, he stopped and got off. Steam rose from her back. He led her in circles in the field for another twenty minutes, cooled her, waiting for her breathing to settle, then removed the hackamore, took sugar cubes from his pocket and laid them on his flattened hand. He talked to her. When she finished plucking sugar from his hand with her rubbery lips, he told her goodbye and walked home.

2

Emma

David walked the streets at night because of Emma. Before he knew her well, David's hands would sweat. Like a shy boy or a coward, he would shiver if she came into the common room and look away if she held his gaze too long. Sometimes he'd leave. She had that certainty over words and delivery that English women have, sure-footed and secure in a crowd. She'd drop her chin and look people straight in the eye. Men felt listened to, but some felt ill at ease. Emma seemed to take pleasure in offending, especially in offending men. She made them feel inauthentic. She'd smirk and make some remark, pretend she knew their secrets, and the slighted man's partner would stiffen with insult, stand back, mouth ajar, and walk into the corridor and whisper to friends about her. Men forgave Emma for these slights and this beguiled David. Emma's insults enchanted him and he woke up one morning in love.

The affair, when it happened, burned white-hot. And when Emma vanished, David fell into despair. He slumped in his office chair all day, windows draped to make it perpetual night-time. During the day, he tried hard to work and at night he tried hard to sleep. But often at night he left the house and walked the streets or walked to the pole corral and spoke with the Appaloosa mare.

3

Amber

A knock woke him. He opened one eye. Shadows of feet pressed in the orange glow under the door. Little knocks came again and he ground his teeth.

Go away, he said.

Three more knocks and he rubbed his eye.

He slipped the bottle into the bottom drawer, jammed his hand into his pocket looking for something to chew, cracked a breath mint between his molars and shouted, It's open.

A dart of light travelled over the carpet.

The girl gripped the edge of the open door and he could see half her face. She said in a small voice, Doctor Chess? The eye was pale green and watching him. Can you spare a minute?

He dimly remembered her face from hallways, or maybe from watching her looking up from the floor of the lecture theatre, her face glowing in the mass of other faces. I can give you five minutes, he said.

She had a bashful smile and glanced down. That'll be plenty.

She stepped in and stood with her blue loafers together. Small feet and a long tartan skirt and cream jumper gave her a wholesome look. She'd knotted a green handkerchief at her throat to match her green eyes and curled her apricot hair in a bun. Backlit in the afternoon sun, she glowed like a live coal. A spattering of pale freckles saddled the bridge of her nose.

I'm sorry, I've seen you around, but, ah, you are…?

Amber. Amber Griffin.

He worked at caring, motioned her to a chair.

Uh, if you don't mind, Dr Chess, I'll shut the door.

Then he regretted letting her in. She'd spin some fairy tale about her

"

crazy sister, or drunken immature boyfriend, or careless, disengaged father and the nasty divorce. How can you be attentive to this drivel?

He glanced at his desk. Printed in upper case letters a note said YOU'RE DEAD. There had been eight such notes over two months. One said, MONGREL, another said, I'LL CUT YOUR BALLS OFF.

Tommy, lab technician in the Psych Department, was standing next to him when David pulled one from his pigeonhole. Tommy looked over at the note and said, There been others?

David shrugged, A few.

Give them to Security.

David shook his head. How could he explain raging hatred to someone as simple as Tommy, and explain why he liked getting notes like this? They brought little surprises to a brain-deadening job, kept him guessing. Someone out there hated him, was bitter, slighted, maybe after vengeance. Maybe a husband. He didn't tell Security because he didn't want Roger Brown, Department Head and wet hen, to know how many enemies he'd made, and didn't want to listen to Roger whine, watch him wring his hands. David collected the hate notes in a little stack in his top drawer. He laid this one on top of the others, shut the drawer and turned back to the student.

Amber pushed the door shut in a way that made him think she wouldn't complain about parents or boyfriends; she'd come to complain about the course. Trying to bury his grief over the disappeared Emma and deal with the coming pettiness of this young woman.

She walked across the office and her walk disturbed him, woke him. The flush in her cheeks, where the freckling stopped, caught the rosy light as she neared his desk lamp.

David angled an open hand towards a chair. Sit down.

She sat and slid the chair too close to his desk, leaned forward in an angle of confidentiality. He didn't lean back, and he wondered how bold she really was, if she would lose her nerve and slide the chair back.

You know, she paused, that some of us are having trouble with Sophie Moss.

David sighed. My, my.

She raised her eyebrows. Pardon?

You come straight to the point.

She smiled. I like to be straight with people.

The phrase, David knew, meant she was probably a trained liar. She would repeat the phrase often enough to a hundred people this year and next, and some would believe her. She might even come to believe it. I like to be straight with people, she'd rehearse in front of the mirror. But she had an innocent face and fine skin, with open truthful eyes, and David had trouble looking into her face when she said, We're suffering. He watched her and wondered, If I do her a favour, will she do a favour for me, come back and entice me, let me see her half-naked? But he was getting ahead of himself.

I've heard this before, he said.

I'll bet you have.

You've spoken to Sophie?

We try. You know what she's like.

He turned his head a little, a sceptic. Know what she's like?

Sophie.

He paused and squinted. Be precise, Amber. What's the problem?

Amber sat back and folded her arms, as if sitting in a cold room with a man she hated. Her breathing was shallow and when she looked away, he watched the rise and fall of her breasts in the cream jumper. She had a scar on the thumb of her left hand, maybe sliced with a kitchen knife, and she kept rubbing it.

After a moment, she unfolded her arms and said, She failed a friend of mine, objected to his opinions.

David sighed. Well, change his opinions.

Amber shook her head. You don't understand.

Then educate me.

His brother's in prison because someone told lies about him.

Lies?

A policewoman stitched him up.

David shook his head. The brother in prison has nothing to do with Sophie, or this course.

He's my friend. He said in his essay that some men are falsely accused of rape. Sophie failed him for saying it.

Well, he shouldn't take it so personally.

Personally?

David watched the flecks of hazel in her green eyes. She brushed a strand of orange hair off an eyebrow with her little finger. Her friend, he thought, must be a fool. He must have known that Sophie was part-time Director of the Women's Shelter, an equal opportunity bully; she bullied men, she bullied women, she bullied children if she got the chance. If Amber's friend was stupid enough to write some men are falsely accused of rape in an essay for Sophie Moss, he deserved to be punished.

So why isn't your friend here?

She maintained her steady gaze. He's gone home. He's pretty upset.

David reached up and pulled at his ear, then looked at her. What's your major?

Law and psych.

As if reading lines from a familiar play, he said, Amber, if you're a law student, you know how to advise your friend. You know the protocol.

I know the unit outline's a legal document. But it says in her unit outline that 'All opinions are respected'.

You have to understand… David tried hard to look sincere, but it proved very hard, so he leaned forward. We lecturers determine what we teach. We're free to teach what we believe.

Amber shook her head. The old goat hasn't changed her lecture notes in ten years.

The protocol, Amber. The protocol. Roger Brown is Department Head, not me.

She glared. Come on. You're telling me to go to Roger Brown?

David rested back in his chair. Okay. Be clear. What do you want from me?

She glanced away, then looked up and held her eyes steady. I'm worried about my friend.

You said that.

Worried about what he might do. Sophie's a nightmare.

What do you want from me, Amber?

She tapped one finger against the top of her knuckle. Can you talk to her?

Talk to Sophie?

Students say she listens to you.

David chuckled, rested back in his chair. Not sure who told you that, but they're sadly misinformed.

Nobody said she got along with you. They said she listens to you.

David leaned back and smiled. I don't know about that. Anyway, look. I'll think about it. If it's any consolation, students have been complaining about her for a while now.

As it came out, David felt his blunder like a hammer. He winced, wanted to shake it off and thought to himself, You moron. You fool. Trying to please a young girl to make yourself a hero, make her grateful so you can see her naked one night. Emma would never make a mistake like that. You're inept. An amateur. Who's working who in this room?

A knot of young students passed the shut door, gabbling over the top of each other, voices echoing in the bare hallway. He waited, the voices faded and Amber smiled.

Thanks David. I'm grateful.

I said I'd think about it. I didn't say I'd talk to her. Take your friend and discuss this with Sophie.

I understand. Thank you. I will. She stood without sliding the chair back and stepped closer to him, reached out to shake his hand, and her skirt brushed his elbow like a bird's wing. Amber's hand passed close to his mouth and he was touched by the scent off her skin. Her thin fingers were cool in his. She stepped to the door, glanced back over her shoulder and smiled. Thank you, David.

4

Sophie Moss

David tapped Amber Griffin's name into Oasis, the student records system, waited for details to pop up – Amber's photo, unit marks. She was twenty, a third year student, born in Canberra. David wrote down her street address and tucked it into a book.

He walked down the hall and knocked on Sophie's door.

The voice inside was croaky and peeved. Come in. Come in.

She hunched over the keyboard and grimaced at the screen. Yes?

It's me.

She stared at the screen and typed.

With his hand on the door, he said, You look busy.

That's right.

I'll come back later.

She nodded and he closed the door.

An hour later, he knocked again.

The same raspy voice said, Come in, come in.

She squinted at the screen. One hand poked into a plastic Tupperware box full of lettuce, radishes, diced carrots, and a food-like paste she ate on days when the others ate takeaway and the staffroom smelled like carrion. Sophie would stand, glare and stomp back to her office.

She tapped and leaned at the screen. What is it? She looked up. Oh, David. What can I do for you? She looked back at the screen.

Must be interesting, he said.

What?

Whatever you're doing.

She watched the screen.

13

David cleared his throat. Sophie, a student came to see me this morning.

Congratulations. The green screen saver tinted her face and black short-cropped hair. She rattled the keyboard. About what?

Fighting the patriarchal theocracy.

She stopped typing and looked up. You trying to be funny?

No. I'm trying to –

Out with it, David. She went back to typing and raked her black stubble hair with her fingertips. Hoop earrings swung on her lobes.

Like a scolded child, David shifted his weight to the other foot. When he visited Sophie, she never asked him to sit down.

Psychology of Gender, said David. A few kids failed it.

Her fingers curled on the keyboard. She glanced up and saw David watching her hands and folded them deep in her lap.

He said, Some failed it more than once, including a boy whose brother is in jail. My –

This department treats students like battery hens. Sheep.

A little unfair, that's all. Get them to surrender their convictions, 'Trust me', you say, then you fail them.

She spun around in her chair and folded her arms. Look. She raised a finger and pointed, Listen carefully. His brother raped a woman. I fight the ideologies that lead to rape. The difference between you and me, David, is that I teach students to think for themselves, make intelligent choices. I defend the defenceless.

David said, Or punish them.

She leaned towards him and cackled, Number one, I teach them that all knowledge is socially constructed, intrinsically value-laden.

Her screeching rose an octave. In the dim room it swirled like a tempest, an impenetrable thicket of thorns tangled between them. A rat couldn't sneak through it, and David regretted coming.

Sophie forced a sort of smile, as if she wanted to hurt somebody. You don't get out much, do you, David? It's part of the job, part of being a grown-up. It's not the Miss Universe contest. Today I'm unpopular, tomorrow they'll come back and thank me. She looked around, pulled a newspaper from the corner of her desk and thrust it towards him. Look at this. Canberra's a vicious town.

She pulled back the paper and began to read out loud. 'He locked his fiancée in her townhouse for eight days and beat her during the confinement. A neighbour heard the man yelling "I'll fucking kill you." When the neighbour knocked on the door to see if she was okay, the man told the neighbour she was singing, an explanation supported by the woman in the house whimpering from a back room. The accused told the neighbour he was sorry and he'd make sure that she sang more quietly. He said that his fiancée drank a lot and if the neighbour heard screaming – take no notice of it. The neighbour bought it. The accused continued to beat her. When his knuckles got sore, he took a house brick and beat her with that, and told her he was going to do it every ten minutes until she passed out. He threw her down the stairs and then jumped off the stairs onto her back until she was bleeding and unconscious again. His lawyer told the court that he had schizo-affective disorder, bipolar disorder, and poly-substance abuse. He was a good person, harmless. He didn't mean to hurt her during her eight-day ordeal. The trial continues tomorrow.'

She stared up at David. Go ahead. Preach balance in your safe little room. She tapped on the newspaper. That's what balance is like off-campus. Big disconnect.

He turned and looked out the window. Students fear you, Sophie.

Her voice rose another octave. Nonsense! Pure sexist nonsense! Misogynist lies. You simple little man. She banged her fist on the keyboard. They let the dregs into these courses, ordinary, mediocre brains, the brothers of rapists, and they expect intelligent debate. I teach them to subvert the dominant paradigm, and I get visits from the Friends of the Rapists' Committee.

David thinking, Why did I come? Trying to remember. What does it matter anyway? What would Emma say? He listened with one ear to student gossip in the hallway, a party some girl had thrown over the weekend, the boy got drunk, ran around naked, smashed a window. Parents weren't happy.

Finally he said, I don't think you understand.

Sophie stood, pushed back her chair and faced him. Oh, I understand all right. You discussed me with a student, that's what I understand. You sat down in your office with a student, shut the door and shared notes about me. That's what I understand. Professional breach.

David nodded. Okay.

No, David. It's not okay. The dean will sort you out.

David smiled and nodded and said, Classic feminist tactic. Get Daddy to sort me out.

He turned and Sophie's mouth pursued him down the hall, bouncing off cinder brick walls, shouting, You just wait, David. You'll be hearing from me. You just wait!

5

Man on the hill

The rain stopped. Streets were polished and black. The man parked his ute under a street lamp and untied his dog, let the dog bounce out of the back and range through forest, sniffing dirt and lifting its leg against trees. The man patted his pants leg and called in a whisper. The dog fell in behind him as he hiked the rising path by torchlight.

He pulled a plastic bottle from his pocket, unscrewed the cap and squirted whisky into his mouth, let a spurt roll around behind his teeth and burn his tongue, trickling hot through his veins. He screwed the cap back on, wiped his mouth with the back of his hand, and tucked the bottle into his pocket. He leaned one hand against a tree and with the lit cigarette between his fingers emptied his bladder.

He and the dog reached the top of the hill and stood in lacy moonlight under wattles, looking down on the house. He stretched sideways trying to see through fire-blackened tea tree branches, the front door and upstairs windows. The dog shook itself and lay at his feet.

The man lay in the dirt next to the dog and lit another cigarette, cupping his hands against the wind. Over five nights the woman had arrived at nine p.m.

Nothing for ten minutes. He watched the street and blew smoke into the trees. A car hissed down the street and turned into the driveway. He stubbed the cigarette in the dirt and watched through binoculars, twisting the eyepiece, swaying from side to side to see through burnt sticks the woman step down from the passenger side of the car. A man stepped out from the other side.

Watching through binoculars, he talked to his dog and said, I'll have her.

From the hill he watched lights flicker on through the house, downstairs and then upstairs in a bedroom. The woman stood by the window and took off her dress. He watched her and patted his dog. He studied her.

In the dark woods, he lit another cigarette, took another swig of whisky, patted the dog and said, Good boy.

6

Student on Black Mountain

A uni student followed a radio-tagged fox in dark woodland on the south rim of Black Mountain. The fox left the path and the student switched on his headlamp to light the forest. On the steep southern flank the student battled tea tree with an elbow in front of him, the aerial held up over the tangle.

At the edge of the forest, he came to a flat opening through trees, a dead-end track. He switched off his lamp and sat on a log and rested, fingering a peppermint leaf, crushing it and holding it to his nose, sniffing its vapours, and listening to animals in the night. Tawny frogmouths boomed over the valley and a sugar glider barked in blue twilight. A glider clambered to the end of a thin twig and launched itself in a twisting glide.

Headlights swerved around the corner and lit trees at the end of the track. Car tyres crunched onto gravel. He knew this track was blocked at the gate and wondered how the car got in. The student crouched and watched.

The driver stopped and clicked on the dome light. The student could see a policeman. The officer searched through his glovebox, then switched off the dome light and smoked a cigarette with his elbow out the window.

The night was quiet except for hissing traffic along Caswell Drive.

An orange ute came around the corner, tyres snapping gravel, and pulled up beside the policeman's car. The policeman got out, walked over, leaned into the open window and said, G'day.

The other man nodded. How ya been?

Busy. And you?

The same.

They were quiet for a time and the man in the orange ute said, Friggin'
cold out here.

The policeman said, Whad ya got for me?

The man bent down and pulled a plastic bag from under his seat,
handed it through the window. The officer took it and said, How much?

Five.

The officer looked up and down the darkened track, yanked folded
bills from his shirt pocket and said, This is a start.

The orange tip of the policeman's cigarette bobbed in the dark.

The man in the ute examined the bills, counted them, and the student
could see the man's fair hair, maybe red or strawberry blond. A big, dark-
coloured dog sat on the seat beside him.

The officer said, Don't phone me at work.

Yeah, I know.

He looked across at the dog. He go everywhere with you?

Why not? We do walkies at night. See things.

The officer flared a match and lit another cigarette. Stay out of trouble.

I always stay out of trouble.

They shook hands.

The officer said, I have to go.

The officer left. The other man waited in his ute, mumbling to the
dog.

The watching student was uncomfortable and shifted his leg; his knee
bumped the antenna and it clanged against the log.

The red-headed man reached under the seat for a torch, climbed from
his ute and walked to the log with the dog trotting behind him. He circled
the log and shone the torch on the student. The student shielded his eyes.

Holding the torch on the student's face, he said, What're you doing?

7

Bill Scott and Nigel Plant

Acting Superintendent Bill Scott leaned back in his chair. Fill me in.

Nigel Plant flipped open his notebook. Pretty vicious beating. The kid can't walk.

Can't walk, but is he talking?

That's the thing. He's on his back in a hospital bed and says he can't remember anything after he sat on the log. Parents say he was doing a project on Black Mountain, watching foxes at night. A cyclist found him in the morning at the end of Rani Road.

Foxes?

Foxes.

Sure. Foxes. You can guess what he was really doing.

He didn't have a car, and he doesn't seem the type. Rani Road is blocked.

Bill said, These kids are all the type, and ACTEW workers hand access keys around to all their friends.

Nigel stood and looked down at his notes. No drugs on him. No money to speak of, twenty-eight dollars in his wallet. His driver's licence is missing. He says he can't remember what happened, but I think he can. Someone beat him bloody, and the kid doesn't want to meet this fellow again.

Bill tapped on the desk. His eyes were empty and black. See what you can get out of him before he leaves hospital. Maybe we'll catch someone using his driver's licence.

There was a knock on the door and a woman in uniform looked in.

Bill shook his head and frowned. Not now. Give me a minute.

The officer shut the door.

Keep me posted. I want to hear if he talks.

Acting Superintendent Bill sat back in his leather chair. He seemed lost in thought, and chewed his bottom lip. Drug deal gone wrong. The kid's probably an amateur, in way over his head. Bill tapped a fingernail on the edge of his coffee cup.

Nigel waited and said, I'll see what I can do.

8

David and Tommy Rose

Sophie passed David with lowered eyes, hugging the wall. Spiky hair stood out like knives, her face compressed into a frown.

David decided to visit Tommy.

Tommy Rose, Tommy the Tech, was the departmental gossip. Tommy was everywhere, heard everything, and he would know something. David stopped at Emma's door. The sign read, 'Dr Bentham is away. Queries to the Department Secretary please'.

Down the hall, David opened the door to the psych lab and saw Tommy standing next to a high black table, his feet apart lifting a plywood maze off a cart. Tommy, a thirty-year-old man-boy, wore shorts in all seasons, running shoes and a sports jersey with red numbers on the back. David stepped across the room and coaxed the wooden frame onto the table with Tommy guiding it from the side.

Any broken? David looked over the mazes.

Tommy grinned. Two. I banged them together.

Anyone else use these?

Tommy shook his head. A bit demeaning, I guess. Rats and rewards. He stopped and looked up. Sorry, I didn't mean that. Tommy shifted the maze on the table and waited. When David stayed silent, Tommy said, You said anything to Security about those notes?

No. I don't think about the notes.

You should say something.

David shrugged. He hadn't told Tommy that he now carried a knife folded in his pocket, but it didn't matter if Tommy knew. David pulled the knife from his pocket, snapped open the blade, heard it click and lock into place, and started to carve the frayed wood from one corner of the maze.

Tommy twisted a screwdriver into one of the boxes and said, Those students see you?

Students?

David finished trimming the piece and slotted the plywood side into place. He folded the knife back into his pocket.

Two in here the other day. One failed his essay, said he was the wrong sex to pass the course.

David watched him. Who were they, Tommy?

Robert Truman, and a girl.

In black watch tartan?

What?

Tartan skirt and cream jumper.

Yeah, that's her.

They stood quietly in the room and Tommy said, His brother's in jail for rape.

I heard that. David eyed him. What did they say?

Who?

What do you mean, who? We're talking about the two students.

Can't tell the truth and pass. To pass, you lie.

David rested his hand on the wooden maze. You sent them to me, didn't you?

Tommy looked away and scooted the maze to the centre of the table.

Tommy?

Tommy's eyes darted sideways as he said, Just seems a little unfair, that's all. His brother's in jail.

Well, Tommy, it worked. She came along, Truman piked out. He's probably her boyfriend. They like to play off one against another, especially when they find a simple one like me. You knew that.

Tommy cleared his throat. Well, uh, Emma Bentham usually handled these things. But she's gone somewhere. They ought to see Roger Brown.

David smiled. Should they?

Tommy's running shoes squeaked on the floor as he worked at the screw. Why do you think Sophie does it?

David shrugged. She loves subjugation.

Subjugation?

Pursuit, subjugation.

Tommy stood with his mouth open.

David shook his head and said, Hard to explain Sophie to someone as house-trained as you are, Tommy.

What?

This place is more savage than you think.

Tommy frowned and said, She'd never hurt anybody.

Oh Tommy, I think she would.

Tommy looked at him and said, You're a little paranoid.

Maybe. But she loves crushing people.

I, uh, I d-d-don't know what you mean. Stammering a little as Tommy often did when he wanted to come across as sensitive and simple.

David picked up another maze and slid it onto the table. I have to go. Thanks, Tommy.

9

Amber again

The tossed pencil clattered off the wall and rolled under the bookcase. He bent his head over student papers and the knocks came again. He touched his forehead and shouted, Yes.

The last card in his letter box said COWARD. He opened the drawer and laid it with the others.

She peeked in, orange hair blazing in the afternoon sun, and said, Hi, David.

He looked away and said, Come in.

She wore a blue jumper over a white blouse and blue skirt. She closed the door and walked to the chair at the corner of David's desk.

He said, You've spoken with Sophie then.

Amber shook her head. No. We saw her but I wouldn't call it speaking with her. She buried us in rhetoric.

David wondered if 'we' meant she went with the boy student Truman, or she went with a friend and they were both protecting Truman.

Amber said, None of us understood a word of it, except that she meant 'No'.

Amber smoothed hair away from its parting. She rested her eyes on David's and said, What about you?

Me?

You know, when you talked to her.

She seemed to trap him with open green eyes. He knew he was tired and vulnerable.

He glanced down and said, Amber, what exactly do you want from me?

She gave him a long empty stare as if she'd caught his cold tone, then folded her arms.

He watched her thin fingers. Amber, look, we try to protect students' rights here. But sometimes, there's little we can do. He leaned back, feigning defeat.

They sat in the room without speaking, arms folded, her eyes shining with anger.

She said, It's an open secret. Nobody holds her to account. Nobody stands up to her.

David said, You stood up to her.

I'm worried about Robert. He won't pass unless he takes that line out of his essay.

Then take it out.

If your brother's innocent, would you say he was guilty?

Robert can appeal.

She put her flattened hand up to block him. Please. Don't insult me. People are frightened of her. She folded her hands in her lap and looked at the floor.

David studied the white parting in her apricot hair. He felt like shouting at her. He felt surrounded. He leaned towards her. Look. I'll talk to Roger Brown, see what I can do.

With an open hand she cleared David's proposal off his desk like dust. Roger? He's spineless. You know that.

He cleared his throat. Look. Be clear. What do you want from me?

I don't know. She raised her shoulders, a little shrug, and watched him. You can write a letter. Why not write a letter to the Vice-Chancellor?

David watched her. You're doing it again, and I'm asking myself 'Why do I fall for this? I should know better.'

She raised her fist between her breasts. Doing what? What are you talking about?

I think you know.

What?

Look, Sophie doesn't listen to me. To be candid, we're not close.

You can write to the Vice-Chancellor.

He grimaced. I could.

Thank you, David. We're grateful. All of us.

Amber, I said I could write to him, I need to think about it. He sat back.

She watched him and waited, You all right, David? You look tired.

I'm fine. It's a little disorienting, that's all.

Disorienting?

Amber, I have things to do.

She looked up and blinked, watched him for a moment and said, Thank you. She reached over and rested her hand on the back of his.

Amber, I'd appreciate confidentiality about this.

Of course. I won't tell anyone. She stood, adjusted her blue skirt at the waist, pulled open the door, looked back and smiled. Thank you, David. We're grateful. I'll see you next week.

David watched her slender back as she stood in the doorway, then listened as her shoes tapped down the hallway.

10

Boy in the street

David walking home from the shops. Under lit street lamps the boy stopped his bike and rested one foot on the ground, looking back with both hands on the handlebars. He spat on the ground. The boy was maybe sixteen or seventeen, short-cropped mousy hair, jeans and long-sleeved T-shirt. David thought he looked too old to be riding a BMX bike. He'd never seen him and wondered how long he'd been in the neighbourhood.

A car hissed by in the rain.

The boy shouted, You don't know what you fucking did. Do you?

David pulled at his earlobe and kept walking, shrugged his shoulders, listening to Fitzgerald in the earphones.

The boy leaned forward and shouted, I'm fuckin' talking to you.

David walked, touched the earphones.

The boy swung a wide circle in the street and came up behind him, passed slowly and waggled the bike wheel against David's leg. You're a fuckin' idiot, the boy said.

Steam came off the street lamps, the road glossy in the drizzle.

The boy yelled, You fuckin' stepped in front of me. I almost ran into a pole.

David gripped his shopping bag and said nothing. The earphones blocked some noise, but he could hear what the boy said. David didn't think he'd crossed in front of the cycling boy when he stepped up onto the footpath. He wondered why the boy was so hostile, spoiling for a fight. He must have ridden ahead and looked back to see if David was dangerous and decided he wasn't.

The boy turned, rode up to him and swung a fist close to David's face.

Next time, I'll fuckin' drop you. He looked down into David's shopping bag, And I'll take these.

David didn't pull back from the boy's fist, he kept his face impassive.

The boy screamed, I feel sorry for your kids. And then he started to scream, You fuckin' paedophile.

Near the corner, the boy exploded. Watch your fucking back. I know where you live. I'm fucking watching you.

David waited for a passing car then crossed the street and walked into a darker part of Cook. Dexter Street curved up a hill. David let the green bag slam against his leg. He didn't turn and look behind him; he wanted to show the boy he wasn't afraid.

The boy continued to scream, I know where you fuckin' live. I'm coming after you.

Off Dexter Street a narrow unlit laneway ran between houses. David turned into the laneway with high metal fences and expected the boy to follow. He didn't, and David made his way home.

11

Letter

In his office, David closed his eyes, opened his fists and rested. He dozed for half an hour then woke and rolled his chair to the computer, brought up the memo page, and addressed it, Roger Brown, Head of Department.

Dear Roger

A number of times this semester students have come to me with complaints about the criteria for passing the unit The Psychology of Gender. They believe that the range of beliefs held by Dr Moss is so narrow that no discussion or range of opinions is allowed, and that she may, at times, fail students because they are male, or because they are females who convey neutrality to male friends or family. That is, if the students do not see males as the root of all evil in the world, as members of a depraved, power-drunk class of subhumans, they fail. Apparently, students are forced into a social constructionist view that all gender is constructed to advantage males, and that suppression of male power is the only antidote to this imbalance. There are two teams, and males are the enemy side that must be crushed. No other point of view is allowed.

Is this a university where free thinking and free expression are allowed? If so, why can't students construct a well-argued, well-referenced essay that contradicts the dominant paradigm held by persons in power, in this case Dr Sophie Moss, and still be allowed to pass? I apologise for the rhetorical question. It deserves a simple, rhetorical answer – because Dr (Brown Shirt) Moss will use her position to punish students as long as they remain independent, free-thinking young people.

Yours sincerely

David Chess

David mumbled to himself, Let's see it in hard copy. He punched the print icon and walked down the hall to the department printer. On the way he thought about words and power. He felt better. He could read the hard copy, destroy the draft and continue to feel better. This one for practice. Brown Shirt, he chuckled.

He bumped down the steps past Bronwyn Williams, the Department Secretary, and stood over the printer. He waited. The machine didn't spit out the document. He climbed back upstairs, brought up the icon and printed a second draft, climbed downstairs and waited near Bronwyn's desk, drumming his fingers on the printer. The draft didn't show.

Damn. He looked at Bronwyn and she continued to type.

Back in his room, he banged the computer. Fucking thing. He pulled down the chooser, tapped twice on the printer icon. The computer blinked and darkened the bar over the words Broom Cupboard.

Broom Cupboard.

He looked away from the computer and tried to think, then he remembered – the paper feed in the Psych printer had jammed.

He walked downstairs and twisted the door of the old janitor's closet. It didn't move. He shook the door, but it held. David struggled and jerked at the knob, spread his feet and pushed with his shoulder. Fucking great.

He climbed upstairs – Bronwyn Williams had left. Upstairs in his room, he pulled the internal telephone directory from the bottom drawer, ran his finger down to Security and punched in four numbers. It buzzed twice, four, seven times, then a recording said, 'This phone is temporarily unattended. For emergencies, please telephone the Australian Federal Police on 000.'

Oh good. Leave the palace undefended.

He left the building, turned and ran over grass searching the campus. Nothing. He saw his words 'Brown Shirt' resting securely on letterhead in the broom cupboard. His running slowed.

He stood under trees and let his deep breathing settle. Drive home. Rest. Keep calm. Tomorrow at 7 a.m. when the cleaners turn up, you come in and retrieve the letter before Sophie arrives.

Simple.

12

Broom cupboard

David lay in the dark. He closed his eyes for a time, held them shut, rolled onto his side, then opened one eye just enough to see the tall red characters – 1 a.m. The harder he tried, the further he fell away from sleep and he saw the words Brown Shirt on the draft memo drifting around the print room. He rolled onto his stomach, fists knotted under his chest and watched Sophie standing at the printer, shaking with rage.

David rolled onto his back, shaky and muddled. He rubbed his nose with the back of his hand. Sun reddened the window and cars rushed by in the street. He rolled back to the clock – 9 a.m. Shit!

He landed on bare floorboards, grabbed the bundle of clothes balled up in the corner, rushed into his shirt and pants, slicked his hair with one hand, reached for his keys and rushed to his car.

He ran down the hall to the broom cupboard and tore open the door. The tray was empty. He threw papers around the little room, searched corners, ripped through the stack of documents that people had printed then forgotten. He stood breathing heavily with hands on his hips.

Someone said, Maybe it didn't print.

David turned and saw a young Master's student smiling. He didn't know her name.

He slipped past her into the hallway and climbed the steps to his office, pushed the chair against the wall, leaned back and closed his eyes with his fingers knotted in his lap.

Oh, good.

13

David and Daniel Bentham

David Chess and Emma Bentham were twins who excluded all others, a closed society, separate from the crowd. Over coffee they sniggered at sociology lecturers who met in the refectory to be intelligent together. People tried to get inside their tight little circle and were squashed like insects. On the first warm night of the year they made love on bare ground in the mountains. On nights when Emma lay in bed with her husband, David ached for her.

Husband Daniel was a technical officer in the department and a good friend of Tommy Rose, Tommy the Tech.

After Emma disappeared, David went to see to Daniel. The Ainslie front yard had no lawn. Black wattles, manna gums, and narrow-leafed peppermints scattered around the house and along a wooden fence.

David shut the Volvo door and strolled to the porch, wrapping himself in his long grey coat before knocking twice. He listened, knocked again, then pushed open the door and watched it swing.

You there, Daniel?

Waiting a few seconds. Daniel?

I'm back here. His voice far away.

David followed the small voice to a back bedroom and saw Daniel hunched in the muffling dark. In the gloom his pupils widened and David saw Daniel sitting in one of two wicker chairs set either side of a scuffed wood and glass coffee table. The room looked hastily arranged and empty. Daniel had the beginning of flaps on his stubbly cheeks, and he seemed caved into the wicker chair. He raised his face and tried to smile, and looked a year older than he had last week.

There was a long silence.

Have you seen her?

Daniel looked up and said, Emma? No. He waved his hand around the room. Not since she left. Place is a bit of a mess.

It was harder to think about Daniel's pain than it should have been, but David tried. It must hurt, he said.

It does hurt. Good script from the doctor but very little sleep in the last two weeks.

Anything I can do?

Daniel hesitated, looked into the corner for a moment, You can get her to come back.

David turned away. She won't make you happy, Daniel, and as it came out he realised how witless and offensive it was coming from him. He watched Daniel slump.

She might come back to you, Daniel said.

David shook his head. I haven't seen her.

Daniel continued to look at the floor. Wasn't much of a match, though, was it?

It wasn't your fault.

Daniel eyed him. Come on. A PhD married to a guy who sets up lab experiments?

David didn't respond.

I bored her.

She wasn't bored with you, Daniel. David watched him.

Why can't women be reasonable? Why are they so vindictive?

David reached up and scratched the side of his nose. You're asking the wrong man.

Funny how things turn out. You and me in the same boat.

David managed a nod. He knew too much about the way life had unravelled for Daniel and Emma.

Some of us don't deserve to be loved, said Daniel.

David thought about the logic behind this and couldn't help listening to traffic in the street. You have anything to drink? he said.

Beer in the fridge.

I'll open a couple.

David returned and slid an open bottle into Daniel's hand.

Cheers, he said and swigged and set the bottle down with a clunk on the glass table.

David said, Nobody at work knows where she is.

Daniel shifted and squeaked in the wicker chair; he lifted the bottle to his mouth, then slouched and stared into the corner of the room. I don't understand why she made the decisions she made.

They sat without speaking.

After a minute, David said, I have to go. Thanks for the beer.

Come again. Daniel's voice was thin.

They stood and walked to the hallway.

As Daniel opened the door, David turned and said to him, Tell me something.

Sure. What?

Do you think she's gone away with someone?

Daniel knotted his eyebrows. I don't know. I thought she was with you.

David reached out and touched Daniel's sleeve. I'll drop by in a week or so.

Yes. Do that.

He left Daniel standing in the doorway.

14

Daniel Bentham knows

David remembered the walk along Bruce Ridge when she said, in a casual way, Daniel knows about us.

David stopped, looking at the ground, then walked beside her without speaking. He looked out over the sparkling city and pondered this news, dampening the shock, imagining Daniel's black anger, how he planned retribution. The department would buzz. Payback was a matter of course. There would be trouble. Daniel would come after him with a knife or an iron bar, maybe a vicious lawyer.

David said, What do we do?

She smiled, He's known for some time and accepted it, to keep peace in the family and keep me from leaving. We can come and go as we please.

They walked and didn't speak. What did she expect him to say?

Emma said, Don't worry, my love.

Don't worry?

This is good news. Daniel's given me permission to take a lover.

David wondered if he'd given permission before, if Daniel had faced this crisis over other men and acquiesced. It was imprudent to ask, and it shouldn't matter.

David would call at Emma's house and Daniel would answer the door, ask David in, always offer him a drink. David would decline, politely. Daniel and David would gossip for ten minutes about people at work until Emma came down, trailing perfume, blonde hair piled up. They would say goodbye, and Daniel would say, Have a good time. He seemed to mean it.

Daniel said later, She did what she needed to do.

David and Emma would go to restaurants. He found places outdoors to undress her, in the forest at night, or sometimes in the car. They were divided about Sophie Moss. On walks, Emma defended Sophie, filled with venom for men who were Sophie's enemies. Emma told stories about men who were liars, cheats, predatory bosses, restraining orders that restrained nobody. Two groups of men lived in this world, Emma said, those bent on wrecking women's lives, and those too cowardly to stop them. There was no third category. On this, she and Sophie agreed. It was an article of faith. A malignancy walking in circles on its hind legs, a holocaust for women. Men filled women with despair, caused women to abandon hope. Men were heartless and self-serving.

Sophie's harmless, said Emma. If you're smart, you can manage her. It's the character of university life. Students know the drill. Give Sophie what she wants. Next semester give the lecturer who hates Sophie what he wants, write the opposite view.

They should be able to float opinions, said David.

Who cares? It's a lesson in handling opinionated people. We're teachers.

Yes, said David, we're teachers.

Then teach them to handle Sophie Moss.

The sun dropped into a pink reef of cloud and she was tired of talking about Sophie.

15

About Eddie Flannery

At Corin Dam they walked but didn't speak, bumping shoulders and crunching stones underfoot.

Near the top of the mountain, Emma said, almost in passing, We're seeing a counsellor.

Who?

Daniel and me.

The wind billowed Emma's white top and David reached up and scratched the side of his face. Why?

Why do you think?

I don't know why. Who?

You mean who's the counsellor?

Yes, who is it? David knew many of them.

Eddie Flannery.

He stiffened. He remembered the bantam Irishman, sandy-haired and smiling about one thing or another, mostly smiling about nothing. Eddie had struggled with essays in the undergraduate psych course, clashed with David, then clashed with Sophie Moss. For a time, David and Sophie agreed on something, even colluded. A miracle – Eddie had to go.

In his first semester, Eddie submitted an essay almost identical to the essay written by a twenty-year-old named Jill Mooney. Jill and Eddie walked through hallways and sat together. An item. David invited Eddie to his office, laid the two essays side-by-side and pointed to the similarities.

Eddie gazed at him steadily, smiled, looked down at the two papers and said, You're accusing me of plagiarism.

David held his stare, mimicked Eddie's smile, and said, I'm asking you for an explanation.

You ask Jill?

No. I'm asking you.

I said, Did you ask Jill?

David leaned back and said, Are you accusing Jill?

Eddie glared. No, you're accusing me.

I'm asking you about an essay that looks remarkably similar to this one. He tapped Jill's essay on his desk.

Whad'ya plan to do about it?

If you can't give us an explanation, Sophie and I will show the two essays to Roger.

So show him.

Eddie –

You're threatening me.

David didn't answer.

Smiling and calm, Eddie stood and watched David for a moment, then walked out, mumbling, We'll see.

Eddie switched to another course and struggled again, fought Sophie Moss, denounced psychologists as frauds, 'semi-educated fakes'.

For three weeks, David found long scratches in the paint down the length of his Volvo, made with an iron nail or maybe a house key. The campus police investigated; David supplied Eddie's name and address but nothing came of it. Eddie called Sophie a femi-Nazi and then she had scratches down the side of her car.

Eddie cut himself free from higher education. To avoid the requirements of the Board of Psychologists, he labelled himself a Lifestyle Coach. Now, a year later, he was back in David's life.

He listens like a thirsty man drinks, said Emma. He'll stay with us all afternoon, listening and working through our problems.

David stared, hiding the tightness behind his eyes, a contemptuous look on his face that he couldn't shake, trying to understand why the news jarred him so badly. He couldn't believe this. So out of character. How could Emma, who doubted the soundest intentions from men, nurtured a pessimism that disabled her trust in anything male, believe in a loser like

Eddie Flannery? Husband Daniel, yes. Daniel was simple, a fool. But why didn't Emma see through this swindler?

In essays, Flannery had written openly about his background, the miserable childhood, a badge of honour. Londonderry, marching season, painted murals on brick wall-ends, men spitting on each other, and Eddie's father, Gerry, telling his children, 'The duty of Catholics is to die for Ireland.'

Bloody Sunday and they moved from Derry to Belfast, lived on handouts from the Church. It was a disgrace to waste the day in low-paying jobs if Ireland wasn't free. Gerry fought Eddie's mother, slapped her, expected her to make do, and she expected Gerry to work as head of the house, father of her children. But he didn't. On long nights away, Gerry took lovers. Eloquent fury against England got him laid, words about liberty and hope and the disgrace of eight hundred years' occupation drew women to his bed.

At twenty, Eddie left his parents in Belfast, travelled to Australia, working odd jobs for five years. He wrote to his loving mother, but gave up writing to his father because he never wrote back. A drunk who warbled songs about victimhood, demanding obedience from his wife and six children. Asleep on the couch with a steel grid barricading the front door against paramilitaries, Gerry woke at midday, maudlin, rubbed his bristly face and demanded to be fed. He was sentimental and he was cruel.

On this walk, David turned to Emma and said, The threatening notes in my pigeonhole. Eddie's on top of my list of suspects. He's never forgiven me for failing him. I expected retribution, a trick maybe, a letter to the dean, but not this.

Emma squinted. What do you mean, not this? You mean I'm the retribution?

Maybe.

She stopped and watched him. You should see your face.

Tell me, did Eddie reconcile you and Daniel?

Emma shook her head. You don't understand, do you? The marriage is dead. What do you think I'm doing here with you? What can Eddie do? What can anyone do? Eddie's helping us with an amicable separation.

David stared. A separation? Are you serious?

She stopped. Of course I'm serious. That should make you happy.

A gaggle of choughs squabbled and turned over leaf litter in the forest.

I didn't see this coming, that's all.

She smiled. You don't like surprises.

Eddie's a con artist.

She flared. He's not a con artist.

But why Eddie?

Why not?

He frowned and they continued down the hill. You don't need a counsellor, he said. You can talk to me.

You're hardly impartial.

He watched her hand swinging at her side and he wanted to touch it. He said, The longer he listens, the more you pay. Right?

Emma's eyes narrowed. What are you so green-eyed about?

He stumbled over a tree root on the path.

Be careful, she said.

You be careful.

And that was the end of it. They didn't speak on the way back to the car.

On their last walk at Corin Dam, he didn't mention Eddie. She'd been cool, one-word answers to his questions, spartan conversation. David tied these brooding patches to troubles with Daniel, or the institution of marriage. He never took the silences personally, and later wondered if this was insensitivity on his part, or maybe Eddie was behind it. She seemed like a woman whose soul was underfed, hunting for scraps, starving. The only person he'd ever loved, and he'd trashed it through his own paranoia.

Emma stopped and turned to him. Branches made lazy shadows over her face. She said, Things are bad.

In yellow-barred afternoon light, she followed him down the path, breeze slipping off the water. Level sun drifted through peppermints. He leaned against the car door and fumbled his keys.

She said, There's only one certainty.

Looking up with one hand on the door, he said, That is?

She looked out over the water, the dam as hard as a sheet of steel. Lately she had started thoughts with some vague remark, then failed to finish them, as if she held a powerful conviction, then decided against it.

With her eyes down, she said, I'm sorry.

He watched her over the car roof, red-eyed as she opened the passenger door.

Coasting down the winding road from Corin Dam, he slowed for crossing wallabies and rabbits. The wrought-iron shapes of wet trees passed in the headlamps.

Emma curled on the seat beside him and slept.

16

Defamation

It was on expensive letterhead, thick black printing on heavy white paper. David rubbed his finger over the raised black letters:

LAROUSSE, COHEN, AND PINCH – BARRISTERS
DEFAMATION PROCEEDINGS AGAINST DAVID CHESS

The first copy arrived by fax and lay for two days in the broom cupboard printer room. Most of the staff had read it. The document bristled with huffy outrage and scorn over the kicking that David had inflicted on Sophie Moss. 'According to our client'…'degradation'… 'deep public humiliation'…'soiled reputation caused by the said memo whose author allegedly intended to malign our client and lower her high standing among her peers'.

Robert Cohen, the defender of said client, had suffered at least as much indignation as had Sophie Moss. He said, 'and I feel a deep sense of personal outrage over the callous disregard for human dignity that you displayed in your memo to Roger Brown'.

David mumbled, For only $300 an hour.

Cohen demanded that David retract, within seven days, the statements in said memo. Damages amounted to $50,000 in stress, medical expenses, loss of career advancement, and loss of professional reputation, plus legal costs. And David must apologise to Roger Brown.

David sipped coffee, squinted and read it again. He picked up the letter, walked down the hall. Tommy the Tech came out of Roger's office, dressed in shorts and a sports jersey. David would have asked him if his friend Daniel had heard anything about Emma, but, not today.

He turned into Roger Brown's office, knocked but there was no response. He pushed it open. Roger sat behind a clean desk in a pink sports coat and grey slacks.

You wanted to see me.

Roger said, Sit down. He held out his hand.

No thanks. David stood facing him.

Roger paused and looked up. I understand there's been some trouble between you and Sophie.

The letter sat in the in-box tray for two days. What's to discuss?

Roger leaned forward. You tell me.

There's nothing to discuss.

Roger sat back. Look. We have a bit of a mess.

It was a draft. I printed a rough draft, to retrieve and think about. Someone locked the broom cupboard – great move. Look, we're a scatter-brained department, we don't retrieve half the pages we print because phone calls interrupt us or we forget what we're doing or it seems pressing at the time but isn't pressing at all. So we leave it. It's too bad people in this department read each other's private mail.

David, I don't think –

Someone retrieved the draft from the broom cupboard before I arrived on Wednesday morning. I hope you're trying to find out who that was.

Your letter was in the staff room, David, under your coffee cup. Nobody said the broom cupboard was locked. Sophie Moss saw the letter, she was understandably quite upset. I mean, Brown Shirt. Sophie removed it and took it to her lawyer. You know the rest.

It's unsigned.

It came from your computer at 17.30 hours on Tuesday.

You've checked, have you?

I had to follow it up.

Then find the creep who did this.

Roger held his hands out like a frog. David, we want to support you.

What's with this fucking we? His words came out in small gritty pieces. We? You mean, 'What's going on, David, so I can make certain that I'm not embarrassed, so my department doesn't get sued.'

Roger twisted a pencil in his hands. David, you need to get some help.

Ah yes, paranoia. Sophie accuses me of defamation, and the whole staff is twittering because they took time to read the letter in the fucking in-tray.

Roger shook his head and put up his hand. I meant legal help. You could be up for tens of thousands of dollars. You could lose your job. He pointed with the pencil. Sit down.

David folded his arms, walked to the bookcase, and turned. Don't worry so much.

It's a mess.

It'll give a third-rate department a black eye for a week but don't worry, nobody will notice.

No. This is grave.

David walked over and leaned his hands on Roger's desk. Don't you think it's important to find out who put the letter in the staff room?

Roger shrugged. I don't know. It doesn't matter any more.

Someone locked the broom cupboard door.

Even if that's true –

Wait a minute. *Even* if it's true?

You –

Of course it's fucking true.

Roger leaned back and folded his arms. Well, ah, your language. I mean really. Brown Shirt. Brown Shirt. Reputation is everything in this university. You cannot soil a person's reputation.

Sure you can.

Roger frowned. What?

Gives her life a sort of physical shape and meaning. Don't you think? Her perfect opus, her little album of bigoted writings and sayings.

Roger shook his finger in the air. Now, you listen to me.

Do you remember a student named Eddie Flannery?

What?

About two years ago, from Belfast. He caused no end of trouble. Put long scratches down the side of my car with a nail, and down the side of Sophie's.

What the hell does this have to do with Sophie?

Eddie's behind this. I know he is. A trick.

You're paranoid.

Good. I'm paranoid. Doesn't mean I'm wrong.

Look, your intention was clear. The letter was meant as a threat, a warning to Sophie, a message that you'll send the letter to the VC unless Sophie does certain things. That sort of blackmail doesn't work in a university.

Sure it does.

What?

That sort of blackmail works really well in a university.

David —

That's not what I did.

Look. You have ideological differences with Sophie. But you don't police standards in this department. I do.

I wish.

Sophie's solicitor telephoned me. Uh, Cohen, I think his name is. I can tell you in confidence, you deeply hurt Sophie by doing this, and, well, she has to stand up for her beliefs. They have a strong case. Legal costs alone could break you.

It's all petty.

I want to broker a treaty between you and Sophie, an even-handed settlement, before this gets out of hand.

It's already out of hand.

David, just keep me informed. I need to know what's going on.

Let's see. What's going on? My ass is being sued by the campus bigot, and I'm going to ignore it because it doesn't matter. That's about it.

Roger shook his head. Goodbye, David.

17

Amber about Tommy Rose

Two knocks woke him. He blinked in sooty light and looked through one eye at shadows under the door, two feet waiting for an answer. David's face lay on assignments strewn over the desk.

Another knock and he rubbed his eyes and turned in his seat. It's open.

She smiled, Can I come in?

A column of afternoon light spilled into the room.

Yes.

She stood in the half-opened door with her blue loafers together. I thought you wouldn't see me.

Why did you think that?

She came close and the desk lamp showed the spattering of freckles over the bridge of her nose, the white skin on her throat almost translucent. I'm sorry.

David looked at her and waited. For what?

Sophie.

He looked away. What can I do for you?

It's about Sophie.

I guessed that.

We heard about the defamation case.

We? Who's we? And heard from who?

Amber shrugged. We hear things.

It seems you do. Look, I need to ask you something.

She stood open-eyed. Of course. Ask me.

You know Eddie Flannery, don't you?'

She squinted. Who?

Eddie Flannery.

Amber shook her head. No. What's this about?'

He watched her for signs of lying. I think you do know him, and I think Eddie sent you along to me, to talk about Sophie. He's got a gift for manipulating young girls.

Young girls?

Like you.

Her eyes widened. That's not true.

It's quite a coincidence. Don't you think?

She looked upset and he wanted to ask her to sit down, but didn't.

I'd like to believe you, but it's too much of a coincidence. Don't you think? You were in a tutorial with him.

Look. I came to see you when my friend's brother was falsely accused of rape. He said that in his essay, and he's struggling with the dogma in Sophie's unit. You know the rest. I'm not going to stand here and defend myself. Listen to your conspiracy theories. Believe it or don't believe it.

Wish I could.

She glared, It's the truth.

He sat and looked up at her.

She stepped forward. We talked to one of the techs.

David looked up. Tommy?

Yes, and the other one.

Daniel Bentham.

Yes. And we talked to Daniel's wife, Emma Bentham, once after class. She's gone now. Amber watched him for some reaction. Emma Bentham told us to see Roger, but Tommy Rose said it wouldn't do any good. We should see you. That's the truth.

She stood watching him, David looking down again, thinking. They said nothing for a time.

Anyway. Now it's tangled up with lawyers.

Yes.

He leaned back and stared at her. Anyway. What do you want?

I know a little about defamation. We studied it as part of a unit. I feel responsible.

Don't.

Amber stood, her green eyes watching him. I'm sorry about what's happened and I want to help. Take you to a solicitor.

David thought for a moment, shook his head and said, I'll find my own solicitor.

She opened her hands. I can help you. I'll come along, take notes. I know the criteria. Defamation rests on three fundamental components. The first –

I won't need a defamation lawyer.

But you do.

No, I don't. It'll blow over.

Not with Sophie it won't. Let me come along and help.

That wouldn't be appropriate.

It's up to you. But you've got to start trusting someone.

David rested back and looked out the window. Not today.

18

David at home

David drove home after lectures and came into work as little as possible. His flat as cold as a tomb. Mornings were desolate. Dirty cups and glasses were scattered over the sitting room floor and the kitchen table, stained with milk or wine; cracked dishes in the sink were crusted with food. Bits of soggy cornflakes plugged the drain hole. The vacuum cleaner never left the closet and cobwebs spread from ceiling to floor in every room.

He lay awake over most of two nights, then three. Around midnight on the third night, he turned onto his side and drifted into the middle ground, a part-dream set in a stone courtyard; a black dog bristling at the side of the King of Sweden, barking at a raven on bare ground. The king knelt and patted the dog and told the strutting raven he was safe from the hostile dog, told him not to fly to the top branches of an oak tree inside the walls of the courtyard. The raven stepped up to the king, took meat from his hand, and David watched them vanish. Red characters on the clock said 2 a.m.

David set his feet on cold floorboards and walked downstairs. It was chilly in the sitting room and light rain speckled the roof and windows. He dressed, climbed into his car and drove under smoky street lamps. Roads were empty. He left his car a block away from Emma's house and walked down the middle of the road in light rain. He stood in their darkened front yard. A dim light shone behind the sitting room curtains.

His lecture the following day had sparkle. Fatigue had focused his delivery and given him a strange presence. Students didn't look at their watches too often; some raised thin arms and asked questions, squinted, challenged him and then scribbled. Some of the lecture embedded, he thought.

Students standing around, girls in knots around the exit. What do you have next? Frowning about assignments, pushing through the door.

Some thanked him for points made in the lecture, but he mistrusted the charm in their sweet voices, their fake smiles. Their smiles especially were suspect, and their dead glances.

He noticed Amber Griffin standing in a back corner watching him, orange hair glowing like a hurricane lamp. Her cream jumper stood out in the ragged huddle of sweatshirts and jeans. She and David watched each other for a moment then she turned and left through a side door.

19

Nigel Plant about Eddie Flannery

On the bottom floor, Nigel passed a handcuffed prisoner flanked by two officers. The prisoner glared.

Nigel climbed the stairs, tapped on Acting Superintendent Bill Scott's door, and heard, Yes.

Bill waved his hand, Come in. How did it go?

Nigel cleared his throat. Not so good.

What do you mean?

Same story. Husband complained to us about Eddie Flannery –

I'm aware of that, Bill snapped.

The wife didn't back the husband's story.

Bill sat back, fiddled his thumbs and looked out the window. Did you see Flannery?

Yes.

Where?

In his flash office in Braddon.

What'd he say?

Nothing really. Said he's a professional trying to help the downtrodden.

Handing out bad advice without a licence.

That's not illegal in this town. So far. We'd be busy if it was.

Met his lawyer yet?

He hasn't hired one. Says he's within the law. He's not afraid of us.

Bill tapped his finger on the desk. He's not afraid of you.

Maybe.

I need to pay him a visit.

Nigel touched his red moustache. You said that before. But I'll say what I said before. Watch him. He could lodge a complaint against you, and the department.

I take it he confers with Sophie Moss.

Nigel snorted. Hardly.

What?

They don't speak.

What do you mean they don't speak? They're on the same freedom bus. They hate us.

They hate each other. Call it territorial.

Bill shook his head. Flannery convinces women to leave their husbands, and Sophie doesn't like it?

That's right.

We're stuck in the middle.

Something like that.

I'm tied up with paperwork. When my desk is cleared, I'll go see Flannery. He's turning into a headache.

After a long pause, Nigel said, Is that all?

Bill continued to look out the window, then waved his hand. For now. Leave your notes with me.

20

Carolyn Scott

Carolyn Scott wrote in her diary, 'The summer is ended, but we are not free.'

She'd come into work glassy-eyed, her blue-black hair tangled, an unsteadiness in her gait, her face covered with make-up to hide rust-coloured marks on her skin. She stood behind the oak reception desk at the hotel moving slowly, nursing sores on her back and arms with her collar turned up to hide marks on her neck and breasts. Hotel guests thought she looked beautiful but perishable.

Bill came home at 2 a.m., tilted into Carolyn's face and whispered, What's your excuse?

What do you mean?

I want the place clean. Get it? Clean.

Carolyn sucked in a breath, waiting for his fists. Bill's rancid breath caught in her throat. She stepped back and looked down to vomit, held it in and said, The girls, and work. There's not enough time.

Bill leaned back and sat on his anger, squinted into her bowed head. Fuckin' pathetic. Look at me when I talk to you. That's right. I'm sorting out criminal scum in this town from 9 a.m. till 10 at night. What the fuck do you do?

Then the hitting started.

Carolyn's friends had warned her, If you leave him, he'll punish you. He's a big man in the city and payback is on the cards.

Carolyn knew this was true. She knew Bill would deliver.

Standing at the reception desk, Carolyn drifted, remembered how they'd met seven years before and she fell in love with his strength and serenity, his quiet and peaceful demeanour. Attentive, he brought her flowers for no reason. Carolyn's parents liked him, though Carolyn's mother wondered about his long empty silences in the sitting room while he waited for Carolyn, his thousand-yard stare at the dinner table on Sunday afternoons, eyes as blank as a cat's and thoughts elsewhere.

At first, the marriage travelled well. Carolyn bore them a daughter named Clare, and he moved through a chain of promotions in the department driven by his talent for solving the impossible, his knack for manipulating friends and enemies into disputes then patching up the conflicts that he'd secretly created. Bill took care of Bill.

On the birth of their second daughter, he started to unravel. Though he'd been odd from the beginning, most saw this as eccentric brilliance, part of the package. Bill concealed his madness then unleashed it when the coast was clear, tossed a knife at Carolyn if dinner was too hot, screamed if she left his soiled clothing on the laundry floor.

Home late after drinking, breath fetid with stale beer, he read the mail left by his leather chair, climbed into bed, lay on his back for a moment, then took Carolyn, tearing at her nightdress, clamped his hand over her mouth, forced himself into her and whispered hideous threats. Stinking rancour filled the room.

Sex enraged him and bad sex was Carolyn's fault. Backward and frigid Carolyn had wrecked their marriage and wrecked his happiness, or so he told her.

We're going to try new things, he said. Three in a bed. Your friend Sarah March. Invite her over.

Carolyn refused and Bill moped and slammed doors. He needled her and said, I'll get my cunt elsewhere.

In police uniform, he dropped into Carolyn's hotel, studied the managers, cooks, clients, cleaners, bellboys. Carolyn gave a nervous smile, trying to serve people while he paced the lobby watching customers.

Who do you speak to? he said. What do you do all day?

At home, Bill watched Carolyn fix dinner and tend the girls. When Carolyn spoke on the telephone, he sat close, read the newspaper and listened. Carolyn put the girls to bed and lingered in their room, sat on Clare's bed until Bill came in. To spare the girls the ugliness she knew was coming, Carolyn left and got ready for bed. He leaned in the doorway and watched her undressing, on the toilet, in the shower.

At work, Carolyn made friends with an assistant manager named Wally Clough. Carolyn was small, dark-haired, and he told her she had delicate cheekbones. On a freshly made bed, he ran his hands over her and she let him. They met in empty rooms and let passion run them.

After a month she stopped him, afraid of snoopy maids who might catch them. But mostly afraid of Bill.

Bill suspected treachery because he was sleeping with a secretary at work. He slapped Carolyn in front of the girls. When she didn't admit to the affair, he slapped the whore, the betrayer of his trust. He slapped her for holding out, he'd slap her again if she admitted to the affair, and he slapped her when she denied it. You have the stink of another man on you.

He sat in his chair with a bottle, his throat ragged from shouting, a man stumbling in a world he didn't quite understand but knew he wanted to wreck. He cut and discoloured Carolyn's face, drove her once to the emergency room and watched the doctor loop four stitches into her bottom lip. Carolyn and Bill lied. She'd come home tired from work, they said, and she'd fallen downstairs. Doctors nodded and scribbled down the story and glanced at each other after Bill and Carolyn left.

Bill said, I'll kill you if you telephone the police. He pulled out the revolver he would do it with, held it against Carolyn's temple and forced her to have sex, rode her with the barrel of the cocked pistol in her ear. Carolyn's white face and bone-shaking fear made him come.

Carolyn painted cuts and bruises with blush and foundation stick until a morning in May. It was a small thing, a remark from a cleaner.

Why do you hide such a beautiful face under pancake make-up?

The next morning she waited for Bill to leave, stuffed clothing into three suitcases, scooped the girls into the car and landed them on her parents' step in Ainslie. Her white-haired parents hugged the girls and told Carolyn to stay as long as she wanted.

21

Eddie Flannery and Carolyn Scott

Carolyn's mother recommended a skilled counsellor to guide her decisions. He doesn't fear the police, said her mother. He doesn't fear anyone. He doesn't fear the devil. He'll give you tactics to sleep at night, tactics about legal representation. When Eddie listens, you're in strong hands.

In his Braddon office, Eddie Flannery sat next to Carolyn, listening to her stories. He reddened with anger. He consoled her as she wept, laid his hand over hers and said, I'll take care of Bill. Leave Bill to me.

When Bill Scott learned that a 'lifestyle coach' was helping Carolyn slice Bill out of her life, he smashed a lamp against the wall. He drank through the night, the revolver on his lap, cocking the hammer and releasing it over and over, listening to the hammer click. She was scheming with a 'lifestyle coach', an Irish faker who pretended to be wounded by Carolyn's made-up stories.

I'll kill him, he mumbled.

Eddie Flannery recommended to Carolyn a lawyer named Judy Wells, who was stony and heartless enough to defeat Bill Scott. A year before she had faced Bill in court, defended a woman. Bill had charged the woman after a drug bust in Charnwood, and Judy Wells beat him in court, set fire to the police evidence and set the woman free.

What could be better? said Eddie. Ready-built shame and humiliation. Tailor-made loss of face.

Carolyn shrugged, wet-eyed and stiff. I don't want any more trouble.

Trust me, said Eddie.

In their second week of meetings, Carolyn looked sunnier. Then Bill threatened Carolyn over the phone, promised to block her meetings with

Eddie Flannery and raised his fist to the mouthpiece. You fucking listen to me. I'll drive him down to the lake and hold his head underwater with my boot. Hear me?

Carolyn told Eddie and Eddie laughed.

She said, Please. Be careful. He's dangerous.

Eddie laughed again, rested his hand on the back of Carolyn's wrist. He doesn't know what dangerous is.

22

Ethics meeting

David stood against the wall reading students' assignments. Department Head Roger Brown sat in his tan sport coat, elbows on the hardwood table. He stood and opened the door to release soupy air trapped by an earlier meeting.

Roger touched David on the shoulder and said, Relax. People aren't coming to attack you.

Vice-Chancellor Jim Stuart, in a grey blazer, white shirt and red tie over blue chinos, swept in. Jim Stuart's eyes were dove-grey but not so soft, and he was laughing to himself about something. Silver hair swishing over his forehead gave him a boyish look and he sat at the head of the table. David knew Jim set meetings around the hardwood table where he could watch people come and settle, note who sat next to whom and who avoided eye contact.

Senior Lecturer Susan Frith came in, a squat woman in a plaid jacket and red skirt, her pageboy haircut freshly trimmed. Sophie Moss followed with her black hair gelled and spiky. Sophie's hoop earrings bobbled. She wore a loose brown pants suit and carried a Tupperware container.

David was startled; he glared at Roger, and this turned to anger.

Roger lifted an open hand. Sophie asked Susan to come along, and I said fine. Roger Brown leaned back and smiled at Vice-Chancellor Jim, How's your friend the minister?

Friend or not, he's starving us little by little.

Roger laughed. The others were frowning and tense.

Sophie Moss and Susan, with shoulders touching, faced David and Roger Brown across the table. The women looked pleased, the meeting was a small formality, and Vice-Chancellor Jim was their man. The draft memo about Sophie that had caused all the trouble was addressed to Vice-Chancellor Jim Stuart.

From the head of the table, Jim glanced at his watch. Who starts?

Roger Brown said, I can. Sorry you're missing your lunch. Our purpose today is to resolve this question of lecturer autonomy, before it turns into a mess. I think David and Sophie agree. He held out his hands in a pleading gesture. Nobody wants conflict.

Jim watched.

Roger said, I'm here to expedite a solution, to help you, Susan and Sophie, consider David's new proposal. He nodded to each of them as he spoke their name. If it's a fair proposal, we'll send it along to Faculty Board with the blessing of the committee. If not, David can try again. Simple.

Susan and Sophie Moss sat whispering behind hands until Roger said, I think you've all read the proposal, but maybe David can summarise.

David cleared his throat. The appeals process is a sham. We need protection for students whose beliefs differ from the beliefs of the lecturer. If a student argues cogently and supports the argument with conclusive research, the Appeals Board should overturn the fail mark given by the lecturer.

Sophie sat with her eyes down. She poked one hand into her plastic Tupperware container and crunched on pieces of lettuce, radishes, and a split carrot.

Vice-Chancellor Jim brushed his silver hair with a little finger, studied the side of people's faces. Thanks, David. Can I hear from the others please? He looked at Sophie Moss.

She stopped chewing, glared at David and said with her mouth half-full, Let's be honest here. This is a piece of retaliation. Against me. Defending men who beat up and rape women. My unit is progressive. I move students away from mainstream thought, reject dominant paradigms. Men don't like this. They want to pull me back into the fold. In this male-dominated university, David's proposal means punishment for a minority. For minority, read 'women'. If you force lecturers to write this falsehood into their unit outlines, it will hamstring free thought. I try to push students forward. David's proposal holds them back, dictates that if a student wants to stay in the 1970s and quote some slanted crackpot who's managed to get himself into print, the student can pass. They can argue fascism, slavery, anything they like and the lecturer is compelled to pass them. If a student finds some neo-conservative running-dog lackey of Andrew Bolt who presents 'evidence' – she held up her fingers as quotation marks – that men are more intelligent than women, the essay passes.

David said, No. The proposal says 'research that convinces the Board'. That proviso works in your favour. If the prime minister spouts 'evidence' that two woman can't partner and successfully raise children, we point to good research comparing female couples to hetero couples, and we prevail.

Sophie leaned back, closed her eyes and gritted her teeth. I see what you're doing here. Look. This is a moral position, nothing to do with research. She pointed with a piece of carrot. You know that, David. And I know where you're going with this line of rhetoric, straight to the lies about False Memory, as if a woman would ever lie about being raped. Come on. It's like denying the holocaust. I will not accept falsehoods. Never. She folded her arms and leaned back. I know these things. I know that children never lie about being abused, and women never lie about being raped or beaten. Never. I won't pass any student who writes otherwise.

Vice-Chancellor Jim nodded. Thanks, Sophie. Look, I don't want to get bogged down in specific cases. Let's examine David's proposal at face value.

Sophie shook her head. Face value. Come on. That's exactly what I'm doing. You can prove anything with reductionist, linear bean counting. Have you read *How To Lie With Statistics*? Someone needs to take an ethical stand for women, and that someone is me. The ground women gained in the 1970s is being eroded.

They waited and watched Jim.

He said, Susan, you're a senior lecturer in the department. I need your thoughts.

Susan shifted in her chair. I agree with Sophie. It would be a travesty, dangerous and narrow. It removes the onus from lecturers to embrace and teach what they believe.

David shook his head, No. They can embrace and teach whatever they like, they can teach anything. They can believe anything they like. This doesn't interfere with academic freedom. The onus is still with lecturers. But lecturers can't fail a student who refuses to embrace that lecturer's beliefs.

Vice-Chancellor Jim watched Roger and said, Is that your understanding?

Roger said, Well, I think we all want a solution to this problem.

Jim shook his head, Obviously, Roger. But what do you think?

Roger looked down and mumbled, I encourage debate in my department. It leads to better teaching.

Sophie leaned forward, earrings bobbling as she pointed at David with another piece of carrot. Do you know there's some fellow arguing that blackbirding slaves from the Solomon Islands to Queensland sugar fields never happened? Slaves came voluntarily looking for work, but the myth is so embedded in the Australian public that Australians can't accept the truth, or so this fellow says. What do you say to reactionary lies like that?

Jim looked at her. It depends on the evidence.

Sophie glared. That's hardly the point. It's revisionist. She pulled her Tupperware container into her lap and looked down into it.

Jim watched her. Fine, but what is this man's evidence?

David said, He wrote his PhD on it.

Jim looked at Roger. Okay, let's take up Sophie's point. What happens if a student writes an essay arguing that blackbirding or the stolen generation are myths?

Roger said, We resolve it as adults, as professionals.

David shook his head. Roger, that's not what Jim asked.

Roger squinted, sloped away from David and said, David, I'm fighting in your corner. We need to workshop some proposals, stitch together a solution. I'd like to hear more from Susan.

They waited, Susan blinked and said, David's proposal compromises academic freedom. I say no.

David said, It's *for* academic freedom.

Roger held up a hand. David, settle yourself.

No, I won't settle myself. This is pure dishonesty.

Sophie leaned over the container in her lap, resting her elbows on the table; she raised a finger and stared at David and said, You be careful.

Vice-Chancellor Jim said, Look. I see no problems with the proposal.

Sophie's mouth fell open, her face gone white. She put her empty Tupperware container where she thought the edge of the table was, missed and it tipped onto the carpet. She leaned back and folded her arms.

Roger, poised with his open hands on the table and said, Uh, Jim, I thought we'd have a little more discussion.

Vice-Chancellor Jim rested his elbows on the table. I've heard enough discussion, and I know how each of you will vote. Roger, you'll abstain.

Roger forced a smile. Look, uh, I want us to move forward. But we need more discussion.

Jim looked bored. We've had discussion. Now we send the proposal to Faculty Board.

A muscle twitched in Sophie's upper lip. That's hardly fair.

Roger, startled now, looked at them one by one. Look, I know it's a poor tactic, but I want to make a concession here, on Sophie's behalf, an offering to David. A compromise.

Jim nodded, Make a concession, Roger.

How about this? He paused, opening his hands on the table, looking towards David, A panel of three lecturers chosen by the unit convenor examines the Appeals Board decision. They support it, or they overrule it.

Jim said, Overrule what? Overrule the Appeals Committee?

Roger was smiling at Sophie Moss. Yes.

David said, That cancels the point of the ruling.

Roger shook his head. No, no, David. Think about it. Let me explain.

Vice-Chancellor Jim looked at his watch. Explain quickly.

Roger lowered and raised the edge of his open hands, as if cutting a birthday cake. My solution is win-win. Roger beamed.

For a time there was quiet around the table; all five stared past each other. Sophie put her toe into the Tupperware container and looked under the table to locate it. She picked lettuce off her shoe.

Susan was chewing her bottom lip. She leaned back and folded her arms again.

Jim said, No.

Roger shrugged his shoulders at Sophie, signalling 'I tried.'

Jim brushed back his silver hair. Okay. Done. I'll put it to the Board.

David was scribbling something in the margin of his notes and Roger peered over trying to read it.

Sophie Moss raised both open hands off the table. What? This can't be the end of discussion.

Jim said, It is for now.

Sophie folded her cloth bag, reached under the table and groped for the plastic container, leaving a pile of chopped vegetables on the floor, stood and walked to the door. Susan followed her out the door, mumbling sharp words in the hall.

Jim collected papers, stood and nodded, Thank you, Roger, David.

They left David at the table. Alone in the room he rubbed his finger over the deep letters EMMA that were penned in the margin, felt the shape of her name and the warmth it brought to him. Thinking about redemption.

23

Second letter

David gulped from the bottle, waited for the drink to burn down his throat, warm his toes and fingers. He gulped again, stood the bottle in the bottom drawer, and slid the drawer shut. The lamp fastened to the edge of the bookcase threw a rectangle over the white paper stamped with heavy black print. David hooded his eyes, thumbed his temples in the dank smelling cave and read the letterhead again –

LAROUSSE, COHEN, AND PINCH – BARRISTERS
DEFAMATION PROCEEDINGS AGAINST
DAVID CHESS – 2ND LETTER

He switched off the desk lamp, sat in the dark, but someone thumped on his heavy wooden door. With the lights off, they should have stayed away, but the metal handle clattered and Tommy stuck his curly head in. The afternoon sun caught his blond hair and made his head glow.

Hey, David. He squinted. You there? In hockey shorts, and with the number 79 printed in red letters on his jersey, Tommy the Tech waited with his hand on the door.

David thought about the hockey stick standing in the corner of Tommy's room in his workshop in the basement, how Tommy beamed if his team won, moped with his arms drooping if they lost. David thought about his own 24/7 morose and prickly demeanour. Tommy's grinning face must be a welcome contrast. Tommy tipped his curly head to people, a thirty-year-old man-boy too sensitive to openly fight, too compliant to disobey, always eager to please. Toss out a ball and Tommy would chase it.

Yes, Tommy.

Tommy looked through his blond eyebrows, gave a wolf-pup smile. You wanted me to set up the galvanic skin response today?

Go ahead.

Tommy glanced down the hallway. Okay, I'll make a start. He turned and rushed out the door.

David grabbed the solicitors' letter, stepped into the rose light, squinted and walked down the hallway to the reception desk and the woman guarding the door.

Roger in?

He's fairly busy.

I doubt it. David opened the door.

Roger sat behind an immaculate desk.

You wanted to see me.

Yes, David. Sit down. He held out an open hand.

I'll stand, thanks.

How are you?

David paced with hands behind his back, turned, and said, How do you think?

Roger glanced away and cleared his throat. Uh, David, look, why don't you sit down?

David paced with the defamation letter flapping in his hand, turned and said, No.

Look, David, I know it's been hard.

Get to the point.

I warned you. Didn't I? If you took that proposal to the Vice-Chancellor, she'd have you. There'd be hell to pay.

David knew Sophie had been there first, a copy of the solicitors' letter sat on Roger's desk. He pointed.

Roger cleared his throat. Yes, oh that. We'll support you.

I doubt it.

Roger shook his head, David, you're too brittle sometimes.

You're as scared as I am, Roger.

No, I mean, it's not in the newspapers yet —

What? Newspapers? Come on. David chuckled. Why would the newspapers give a fig about a third-rate psychology department in a second-rate university?

Look, I –

David pointed at the letter. Someone in your department took the coffee cup from my office, and put the draft letter under it in the staff room.

Roger shook his head. Always jumping at shadows.

David turned in the middle of the room. I'm not jumping at shadows. Please. Sit down.

What do you want, Roger?

I warned you. Didn't I? Win the battle with the Vice-Chancellor, and she'll have your cojones. What is wrong with you? You'll lose your job. She wants you sacked.

It's petty. None of it matters.

I don't see how you can say that. Try to yield a little. Don't be so recalcitrant.

David leaned forward and laid his palms on Roger's desk. Recalcitrant? David turned and continued to pace. You won't raise your fists when the battle heats up.

Roger lifted a shaky finger. Now, you look –

At the end of the room, David swung round with a jerk, slammed his forehead into the edge of the hanging bookcase. Fuck, he yelled. Fuck. He bent over and reached above his eye.

Roger stood. David. You all right?

A hand pressed on his brow, David tipped his face down. No.

David, let's walk over to the clinic.

Drops of blood fell on the carpet. Roger pulled a wad of tissues out of a box on his desk. Put this on it.

David said to the floor, Stop fussing. He reached out for the wad and pressed it against his brow.

Let's go to the clinic David, or get the nurse to come here.

David pressed the tissues, studied the drops of blood on the solicitors' letter.

Roger said, Stop this act, this pretence of being all dark and wounded.

I am wounded, thanks to your fucking bookcase.

Listen, I've worked hard on this all morning, organised a meeting between you and Sophie. Let's untangle this mess before they drag in more lawyers.

David looked up from under the wad of tissues. Blood trickled from under them. He said, Read the letter in front of you. He wiped blood from the bridge of his nose. I'm wasting my time here.

David walked out the door and Tommy the Tech stood next to Roger's secretary.

Tommy mirrored David, pressed his hand to his forehead. You hurt, David?

No, Tommy. And stop looking like it's your fault.

David walked down the hallway, head bent and Tommy watched him, puzzled by this man he no longer knew.

24

Boy again

In light rain, the boy stopped his bike next to David and rested one foot on the ground. He spat at David. The boy shouted, I fuckin' told you to stay off this road.

David kept walking, shrugged, pushed an earphone into his ear.

The boy leaned forward and shouted, You fuckin' deaf?

David walked, touched the bandage on his forehead.

The boy came up behind him, slammed the bike wheel against David's leg and said, You're a fuckin' meathead.

Yellow glow off street lamps in the shopping centre lit the road.

The boy mumbled, Remember? You almost ran me into a pole. The kid pinched his nose and blew snot onto the road.

David gripped his shopping bag. Maybe glare and shout and try to scare him off, he thought.

The boy turned and came back, rode in circles around David, sidled up to him and swung a fist close to David's face. I'll fuckin' drop you. He looked into the bag. I'll take these. Anything good to eat in there?

David brushed away the boy's fist, and kept his face blank.

The boy screamed, I feel sorry for your kids. Screaming, Fuckin' paedophile.

Near the corner, the boy screeched, I'm comin' after you.

Dexter Street curved up the hill. The shopping bag banged against David's leg as he walked. He didn't turn and look behind him; he turned off Dexter Street into the narrow unlit laneway bordered by high metal fences between houses.

The boy followed and said, I'm gunna check out your house.

David turned and said, How'd some mother raise such a loser?

The kid said, Now you've fuckin' done it. He rode up behind David and slammed the bike wheel into his legs.

David buckled for a moment then looped the groceries in one arm, fished the knife out of his pocket, unfolded the blade, and walked with the open blade against one leg. Behind him he heard the clatter of the bike as the kid dropped it in the laneway. David turned his head and the boy had a knife pointed at him.

David swung around and said, I've got a knife. He pointed it towards the boy. Leave me alone.

The boy laughed. You fuckin' scare me. Nobody disses my family.

Suddenly the boy was low in front of him; a blink of light came off the blade. He swung the blade in a flat arc at David's waist and David arched back like a cat, dropping the bag of groceries.

The boy lunged again, David leapt back, twisted and shouted, Fuck off.

The boy laughed and hissed, Scared now. You started this.

David circled with the knife, showed he wasn't bluffing. Fuck off. He swept the knife like a scythe and cut the boy. An accident. David backed away and said, I, I'm sorry. I…

The boy grabbed his cut arm, blood running through his fingers. Now you're fucked. The boy jumped forward, hacking with the knife, grabbed at David's sleeve with his free hand.

David skipped backwards. The boy circled and came at him.

David held his knife between them. The boy tripped over the bag of groceries and David's knife caught him in the throat.

The boy fell to his knees, rocking, gurgling, then onto his side, drawing long breaths, trying to get air. He crawled towards the road, then folded onto his side as if suffering terrible cramps. He dragged himself to the fence.

David stood back as blood gurgled into the laneway and watched the boy twist on the ground. Lights glimmered in houses. In the distance a dog barked. The rain had stopped.

The boy tried to pull in deep breaths, he started to shudder. He kicked at bushes in the laneway.

David was panting now, looking at the boy. Are you okay? He knelt and put his hand on the boy's arm.

David waited. The wild kicking stopped.

David watched the still boy for a time, he didn't know for how long, then grabbed his shopping and ran.

25

Nigel Plant arrives

The white circle of Nigel's torch fell on flattened grass. Cords of blood strung over concrete onto bushes.

Nigel turned to the others. Don't touch the bicycle. Spread out, search Dexter Street, the park, and both ends of the laneway.

Two uniformed men and three women shone torches over drips and smears where the boy had crawled towards the road, then twisted and dragged himself up against the fence.

Up and down Dexter Street in front and back yards they hunted. Neighbours stood in knots and talked quietly. Nigel spoke to men and women over fences in the laneway.

The air was sharp and clean. An orange cat peered from under a banksia. At the south end of the laneway, two officers crunched over stones into a grassy park flanked by black trunks of ironbarks and tan casuarinas; they searched for patches of damp and tracks matching the bicycle tyres, or weapons.

Nigel picked up a plastic bottle lying against the fence. Moisture leaked out of its neck. He sniffed alcohol in the lip of the bottle and shook his head.

Bloody kids.

26

Mountains

The road to the mountains was thin and gravelly through dark forests of owl trees. Chocolate-coloured bark, narrow-leafed peppermints, ribbon gums and brown barrel along the road to Mount Franklin. The Volvo straddled the rocky spine between the capital territory and New South Wales, potholes filled with standing water, naked woodland, high clean air. In the headlights he flushed a dozen yellow-tailed black cockatoos slow-flapping, squawking like rusty iron gates, flying off in the night. He pulled alongside a huddle of snow gums.

A slight breeze stirring through eucalypts, rattling their hard leaves like rosaries. A sugary scent wafting up from the earth. He lifted the shovel and plastic bag full of clothes off the back seat and searched with the torch for a bare place to dig. The stony ground was hard. He stabbed with the shovel and scraped and cut at three other places and knew it was no good. He tossed the plastic bag and shovel into the back seat and turned back down the track. At Two Sticks Road he drove the muddy one-lane track for ten minutes. On a steep bank under the road he found softer ground under a log and buried the bloody clothes and the knife, thinking about stupid criminals who tossed murder weapons into the first lake or river they found, the first spot police would search.

27

Aftermath

David lay in bed over most of two days waiting for the knock on the door. On Wednesday he took his first food and said to the empty room, Go to work. Act normal. Act like David.

That afternoon, two police officers came to the department. David's stomach dropped, cold and heavy as lead in his gut. David smiled in the hallway and noted the first officer's name tag – Nigel Plant.

The officers knocked on Sophie's door.

In his office, David wrote down the name, fighting paranoia and thinking about the boy in Dexter Street. He tried all afternoon to change his mood, let a tutorial run itself, his mouth dry, he said little. Students with their heads down drew graphs and copied notes. He leaned over shoulders, mumbled, tried to teach them how to record each trial in a notebook, but his speech lay deadened, his tongue thickened as if anaesthetised. He forgot in mid-sentence a needed word, a researcher's name, the point. He drifted and looked out the window at slender wrists of eucalypts, the pewter colour of the sky and the tutor in the room opposite laughing as she pointed with a wooden stick at a word on the board. Students talked and giggled. He turned his back and they muttered his name, or so he thought.

Mercifully, the two hours finished.

In the hallway, he passed Sophie Moss. Each looked the other way.

In his office he dropped a yellow pillow on the floor, stretched out, and slept. He drifted face down like a body in a muddy river until someone whispered 'Nigel Plant' in his dream and he slowly opened his eyes, rolled his head, and looked at the orange crack under the door. Shadows of feet drifting by. An anvil sat on his chest and blocked his breathing.

David stood and took three deep breaths. He watched himself from above and mumbled, What would David do? He leaned back in his chair and thought about this. How would David act? How do you look and act like David?

He walked to Tommy the Tech's room, settled his breathing, and opened the door. Daniel not in today?

Tommy's look showed that he knew something. No. He's still in bad shape about Emma leaving.

They were silent for a time, and David said, We had police in the building today.

Tommy kept his head down. Yeah. Tommy was quiet, milking the moment.

What's it about?

Some ex-husband tried to break into the Women's Shelter last night. Decided to retrieve his wife.

David thought about this, and said, Why didn't they visit Sophie at the shelter?

They?

The police.

Well, she's not at the shelter much and she's here today, isn't she? You know what she's like. People do things on Sophie's ticket in Sophie's time, where Sophie dictates, even the police.

David nodded, thought about this for a moment, and left.

28

Nigel Plant about the kid

Acting Superintendent Bill Scott leaned back in his chair and said, Talk to me about this stabbing.

Nigel stood in front of Bill's desk and said, Nothing yet.

Bill studied the open file. What else do we know about the kid?

He was a punk. Friends were punks. Single mother was a typical punk's mother, series of punk boyfriends.

So it was a neighbourhood kid, a gang thing.

Maybe. Some think so.

Bill looked up. Do we have a knife?

No. We checked drains along Dexter Street, bike paths, the park nearby, front and back yards, interviewed a dozen families.

The idiot still has it then.

Probably.

Find the knife, you find the stabber. Any names yet?

No. Mother's in bad shape, says she has no idea, no names. His friends have no idea. One fellow living nearby said he might have seen the kid that night or another night arguing with an older guy, thirty or so, riding his bike alongside this man.

Thirty's old?

It is to a kid.

Thirty years old means one of Mum's boyfriends or a stray uncle, maybe his dealer. Did you get a description?

Vague. The neighbour said he had a black baseball cap hanging from his belt, from a hook or something.

Bill thought about this. All right, follow it up. Find that knife. It'll be around.

We'll find him.

Bill closed the file and pushed it to the corner of his desk. How'd you get along with Sophie Moss?

Nigel smirked. How do you think?

Still blaming us?

We arrived at the shelter five minutes after the call. The husband was drunk, pounding on the door. He didn't get in. We arrested him. Workers at the refuge were fine, including the real director.

So what's Sophie's complaint? said Bill.

The husband shouldn't have been near the shelter.

Bill shook his head. That's our fault? AVO in place, he violates it. Nobody hurt, we arrest him, and that's not good enough. He shook his head again. Shit. Did she invite you in for tea and bickies?

Nigel stroked his red moustache and smiled. She was at the university. And no.

How'd you like to sit in that class once a week?

No need to. We've heard the lecture. Plenty of times.

Anyway, said Bill, she didn't make a formal complaint, that's something. You seem to know how to handle her.

Nigel shrugged.

Bill looked out the window. She doesn't like me.

Nigel watched him. Don't take it personally.

Okay. I won't take it personally. Keep me informed.

Will do, said Nigel.

Bill leaned back and stared out the window again, tapping his finger on the desk. Things are getting worse out there, aren't they?

Nigel nodded. Partly an increase in reporting rates.

Bill continued to drum his fingers on the desk. For what? For stabbings?

For domestics. Women call us more often than they used to.

Still, no politician wants to be king of a small town. They wanted their big city, didn't they? They got their big city and they got more crime. Bill drummed his fingers again.

There was quiet in the room and people were talking in the hallway. Voices faded as they passed.

Nigel stood and waited. Is that all, sir?

Looking out the window, Bill said, That's all.

29

Nigel Plant and Lisa Charles visit the Kellys

The marked car sat in the driveway. The tiny house was feebly attended, brick and fibro with a scabby lawn and a weedy garden stretched along one side.

Nigel killed the ignition and shook his head. This is the part we get that high salary for. What does the manual say?

The manual? said Lisa.

About asking the mother if her dead son had enemies.

Haven't you committed the manual to memory?

I can't remember a thing from the manual. At the academy my eyes would glaze over during role-plays. Half a page into the manual and I'd get the nods. Anyway, Mrs, uh, Brandy…what's her name again?

Mandy. Mandy Kelly. Bad pun.

Accident. Clever word play is too hard for a policeman. English at the academy gave me the nods too.

Lisa watched the house.

Name one case we studied, he said.

A stress manager had a neighbour with a barking dog. He knocked on the neighbour's door, argued with him, and knocked him unconscious with a flower pot.

I don't remember that one. And this isn't a barking dog, otherwise we'd be sniffing – sorry, I did it again – a lot less paperwork, fewer battles with the likes of Brandy.

It's Mandy. Have you spoken to the little brother?

No. She won't let me near him. When the cry went up around the neighbourhood, he ran into the laneway, found his brother dead, smeared with blood. He stood around the whole time I was there. Dead silent. Wouldn't speak to anyone.

The point of today's visit?

Bill thinks the kid'll speak to us at home. They refuse to come into town.

Where they from?

Queanbeyan.

Why didn't they stay in Queanbeyan?

Good point. To not love Queanbeyan is to not love life.

Let's go, she said. Lock the car.

This woman, uh, Randy –

Mandy. What's the brother's name?

Shannon.

The dead one? said Lisa

No. The dead one's Rodney. There's two boys. Shannon's about twelve, or maybe fourteen.

Apparently Mandy and young Shannon spent a few weeks in the Women's Shelter, hiding from him.

Hiding from who?

Hiding from Rodney.

The one who was killed?

That's right.

Nigel shook his head. People in this city don't understand how low-lifes stretch right across town, north to south and east to west. And they all know each other. Quite a few hate each other. Now she's broken-hearted and blaming the police for her son's death.

Yep.

He shook his head slowly. You couldn't make this stuff up. The woman gets beaten up, hides from him inside the shelter, then tells people the little thug was a saint all his life and the police should have protected him. The mysteries of the human heart.

I take it Dad's off the scene?

What do you think?

They locked the car and mounted the step. The curtains were drawn. Nigel knocked three times and heard rustling inside. The latch clattered and the door opened just enough to cast a blade of sunlight on the pasty face of a freckled boy.

What do you want? His voice was irritable, full of rancour and not frightened. Eyes were a cold shade of blue.

Are you Shannon? said Lisa. She smiled.

His eyes narrowed. What do you want?

Shannon, is it?

I said, what do you want?

Nigel leaned forward. Shannon, I don't know if you remember me. I'm Nigel Plant. This is Lisa Charles. Can we please come in?

A weak voice from the back room called, Who is it, Shanny?

Looking at Nigel then at Lisa, the boy said in a loud voice, Cops.

The springs of a bed screeched and slackened, the scrape of bare feet shuffling on bare wood to the door. Shannon backed into charred light and watched.

A shadow moved in front of him, then a pale round face similar to his. She squinted through the crack in the door; limp brown hair fell over one eye. Yes?

Hello, Mrs Kelly, said Nigel.

She said, You found him?

Mrs Kelly, this is Lisa Charles. Can we please come in for a minute?

Her sun-strained eyes were suspicious and reluctant. In the sliver of light, she regarded the officers. She was slow-thinking and careful, looking back into the room as though dreading what Shannon might do. She waited and stalled, thought about asking again what they wanted. She stared for a moment, then looked back into the darkness at Shannon's face.

With a faint moustache of perspiration on her upper lip, she said, Okay, come in.

She unhooked the safety latch and Lisa and Nigel walked past her into the sitting room. The smell of poor living came at them. Lisa tasted shit on her tongue and wanted to spit, tried breathing through her nose.

Mandy shut the door. It was too dingy to see. When their eyes adjusted, they saw dirty cream walls, a brown sofa, a television, coffee table, stereo, and two wooden chairs.

Thank you, said Lisa.

Mandy walked to a wooden chair and slumped with her hands twisted in her lap. Shannon had disappeared.

Nigel and Lisa stood in the middle of the room.

Lisa said, Do you mind if we sit down?

No, fine. She waved around the room at nowhere in particular.

They sat on opposite ends of the brown sofa against the wall. Lisa could see through to the kitchen, a wooden table and chairs, a muddy blind drawn over the window. Dirt lay in the cracks of the wooden floor. Cream wallpaper with faded roses came away at the seams, along the edges of shabby cupboards over the sink.

A framed photo of the two boys sat on the coffee table in the middle of the room. Shannon and Rodney were smiling.

Nigel and Lisa sat under a poster of Jimi Hendrix and nobody spoke. A soot-coloured pit bull with grey hairs in its muzzle waddled in stiffly from a back bedroom and banged its tail against Lisa's leg. Lisa didn't reach down, and she wondered why it hadn't barked when they arrived. Shannon followed the dog in and slumped in the doorway between the kitchen and sitting room with his knees under his chin, forming a triangle that blocked the way.

Mandy said, What is it?

Mrs Kelly, We've only got one lead so far. Two neighbours saw your son with a man about thirty, carrying a green shopping bag. He had a black baseball cap pinned to his belt. We haven't found him yet, but we're working on it. In the meantime, we'd like to follow up other leads.

Mandy's thin interlocking fingers were deep in her lap. She turned her head a little to the right, away from Shannon.

Slight redness crept into Shannon's face, as if the blood from Mandy's face had drained into his.

Mandy sighed and said, You're nowhere then.

Nigel said, We'd like to follow this lead, Mrs Kelly, but we have no idea how this man is connected to Rodney.

Mandy continued to look away.

Lisa said, We need to know if Rodney had other friends, or family. People who might know this man. Do you have other family in town?

Mandy shook her head. No.

None? said Lisa.

When she didn't answer, Lisa said, Mrs Kelly –

Shannon looked up from the kitchen doorway and growled, She said 'No.'

The look made Nigel shift in his seat. The dog wandered over and started to lick Shannon's face.

Barely parting her lips, Mandy said, We can't take any more. Just find him.

Nigel looked around the room, at an AC/DC poster on the wall by the kitchen door.

I'm sorry, said Lisa. We understand how difficult this is. There are no other friends or relatives close by who can help you?

That's what I said.

Mrs Kelly, Rodney was carrying a knife. Do you know why?

Mandy shook her head.

He would have known it was against the law. Did he talk to you about enemies, people he was afraid of?

She sighed again. Of course he carried a knife.

Lisa opened her hands in front of her. I'm not sure what you mean.

I mean he had enemies, and they were permanent. They all carry knives.

Lisa nodded slowly. We'd appreciate any names you can give us.

Mandy shook her head. You people are so stupid.

Lisa waited, and said, I beg your pardon.

They're not afraid of you. They'd be over here the minute you left, banging in my front door. Baseball bats aren't against the law.

So there was some trouble.

They didn't knife him.

His enemies?

They weren't the ones.

Nigel said, How can you be so sure?

Mandy shrugged. That's enough. Leave us alone. She turned to Shannon slouched in the kitchen doorway.

Lisa said, Mrs Kelly, are there any names of enemies you can give us?

Not till the sun grows cold.

Lisa squinted. Pardon?

Mandy looked at Shannon and said, Leave us now.

From the doorway Shannon glared. He didn't blink.

Mrs Kelly, if you don't mind, I'd like to ask Shannon a few questions.

Mandy stared at her. So ask.

Looking down at him, Lisa said, I understand that you found your brother, after you heard sirens.

He looked at his mother, eyes full of hate, put his arm around the dog and looked at the floor.

Did you talk to anyone in the laneway? After you ran there?

He shook his head.

Shannon, your brother was carrying a knife.

He stared, said nothing. In the quiet, Lisa heard a car rush by.

Through tight lips the boy hissed, So?

Lisa waited, saw he was about to detonate. Okay, Shannon. We can talk another time. She turned to Mandy. Is there any possibility you could help us with a list?

Mandy looked back across the room at Shannon on the floor.

Shannon jammed his feet in the doorway, kicking now, and shook his head.

No, she said.

It'd be helpful if Shannon came down to the office some time, said Lisa. It won't take long. We have CCTV vision from Jamison. There's a blurry shot of a man at the payphone. Shannon could look at it, see if he recognises this man.

Mandy shook her head and said, Shanny stays with me. Her voice was flat.

Out of the corner of her eye, Lisa saw Nigel watching her. She looked over at him. I think Mrs Kelly can decide what's best.

Shannon sat wedged in the door jamb, his arm around the dog.

Lisa leaned towards him. Shannon?

Mandy glared. That's enough. No more.

Can I –

Shannon stood up from the doorway, walked over to the couch with the dog following and leaned close into Lisa's face. She said, No more.

Nigel pushed an open hand towards him. Okay, son. Settle down.

Lisa said calmly, Shannon, we're sorry about what's happened. We're doing our best to find the man or boy who killed your brother. She turned to Mandy. We'll go now. Please tell us if there's anything we can do. A formality, Lisa knew, because there was nothing they could do.

They stood, let themselves out, and backed the car into the street.

30

Nigel Plant visits Sophie Moss

Nigel knocked again.

A voice from the other side of the door said, Come in.

Sophie squinted at the computer. Tapping on the keyboard, she said, What is it? She looked up. Oh, Nigel. You're here.

Nigel stood in the middle of the room and she turned her face back to the screen. Stuffy air in the room smelled sharply of garlic and Nigel didn't know if it was body odour or Sophie's breath.

He looked at his watch. Am I early?

She didn't look up. What?

You said two o'clock.

Oh, right. Workplace collaboration between health professionals. Conference paper. Deadline for participants 4 p.m. tomorrow.

He waited.

She typed for another two minutes then rolled backwards away from the computer. Right.

Nigel said, Mandy Kelly.

Can you believe it? That kid bashing her –

Kid?

Rodney. Sophie shook her head. Come on, who are we talking about here? Didn't you come about Rodney?

Yes. Sorry.

Another woman you didn't protect. Mandy Kelly. Police said, 'He's a minor.' Well, he beat her up, used to take a knife into the bathroom when she was in the shower, push the curtain aside, poke her, play sick games.

Nigel nodded and wrote in his notebook.

And you lot recommended counselling. What is the matter with you? Counselling. Sit the mother and son down in a room at Relationships Australia as if it's some family dispute. Counselling. Treat the participants as neutrals. Come to a settlement. Can you believe it? Counselling. You should have locked him up the first time he beat her up. Domestic violence is domestic violence. Bashing isn't a family dispute. The sooner this government wakes up to these fourteen or fifteen-year-old thugs, the sooner conditions will improve for women in this city. Lock them up. Rodney should have been in jail.

Nigel stared. He's dead.

I know, I know. I'm sorry. But it doesn't surprise me. Crowd he ran with. He started a fight, some other kid finished it. What goes around comes around.

Nigel, standing and writing, said, We were wondering, Sophie, if you could tell us anything about that crowd he ran with, and how you know he started a fight.

She jerked back in her chair as if it was a stupid question. Mandy said there were gangsters in that neighbourhood. Her little thug was happy when Mandy came and stayed with us. Meant he had the house to himself. Perfect. Sophie pushed her fingers through her spiky hair, pulled a Tupperware container off the shelf and began eating with her fingers. Mandy brought the young one with her. What's his name?

Younger brother's called Shannon. Shanny. Inconsolable over losing his big brother. Nigel looked up from the container to Sophie's eyes, trying not to be distracted by her smacking. We tried to get a list of friends from Mandy, but she wasn't forthcoming.

Of course not. They'd be around the next day with clubs.

Well, we still need to find the person or persons who killed him, find them with or without Mandy's help.

Sophie turned away and continued to type with one hand, leaving grease on the keyboard. The computer screen lit her face in the dim room, made her black crew-cut glimmer. Keep talking, she said. I'll just finish this. We're multitaskers.

Nigel stood without speaking, shifted his weight to the other foot.

She ran her fingers through her black stubble again, hoop earrings rocking. She said, Construction of knowledge is the engine of this cancer. Nearly done here. She typed another sentence then said, I teach students to subvert the dominant paradigm. Then I get visits from the David Chesses of this world.

Through slitted eyes, Nigel shook his head. Pardon?

Sophie was licking her fingers. She pointed over her shoulder down the hall. The rapist's friend tried to muzzle me. Muzzle him if you want to do something useful.

Rapist's friend?

Why do you think it's so bad in this city? Hierarchical patriarchy in the police department, patriarchy in this university. Nobody speaks up for the oppressed. She put her fingers into the Tupperware box and crunched more salad.

Sophie, uh…

Come on, Nigel, out with it.

I'd like to get back to Rodney Kelly.

Look. I'm sorry the kid's dead. Terrible business. Terrible for Mandy. No doubt she'll paint him as a victim and, technically speaking, I suppose he is. But he brought this onto himself, sad as it is. Look. Maybe it's for the better. He'd grow into a woman-hater and abuser. His mates cut short a blossoming career of woman-killing.

Nigel waited, but she seemed to be done. Okay, thanks, Sophie.

Nigel left and walked down the hall. He stopped and read Dr David Chess on the door, regarded the name for a moment, scribbled the name in his notebook and left.

31

Airports

It was an accident. David noticed the speakers' list for the 5th Annual Conference on Comparative Psychology to be held at the University of Hawaii. Emma was presenting a paper that she and David had submitted seven months before. He'd forgotten about it, but thought, If they lock me away, I can see Emma one last time. David asked Daniel Bentham, but Daniel hadn't seen or heard from his wife in a month.

Ring me if you find her, said Daniel.

I will.

At the airport, David thought, I can test what they know. If they suspect me of a killing, they'll never allow me out of the country. They'll stop me at the border.

At Mascot, he waited with his bags inside the international terminal, long queues, people staring at palm-held devices. He slumped in a row of chairs and closed his eyes. He opened them and two security guards stood in front of him.

David Chess?

He blinked, eyed them both. Yes.

Can you please come with us?

He slowed his breathing, forced a smile and said, Sure.

He didn't say, What's this about? He didn't say, Is something wrong? He was compliant, friendly.

In a small windowless room, a security guard sat across the desk from him and offered him a chair. A Federal Police officer stood near the door.

The security guard said, Dr Chess, can I see your passport please?

David slipped it from its folder and handed it, open, to the officer.

The officer scrutinised it and said, Where were you born?

Adelaide.

The room was quiet with muffled talk from the hall outside.

Date?

David gave it.

The officer nodded. I see what's happened here?

David waited.

The officer said, There's a David Chess with the same birthday. But he was born in Adelaide Lead, a town in Victoria, different year, and the computer dropped the Lead, left us with two David Chesses from Adelaide. Dumb beasts, computers.

As David watched him, the officer was distracted by the computer screen and David's passport.

What are the chances, the officer said, that another David Chess would be flying to America on the same day? He shook his head and handed back the passport.

David said, You tell me.

The officer shook his head, Wouldn't read about it. Then he looked up. Thanks, Dr Chess. That'll be fine.

David blinked. That's it?

The officer nodded. That's it. If this happens again, just remember there are two of you.

David stood, thanked them and walked into the hall. Nice trick, he thought. They're watching me, toying with me. He sat in the same row of seats and thought about this.

Two hours later, on the plane, he was calm again. He buckled the seat belt and remembered how the scent of Emma's skin would lift him to a state of foolishness, and the stink of the woman sitting next to him made him want to vomit. Waves came off her and burnt his nose. Standing in line, the woman smelled like a male ferret. He stood back and made space. Then he boarded the plane, praying she would be far away, and she arrived, jammed and fought a too-big case into the overhead locker, buckled herself into the seat next to him.

Fourteen hours of this, he thought. While the cabin crew readied the plane there was a blast of BO each time she raised her arm to fiddle with the screen on the back of the seat. She was defiling and sharply offensive. He turned his head away.

It worsened during the flight and he reached up and twisted the air stream down onto himself, freshened a bubble around him. He reached up again and twisted the other nozzle onto the woman to blow the foul air back. She folded her arms and rubbed her hands together, maybe hoping that David would notice and take pity. He opened the air duct more. The woman asked the flight attendant for another blanket and she covered herself and folded her arms and tucked into a ball for seven hours while David lay dreaming about Emma.

The woman didn't say a word.

The captain interrupted the film. David slid the metal buckle into the slot and watched the scattered lights of Honolulu. Hydraulics grumbled, wheels folded down and locked and tyres yelped on tarmac.

He was on a tropical island with Emma.

At 2 a.m., in a ragged grey hall, he stood in a snaking queue. Passengers unfolded passports, signed declarations, looking wide-eyed and honest at the slow-moving, thick-bodied officers who tried to pick smugglers, American flags stitched on their sleeves. David hid his fear, made eye contact with Border Patrol and smiled. They let him pass.

David waded eyeball-deep through unwashed travellers, waited for the chute to cough up his baggage, watching for Emma's blonde head, searching the cafe, dragging his bags up steps and stopping at the top. Scanning the crowd.

Outside, the saccharine breath of Honolulu caught in his throat.

The cabby had an open smile and stood closer than needed. It'll fit in the trunk, he said, and dropped David's suitcase into the boot of a giant black Lincoln Continental.

David opened the driver's side door, and the driver laughed. David shook his head, walked to the other side.

As the Lincoln rolled onto the freeway, David said, I need a room for two nights. Somewhere close.

The Lincoln sizzled down the wet freeway, wipers sloshing water off the windscreen. Ocean wind beat against palm trees in front of low-roofed houses. Rooster tails smoked under fenders.

Waikiki if you like, said the cabby. Yeah, Waikiki Beach. Close enough. And safe, very safe. Lots of police to protect rich white people.

Sounds fine.

Coral Reef Blue Lagoon's a good place. I take many people to the Coral Reef Blue Lagoon. Two blocks from the beach.

Quiet?

Oh yes. Very quiet. No people on the beach at night.

Good, he said. I need quiet. David looked out the side window.

Nobody else swam in the sea at midnight. Moon-washed trees lined the beach. Scavenging gulls cried and spun in a cluster near street lamps. Bats flitted through shadows. Mountains at the centre of the island stood jagged and black. Under a silver dusting of stars, he floated with salt on his lips.

Canberra memories of the scent of eucalypt, smooth-flanked brittle gums in warm rain. Emma walked ahead of him past a storm-ruined piece of ground on Black Mountain. They lay on a bed of soft grass under a tree, slept for a time in the winter sun, and Emma curled into him for half an hour, tucked her warm face into his, kissed the salt off his skin and whispered, I love you.

She woke and raised herself over him, came down with her lips on his.

Coppery sun dropped into the hills.

She kissed the side of his mouth and murmured and touched his cheek with the back of her hand. Then she stood and said, We need to go, and she waited for him to stand. Race you down. She kissed him again and dashed down the hill, eyes straight ahead through bushes and trees with David following.

Emma ran with David in the Honolulu night as he floated in the sea. Warm sea curled round him like a cat.

32

Honolulu

A different light filled the window. David rose, sipped coffee and showered.

The taxi carried him under cerulean sky past couples, brown men and women from pineapple plantations caught out in the crucifying sun.

At the university he stood in yet another queue and lifted a conference programme from a stack, and a cotton bag with pens, writing paper, name badge, a complementary glossy black cup with 5th Annual Conference on Comparative Psychology – University Of Hawaii written in gold. The programme listed Dr Emma Bentham for 11 a.m. tomorrow morning. Until then he would avoid faces he knew, and avoid his own.

A blonde head moved through the crowd and he elbowed past a cluster of people following the head down the corridor, slipped between bodies, half-running, skidded around a corner, wanted to yell out. He shoved people aside and turned another corner but the woman was gone.

In the lecture hall, he stood in the doorway and scanned the backs of heads until lights dimmed and he had to sit down. There was little new in the first two papers. The audience was mesmerised by the first speaker's crippling stammer. During his analysis of facial asymmetry and mate choice in baboons, he stopped dead in mid-sentence, twitched his head and pried the defiant word out of the corner of his mouth – Animals with l-l-l-long generational times are exposed to m-m-many years of opportunities for m-m-m-mutations. The spat-out word ricocheted around the room.

The second speaker, from England, showed slides of herself sweating in the jungle in khaki shorts and a white singlet, contemplating Bonobos through Leica binoculars. Her plum-coloured nipples rose and fell and moved sideways inside her linen shirt as she tapped at the screen with a stick and left the electronic pointer on the table. The audience followed her nipples and missed crucial points about tool use, female alliances, and joint care of offspring.

Midway through her talk, David stood, let the seat bottom squeak and slap, and left. He circled the foyer, hunted the courtyard, the café, out near the swimming pool, and returned to the café and bought a coffee. In the corner of the foyer, he stretched out on two chairs.

A man in a brown suit walked up and stood in front of him. Dr Chess?

David looked up. Yes.

The speaker was a short, colourless man, the sort of man you wouldn't notice in the street. He pushed his heavy black glasses onto the bridge of his nose and tried to smile. Dr Chess, my name's Bruce Dewey. I'm in charge of the conference program.

David stared into his coffee. Congratulations, Bruce.

Mind if I sit down?

David nodded at the chair opposite. Go ahead.

Bruce sat, paused and watched him. When David continued to stir his coffee, Bruce said, I noticed you were in the same department as Emma Bentham.

David stared at him.

Bruce cleared his throat and waited for a response. When there was none, Bruce said, Uh, we expected her, but it's 2 p.m. and she's a no-show. No reply to our emails. We're not sure what to do. Causes some organisational problems.

I'll bet it does.

Never had this sort of thing before. People usually let us know, cancel, give us a phone call. Do you know where she might be?

No idea.

David wrapped his hands around the warm coffee and sat back, looked away from Bruce Dewey and fought the inclination to shift chairs as the man breathed heavily. His breath was rotten like a worried dog fed liver that morning.

Dewey folded his arms across his chest and said, We don't like to drop a person from the programme until we're certain she's not coming. She registered seven months ago.

David shrugged. She's not there either.

Pardon? What do you mean not there?

At the department. Nobody has seen her for a month.

Bruce shook his head. Oh my. I see. Bruce was edgy, looking over his shoulder, then back at David. We had a meeting this afternoon, Dr Chess, and your colleague Sophie Moss is here. She volunteered to give the paper.

Great.

Problem is, she's raised some allegations about you. Bruce paused, and watched David. When David continued to stir his coffee, Bruce said, Dr Chess, we've had a letter from a lawyer in Canberra, in Australia. Solicitors they're called out there, aren't they?

Yes, solicitors or lawyers. What's this about, Bruce?

Dr Chess, they seem concerned.

Lawyers are trained to fake concern.

They claim that based on the joint abstract you submitted to the committee, the ideas in your paper belong to someone else.

As David eyed him, Bruce looked relieved, as though he had practised the sentence for hours in the mirror that morning, and now it was over.

Belong to someone else? What are we talking about here, Bruce?

The letter said, in so many words, that your paper *Modelling Workplace Goal-Setting: What Can We Learn From Comparative Psychology?* with your co-authors, Dr Emma Bentham and Sophie Moss, isn't your work. Is that correct?

The names are correct.

Anyway, the letter said that if you attend the presentation of this paper, Sophie Moss will take legal action against you and, frankly, she might take legal action against us too.

David looked up from his coffee. Nonsense.

Well, Dr Chess, we don't really know that now, do we? We don't know if she's bluffing.

She is.

Well, it wasn't just Dr Moss. She directed lawyers in her own department to carry through. Your own department. She said her department would back her up. And she said the computer programme used in the paper belongs to Dr Moss.

David wrapped his hands around the coffee cup and sat back, looked away from Bruce Dewey and fought the inclination to shift away as the man breathed heavily through a stained moustache.

Look, Bruce. Sophie's department is my department. Somebody's made a mistake.

Dewey folded his arms over his chest. This is a litigious country, Dr Chess. There's no mistake.

My collaborator, Dr Bentham, acquired the data from Sophie Moss. Sophie gave it to her. Emma Bentham and I wrote the paper.

Fine, Dr Chess. Where is Dr Bentham?

David stared at him, smiling faintly. I told you. I'm not sure.

What do you mean you're not sure?

How many meanings are there for 'I'm not sure'?

Bruce shook his head a little. Just a bit odd, isn't it? Tell you what. You give us Dr Bentham's phone number in Australia and we'll call her.

Can't do that either.

Why not?'

Haven't got it.

Neither do we. There's no phone number on the paper. Bruce tried to look baffled, practising the tactics he'd been taught for dealing with liars. I'm a little confused, Dr Chess. Dr Moss's lawyers are lying, directed by Sophie Moss to lie, and there is no co-author to back up your story. What am I missing here?

Doesn't look good, does it?

I'm sorry, Dr Chess, it doesn't look good. I'm afraid we can't allow you to be present during the session.

Look, I realise there's a cultural abyss here, Bruce, so I'll try to use words we can both understand. Does cowardice mean anything to you?

Bruce was nervous, like an otter, squirming, looking over his shoulder, then back at David. We had a meeting this morning, Dr Chess. He pushed his glasses back up onto his nose, At length we discussed this, and we decided to alter the program. Sophie Moss is sole presenter.

David nodded. So I came here for nothing.

Well, that's a little harsh. I'm sorry you feel that way. It's quite a good program.

David shook his head again. No fighters for justice in the US any more, except in action movies.

Well, uh, the difference is that real life is full of lawyers.

Yes, well, real life *is* full of lawyers, Bruce. Rather like flooding the world with dysentery.

Bruce shook his head. Look, Dr Chess, sorry if I'm being presumptuous, but ex-research partners in revenge mode can kick like a mule. She's damned angry at you.

David sighed. That's none of your business, is it?

Bruce raised the palms of his hands. Sorry, sorry, forgive me. You're right, it's none of my business. But you're an intelligent man, you can understand that Dr Moss is shooting bullets at you, and she could miss and put a hole in me.

Great metaphor, Bruce, sort of urban American, isn't it? And, of course, I understand your position. You're a shivering spaniel frightened of a rolled-up newspaper.

Dr Chess —

I didn't steal anyone's data.

I…

And, Bruce, try to educate yourself about oral hygiene. The basics.

His eyebrows knotted. What?

Especially on days when you know you're going to be frightened.

Frightened?

You have uncommonly bad breath. Try another brand of mouthwash.

Bruce covered his mouth and sat backward. He waited and David didn't speak.

David stood and looked down at him. Thanks, Bruce.

David walked out, turned and saw Bruce sitting alone next to David's untouched coffee with a tired look on his face. He dropped the conference program in the bin.

33

Zoo

He pushed through turnstiles at the Honolulu Zoo, studying coins in his hand, trying to remember which were quarters, nickels and dimes.

The smiling girl at the counter said, I've seen more of these than you have, and lifted three coins from his open palm.

Under red flowers covering a fat-trunked tree, he spread the map over a bush. Bonobos were at the far side, near Paki Avenue.

A woman held the hand of a little girl and the girl watched David. She huddled close to her mother's leg. He looked behind him and saw two men in suits. He knew he was being followed. He rushed down the path, eyes hooded, around a rock wall, and was stopped by a yellow barricade that said 'Closed to the public'.

Zoo attendants in khaki slacks and short sleeves ran through a gate in the African display. He slid sideways around the yellow barricade, crept towards them, but he couldn't see what they hid. He looked behind him and the two men were gone. Further along they had blocked the road with a second yellow barricade that said 'No Entry', and had erected a hessian screen around a dry moat. The attendants rushed about and didn't notice David as he edged around the second yellow barricade and watched them scurry with ropes and bags, down the cemented rock wall into the moat and back up the rock wall again.

Two men on top hauled on ropes tied to a bulge covered with canvas. It slid out from under the cover, a tawny carcass with spiral liquorice-coloured horns, a rope looped around its throat. The antelope skated out head first on its side, neck stretched by the rope, jerking up the wall onto a wooden plank. He looked at the antelope's face and dead black eyes, and thought about the boy.

On top of the moat, two attendants laid the canvas over the antelope body next to a parked van. The antelope, he guessed, had fallen into the rock moat and broken its back. The attendants would have killed it with a rifle shot to the brain and set up a subterfuge to shield the death from the public. They lowered the tailgate, lifted and swung the carcass into the back, and closed it. Blood dripped from the antelope's mouth onto the path.

He thought, We're all assassins. He stood wondering why crimes were so badly conceived and concealed, so easily detected. People were caught out because of a failure of willpower, or a failure of reason at critical moments.

The attendants jumped into the van and drove away. David had glimmerings of the trouble he was in. Police would describe him as a loner, paranoid, troubled. But nobody knew him, except Emma. And Emma was gone.

They would catch him in Honolulu, or maybe in Sydney, and he would be alone.

34

David reports back

David shut the Volvo door, stepped onto the Ainslie porch, and knocked twice. He listened, knocked again, then pushed the door open and watched it swing.

Daniel? Waiting a few seconds. Daniel?

A small voice came from a back room, Here.

He found Daniel hunched in the dark.

Daniel raised his face. He'd aged a year in the week that David was away. How was your trip? he said.

David shrugged. Not so good.

Did you see her? The naked walls gave Daniel's voice a hard echo, like a forgotten child in an empty cave.

Bad conference.

Daniel raised his eyebrows. But was Emma there?

No. Sorry.

Daniel slumped in the chair. He was unwashed and smelt like dirty feet. Daniel shook his head, Sorry. She's angry at both of us. Not sure why. Somehow we've disappointed her.

I went to the zoo.

Well, that's something.

Pleasant enough.

Why are women so vindictive?

David looked down. He knew too much about Emma and Daniel's union built on stupidity. Maybe each failed relationship with Emma was unique, or maybe in Emma's eyes Daniel and David were the same weak-willed man.

David said, Do you think Eddie Flannery had anything to do with this?

Eddie? Why Eddie? He helped us. Things would've been worse without Eddie.

I don't see how things could be much worse.

Daniel frowned, Why?

Why did she leave? said David

Daniel shifted as if his backbone rubbed on the wicker chair, then he stared into a corner of the room. Can't do much about that now.

They sat without speaking, and after a minute, David said, I need to go.

Yeah. Come again sometime. Daniel's voice was thin. He opened the door.

David paused and turned to him and said, Tell me something.

Sure, what?

Things have changed, haven't they?

Daniel thought about this. I guess so.

Kids carry knives.

Yeah, well, tradesmen carry knives.

Kids carry knives to stab other kids.

Yeah, well, I guess.

Daniel reached out and touched David's sleeve. Drop by in a week or so.

I will.

He walked to the car.

35

Bill Scott's vengeance

Bill Scott telephoned Carolyn's parents in Ainslie. He drove to Ainslie and took his wife aside, poked his finger into her chest, bruised her and said, Think about what you're doing. You're making a serious mistake.

At work he was hounded by demons. Vengeance clouded his decisions, burned his eyelids, buried him in smoky nightmares in the middle of the day. Ghosts shouting in the middle of the room, grinning from corners, tainted his aptitude for a job he'd done easily for seven years. Dreams of vengeance made him sweat.

He decided to break her, make her fold. His solicitor wrote punishing letters and Bill increased the number of phone calls, visited the Ainslie house more often. He would stand on the porch and watch Carolyn shudder and acquiesce to his threats. Then return to his office and breathe easily. Done.

Then she'd recant, as if Bill had never visited and shouted and stabbed his finger into her chest, or paid his solicitor to write menacing letters. How could this happen?

Standing in uniform on the top step in Ainslie, he demanded to see his daughters, resting his thumb on the butt of his pistol. Carolyn shivered, head down. She agreed.

But after he left, Carolyn recanted.

Bill exploded. What gives you the right to stand against me? You've got some nerve.

He asked around, gained intelligence, traced Carolyn's movements to Eddie Flannery.

Carolyn drove to Eddie Flannery's office in Braddon, crying and frightened. She sat on the floor in the corner with her face on her knees.

Eddie promised her victory and sent her back out to stand against Bill.

36

Bill Scott about Eddie Flannery

It's illegal, said Bill.

Nigel hesitated. I'm not so sure.

Bill studied the open file. Tell me again. What do we know about him?

We questioned Flannery because two husbands said he had sex with their wives, then brainwashed them into leaving home.

Bill closed the file and pushed it to the corner of his desk. That can't be legal.

It's legal when our questioning comes to nothing.

How many times did you question him?

Three times.

And nothing came of it?

Nigel stroked his red moustache. That's what I'm telling you. The women refuse to file complaints.

He causes women to leave home, said Bill, and nobody complains.

That's right.

You're telling me you can't charge him with anything?

Yes, sir, that's what I'm telling you.

Bill knitted his brow and looked out the window. Maybe I should see him.

You can try, sir.

I can do more than try.

But I wouldn't if I were you.

Wouldn't what?

See Eddie Flannery.

Why not?

With respect, sir, he might lodge a complaint against you, claim that you've got an agenda.

This fellow's jerking us around. I'm a policeman with responsibilities to the people in this city. I'll pay him a visit.

Nigel gazed at him steadily. Be careful, sir.

Careful. Of what? You sound worried.

He knows his rights. Boys from Belfast live on borders, sneak around dark neighbourhoods and cut up police without getting caught. They're practised.

Damn it. This isn't Ireland. He won't cut up this policeman. What's he like to talk to?

Nigel smiled. Let's put it this way. If I had Eddie's banter and talent with words, I wouldn't be on this pitiful salary.

Bill leaned back and stared out the window, tapping his finger on the windowsill. How does a man who lures women away from their husbands, then rapes them, how does a man like that escape punishment? And poor husbands paying his salary. Do you realise that? How does a thing like that happen?

Nigel shrugged. Bigger balls than us.

Bill stared out the window and drummed his fingers on the sill. We'll see about that. He drummed his fingers harder. We'll just see about that. He looked up at Nigel and said, I've seen his type before.

There was quiet in the room and they looked away from each other. Two officers walked by in the hallway, talking; their voices faded as they passed.

Nigel broke the silence. With respect, sir, I don't think you have seen his type before.

37

Bill Scott visits Eddie Flannery

Bill arrived in uniform.

The office door fell open and Eddie smiled and said, Bill, come in.

Bill stepped past him and eyed the space above Eddie's desk. A line of six diplomas spanned the wall – from the Southern Cross School of Hypnotherapy, the Life Skills Institute, the University of the New Age, each framed in wood and metal edge, some with gold inlay. The room smelt of Pine O Cleen.

Eddie looked up at Bill, shook his hand then turned and sat behind his desk. What's it like out there? said Eddie.

The weather, you mean?

Yes. We don't get much sign of it in this tomb.

Fairly warm, pleasant.

Bill watched Eddie's hands and eyes and body shape for signs of fear. Eddie motioned Bill to a chair opposite his desk, and Bill sat and removed his cap.

Eddie said, What can we do for you today?

Bill cleared his throat, looked around the room and back at Eddie. I understand that Officer Plant came to see you a couple of times.

Eddie smirked. More than twice, Bill. You should know that. Should be five visits on your file.

Yes, well.

Bill noticed Eddie's stubby fingers, as if all were sliced off by a buzz saw.

Eddie opened his hands and said, You do keep files down there?

Of course. I don't want this to descend into anything too formal, that's all. Maybe it was five visits.

I enjoy Nigel's visits. He's welcome any time. Not the sort of fellow who's gunna come along and test you on your Nietzsche now, is he?

Well, I wouldn't know about that.

And you came all this way to talk about Nigel?

Well, it's not that far to come, Eddie, and you know why Nigel made five visits.

Remind me.

Bill thumbed his cap. To discuss your work.

My work.

Well, I looked over the files, Eddie, and I…

Eddie shook his head. Let's not waste time here.

Bill stared. Pardon.

The purpose of your visit.

Bill leaned back and gripped his cap. What?

The purpose of your visit, Bill. Eddie was smiling and calm.

Meaning?

Your wife, Carolyn.

Bill was quiet. He took a breath. As he exhaled, it whistled through his nose. Now, you listen to me. He pointed.

No, Bill, you listen. You came to talk about your wife's visits to my office. Why not come out and say it?

Bill folded one arm over his chest and gripped his elbow. You brought this up, not me. You want to talk about my wife, go ahead.

Eddie shook his head. Sorry. Bound by confidentiality.

You…

If you wanted to talk about my general work, you'd've brought along a friend, probably Nigel Plant.

Bill watched him.

Anyway, now that you're here, criminality's a little hobby of mine. Let's talk about criminals.

Red anger filled Bill's cheeks. He shifted in his chair and transferred the cap to his other hand. Eddie noticed a wet thumbprint on the rim.

The other night, said Eddie, I was reading about serial killers. You know the key psychological feature driving serial killers?

Bill didn't reply.

Fantasies.

Bill nodded. I heard something like that.

The killer has vibrant fantasies about killing and maiming people for months, even years. He battles them, tries to drown his fantasies in the bathtub, toss them over the fence to hungry dogs, rallies Christian teaching against these terrible visions, but the visions win. The killer tires of his own feeble tactics and succumbs to his fantasies.

Succumbs?

Yes. Kills somebody. Fulfils his fantasies.

I'm not interested in talking about serial killers.

What about alcoholics?

We deal with alcoholics, yes.

Eddie turned his head slightly and watched Bill with one eye. So do I. Women tossed against walls by alcoholic men, driven to the hospital, stitched up by doctors. Broken.

Bill sat forward, What's the point of all this?

Alcoholics don't get married, Bill, they take hostages.

He stared.

How come this city allows drunks and wife-beaters to carry guns?

Bill leaned forward and pointed again. Now you be careful, son. Bill's other fist was tight in his lap. You're only listening to one side of the story.

Okay, Bill. Tell me your side of the story. Tell me you never came home drunk. You never beat her up.

Bill stood and glared down on the little man.

Eddie smiled, looked up and said, You learned that trick at police college.

Bill's nostrils flared.

You know, said Eddie, hate does interesting things to the physiology. Pupils dilate to make us look menacing. Heads tip back to protect the nape of our necks from sword blades. It's all unconscious.

Fucking bog Irish.

Now that's disappointing, Bill. Police showing open bigotry. Eddie smiled. Let's not do this. I'm happy to hear your side of the story.

I took out a restraining order to keep her away from my house.

Eddie chuckled. Conventional trick.

Trick?

Sure. Carolyn tries to retrieve her clothes, you punish her by not letting her in. A little childish, but effective.

The law's not childish.

Well, I don't know. The men in your department still need adult supervision.

You little Irish prick, nobody talks to me that way.

Report me, Bill.

I will. And I'll charge you with –

Charge me with what, Bill?

We'll find something.

I've seen this before. Look, you're annoyed. And I understand that. You're seeking reprisal. You know, I heard stories about you. Your aptitude for solving problems came from your skills at emotional detachment. Emotion never clouded your reasoning because you had none. You were a calculating machine, a chess player. Cops trusted you. You got ahead, kept your hunger for vengeance in check, caged it for seven or eight years. But now it's breaking loose, Bill, starting to seduce you, offering you sweets, little rewards.

You're talking nonsense.

Hatred's off its lead, Bill. You and your vengeance are an item again. Tight. A team. And she'll finish you.

Staring, Bill said, You evil little bastard. You lure wives into this room, pry secrets out of them. Take $100,000 a year for spouting self-righteous clichés that I could read for $4 in *Woman's Day*. You're a disgrace.

Eddie smiled. You're right there, Bill. A disgrace. But let's not get ahead of ourselves. A night of judgement is coming.

Bill realised he'd been standing over Eddie for some minutes. Eddie continued to look up and smile.

Bill said, We'll meet again.

Eddie smiled and said, Oh, I'm sure we will.

Bill turned and left.

38

Daniel Bentham angry

David arrived and found Daniel changed and drinking. The sink was full of empties.

Daniel sat in his chair, tipped up the bottle and swallowed, and said with his throat full of bubbles, Emma. I hate the name.

I wish I could do more to help you, said David.

Help me? A glimmer of hostility ranged over his face. Then kill Eddie Flannery. If I had the bastard here, he pointed at the floor, I'd spill his blood.

David was taken back. Eddie gave out some patently bad advice, I know.

Daniel shook his head, anger in his face. You don't know the half of it, mate. He glared damp-eyed at David, sniffed and rubbed the back of his fist under his nose. Siding with her's one thing, fucking her's another, isn't it? Fucking her is siding with her a little too much.

David jerked backwards. Eddie had sex with Emma?

I trusted every word out of his slippery mouth. We'd go in there, you see. He was on my side, he was Christ listening to every word coming from this poor sinner. Saw us together at first, listening and nodding like they do, getting you to spill your guts. Then he saw us apart. Always listening. Decided we should split, amicably of course. We'd never make it, he said, so we should split and lessen the torment. His very words.

Daniel drained the bottle, set the empty on his knee, looked at the floor. Then Eddie saw me alone, twice a week listening, my great buddy, my one true friend and brother. Sometimes I didn't even pay him.

But he had sex with Emma?

Daniel nodded. I know the signs. I was in denial. My great true friend, giving me free advice about Emma and screwing her twice a week on his office floor. Daniel slumped deeper into the wicker chair and stared past David, as if he could see Emma and Eddie in the room.

David folded his hands tightly around the bottle, stifled vomit rising in his throat. Eddie can be charged with having sex with a client.

Daniel was slow thinking, but his eyes quickened. She'd deny it.

But did she actually tell you?

Daniel shook his head in anger. It's all come back to me. I've been thinking about the day she left. She wanted something from me, but I couldn't work out what.

David said, Exactly what did she say?

She said she had a lover. And I said, 'I know. David.' And she said, 'Not any more.'

This hammered inside David's chest.

I settle the whole thing in my brain, and for a day or so learn to live with it. Then pictures come back into my head and I go for the gun. I'll kill him.

David's mouth was dry. Tell the police. Don't do anything silly.

Daniel's lips tight and pale. Do anything silly? *Silly?* Telling the police. Now that's silly. It's no police matter.

Counsellors are licensed. It is a police matter. Tell the Board of Counsellors.

The wicker chair squeaked and Daniel folded his arms with the empty beer against one shoulder. He pointed at David with neck of the bottle. Now you know.

Eddie's hurt other people.

Daniel stood and opened another beer, took a long swig. A dog barked over the road.

David stood and said, I need to go.

Daniel sat with the beer on his knee. Bits of wicker lay under his chair. He said to his shadow on the floor, You go see him.

What?

Daniel said, like a pleading child. He'll be scared of you. He'll stop screwing Emma. She'll come back.

I don't think so. We don't know where she is.

Right. I don't have a clue. Boneheads are slow.

I'm not saying that. A minute ago you said you never wanted to see her again. I'm confused.

With his hands tightly gripped around the bottle, Daniel glared, hissed through his teeth, Eddie used that one.

Rocking his head from side to side, he caricatured Eddie in a thin falsetto voice, 'I'm confused, Daniel, tell me more.' That was Eddie, leaning forward, looking quizzical. 'I'm confused, my friend. Help me out here.' A trick they use, isn't it? He glowered. Isn't it?

No, Daniel, I –

Daniel glared at David. Go see him. He stretched his feet into the middle of the room, chin resting on his chest.

David said, I'll think about it.

Daniel studied his shadow on the floor, looking into some black ugly vision, murmuring a rebuke to Eddie, or maybe to Emma.

David let himself out and stood in the street and reflected on this pattern, so common in loving couples, in ancient times and modern days too. One is simply too decent to understand the other.

39

Finding Eddie Flannery's house

On the phone, Daniel said, Do something for me.

What?

Find out where he lives.

David hesitated. Why?

I'll knock on his door. Talk to her.

Leave a message at Eddie's office.

I've been to his office. Now he won't even answer my messages. Says he doesn't know where she is, acts like my enemy now. She's at Eddie's house. I've tried her family and friends and she's not with them. She must be at his house.

David paused with the phone in his hand, trying to work out if any of this was sane. He rolled the statement over in his head, trying to look at it from another angle, see madness or sanity or delusion. I'll see what I can do.

He scanned the white pages for Eddie's professional entry – EDDIE FLANNERY – LIFESTYLE COACH, with his office number, and some initials after his name related to New Age diplomas. There was no home address. He typed Eddie's name into the student management network, found his old home address and phoned the number. A woman answered and said, No, he left a year ago, but I still forward his mail to an O'Connor address.

David marked the location on a street map and walked out to his Volvo.

In the street he found the mailbox. The two-storey brick house sat among trees on Dryandra Street. He drove by twice, circled the block to look from another side. He could see a fenced veranda out back, a balcony on the second floor. David studied the neighbouring houses and the forest nearby. He realised that someone could watch Eddie's house from the wooded hill over the road.

He phoned Daniel. If she's staying with Eddie, you could sit on the hill opposite, watch with binoculars at night, figure out when she arrives or leaves, catch her and speak to her when she turns up.

The first night, David came with him. He said, Eddie knows our cars, and so does Emma. We'll park at the CIT and walk through woods to the hill overlooking Dryandra Street.

They walked for ten minutes carrying pocket torches. A bone-white half-moon lit the forest, and the sky was touched with blue. On the ridge overlooking Dryandra Street, they settled under a tree. Cars hissed by beneath them but nobody pulled up to Eddie's house.

They stayed for two hours, then left.

The following night, David couldn't sleep. He dressed and drove to the woods overlooking Eddie's house, watched. In three hours of watching, he saw Eddie walk into one of the upstairs bedrooms, then out again; an hour later, Eddie pulled the curtains. He waited and scanned with binoculars. A couple was arguing in the house next door, and a man dressed for bed in the house on the other side.

Late at night there were no cars and the sky stayed navy blue with a bite in the air; David huddled in a jacket and concluded that Emma wasn't there.

Eddie, or what looked like Eddie's shadow, switched off the light behind the drawn curtain and the house went black.

He drove home on empty roads.

For two weeks, Daniel watched the house, alone on the hill, crouched at the base of a tree waiting for someone to enter or leave. Twice he saw figures in the woodland behind him; one looked like a policeman, the other was a woman jogging in track pants and hooded coat. He thought the woman was Emma. He stood and called out, but she ran into trees.

Only Eddie's red four-wheel drive came and went through the electric roller door, and the vehicle's tinted windows stopped Daniel from seeing whether Emma arrived or left with him. Daniel watched the sitting room windows, and bedroom windows on the second floor.

At home in the middle of the night, Daniel woke and thought about Eddie's house. He dreamed about standing watch.

Daniel said over the phone, Eddie's holding her captive.

What?

She's locked in a room and can't get out.

No, Daniel. That's not how Eddie works. She'll phone you in due course.

We need to get inside that house.

David stood holding the phone, shaking his head. What?

See inside the house.

No, Daniel. Don't even think about it.

I know she's in there. We could sneak in.

She's not in there, Daniel. That's crazy.

Daniel rattled on and David tuned out. He pictured Daniel last year, a kind and even-tempered man with an open, sunny smile. Unbroken. A woman should be lucky to own such a man, a kind, generous, loyal and steadfast man with a single shortcoming. He needed help to make any decision, big or small.

40

Bill Scott meets a friend

On Friday morning at three a.m., high on coke in front of the TV, Bill hit on a plan to fix the lifestyle coach. Freddy O'Rourke would take him out. Freddy was an Irish bouncer and drug dealer, a bearded haystack with stubbly red hair, a steroid abuser who liked to fight. Irish on Irish. How poetic. World history was full of Irish on Irish – England, America, Australia, Belfast. And Freddy would leap at the chance to stomp Eddie Flannery. He would disable Eddie with a tyre iron.

In the dark, they pulled their cars next to each other at the bottom of Stockdill Drive on the Murrumbidgee River. They greeted, used a few customary niceties, then both sat in Freddy's orange Holden utility. Freddy's Rottweiler lay tied in the back. Freddy snapped the caps off two bottles of beer.

They swigged them for a while until Bill said, That kid is still in hospital. I'm glad you didn't call me.

You said not to.

What happened?

He'd been watching us, sitting on a log in the dark. Don't know for how long. Don't know what he saw. Don't know what he was doing there in the middle of the night with no car.

Why did you keep his driver's licence?

Because I said I'd visit his sister in the middle of the night if he talked to the police. I guessed he must have a sister.

He didn't talk.

Good. He has a sister then. I like a good outcome. Freddy lit a cigarette and said, Anyway, whad'ya need? More controlled substances?

I've got a bigger problem.

Shoot.

Teach a lad a big lesson.

A lesson? Who?

A cheat. He steals other men's wives. A pimp. You heard about white slavery. Prostitution racket we busted in Campbell.

Sure did.

This guy's pimping women, making slaves.

Freddy listened in the dark, sucked at the bottle and made his cigarette glow. He nodded and rubbed an oily hand over the red stubble on the crown of his head. Sounds like you've got a problem all right.

I do.

What's his name?

Eddie Flannery.

Freddy snorted cigarette smoke through his nose. Yeah, I know him. Poncy little fucker. I won't need tools to break Eddie's legs, if that's what you want.

Does he know you?

Come on. We run in different circles, to put it mildly.

We can't do this if he knows you.

Stop fussing. He doesn't know me. What's the arrogant little prick doin' to bother an acting superintendent? Why not fix him yourself?

It's not that easy.

He must have plenty of enemies.

He does. That'll make it easier for you. Police will think it's one of them.

Freddy said, You know, one thing's sort of a mystery, Bill.

What's that?

He took a long swig of his beer. When'd you take such a disliking to midgets?

He's the first.

Freddy rubbed his head again, blew cigarette smoke into the cab. How bad do you want me to hurt him?

Bill sucked on his cigarette looking out over the river. Shining ripples in the moonlight. He's a fancy-talking little prick. Talk that's dangerous. He strings pretty words together. Work on the left side of his brain with a tyre iron, baseball bat, you choose the tool. Pulp the left side of his brain.

Freddy rubbed his knuckle under his nose. I can do that. And crunch the right side too.

Bill's cigarette glowed and faded. He exhaled. Whatever. Just be smart about it. Don't be seen. Don't be heard. Don't talk to people.

That's fine.

And I can't go near you any more.

Understood.

We never had this discussion. You know the rules.

Yeah, yeah. I know the rules.

41

Daniel Bentham watching

Daniel slept curled in a chair. The light brushing of rain on the roof, wind blowing through she-oaks in the yard, and the water running in gutters woke him. He rose from his chair and shut the window before showering and crawling into bed.

For an hour, Daniel rehearsed how he'd put a knife into Eddie's throat, finish the evil that had rolled over his life. He turned onto his left side and drifted into the middle ground, a dream about Emma sleeping in Eddie's double bed in the house on Dryandra Street.

When the telephone buzzed in darkness, he woke in deep melancholy. With feet on the carpet, he pulled a white robe around him that he laid each night at the end of his double bed. It was cold in the sitting room, light speckling of rain on the roof and windows.

Daniel lifted the receiver. Hello, and glanced at the clock over the television – 1 a.m.

A faint whisper, barely audible.

Daniel wondered if he was asleep. He waited.

Another whisper.

Hello, he shouted.

The line went quiet.

Hello.

He didn't know the low female voice, he didn't hear what she said, an overseas call, a misdialled number, maybe a hoax.

Nothing.

Emma?

There was silence.

He waited and the caller hung up.

Daniel lay in bed for a minute, then dressed and walked to the car.

He drove through tidy neighbourhoods, no beaten-down houses or ragged cars or trash in the gutters, only Canberra wealth. The wipers snapped back and forth and cleared mist from the windscreen as he passed dark porches, misty eucalypts in front yards, steel-coloured ribbon gums with cut shreds of bark hanging in forks and trickling rain. Hayden Drive was a dripping street full of black trees, empty of car lights. Daniel steered into the access road at the CIT weaving across the car park. He shone high beams onto a solid wall of trees along a wire fence, the edge of Bruce Ridge. Yellow lamps over the car park smoked from the rain; no cars moved, no people entered or left the sliding glass doors at the back of the CIT. Daniel rolled the car towards the back row and sat with the motor running, shaded from high moonlight by lanky ribbon gums on the border. He walked through woodland and through more woodland to spy on Eddie's house.

At the top of the hill, he stood looking on darkened windows. He shifted between fire-blackened tea tree branches and sought a better view.

Below him, the house was quiet, curtains drawn. He lay in the dirt and watched. With eyes closed, he saw Emma inside the house. With eyes open, she was gone.

Lights flickered on in the neighbouring house, in an upstairs bedroom. He switched his gaze and studied the neighbouring house.

Nothing moved in Eddie's house until 8 a.m., when Eddie left through the front door, climbed into his red four-wheel drive and drove to work.

42

Daniel Bentham hatches a plan

You there, Daniel? David pushed open the door. Daniel?

Back here.

David followed the faint voice to the back bedroom. In the gloom, he saw the two wicker chairs set either side of a glass table.

Collapsed into the chair, Daniel raised his face, bags under his eyes and stubble on his cheeks. Thanks for coming, he said.

David shrugged. Any time.

They sat for a moment and David said, Sorry I'm late.

Daniel said, Something's wrong. She's in there. She tried to call me.

David shook his head. Daniel –

You need to get into that house.

I need to what?

Get into Eddie's house.

No.

We need to see inside.

You're crazy.

We can get inside.

How?

Just knock on the door.

Then what? Pose as plumbers? Come on, he knows us.

You could get in.

David stared and shook his head. No, Daniel.

He probably leaves the balcony door unlocked.

He probably does. So what? I'm not going to break in, and neither are you.

David sat thinking about his own part in Daniel's suffering, listening to his own sense of guilt, feeling solidarity with the man he had betrayed. He wondered, How do men decide to do such brainless things? Break into someone's house? Foolish ideas that begin to sound intelligent after enough time. A kinship of insanity.

He'll have us charged.

He won't, said Daniel. Eddie hates the police as much as the police hate Eddie. He'd see it as a failure of Irish manhood.

David said, I don't know.

He won't be home in the daytime, and if he shows up, it would only be you and me. Nobody else.

And Emma.

Yes. And Emma.

David thought about this and understood that Daniel was demented.

Daniel's voice was sharp and pleading. I'd do it myself, he said, but I can't climb that balcony. I get dizzy spells. But you can. He looked at the bandage on David's forehead. Your head's okay, isn't it?

Clear as a bell. That's why I'm not going to do it.

I'll sit on the hill over the road with a mobile phone and warn you if anybody comes.

No, you won't. I'm not breaking in to rescue Emma. Stop reading fairy tales. If you think Emma is locked up in Eddie's house, call the police.

I have called the police. You know I have. They want to stop Eddie, but they can't figure out how.

David said, Emma probably isn't even in town. I'll talk to you tomorrow.

He left.

43

Break-in

At nine the following morning Daniel woke, rested his face on the pillow trying to stop the banging in his head, like a hammer on tin plates.

He rested in a chair with his head down, then dressed and slipped a folding knife into his pocket, drove to the CIT car park, left his car and walked through long shadows in the forest. He picked his way downhill through tea tree, stepped between two wooden posts that led onto the road. He wandered over Dryandra Street, circled through Eddie's side gate into the backyard and knocked on the door.

Daniel expected Emma. He stood waiting for Emma's face to appear in the doorway but nobody answered. Eddie's back fence stood two metres high, tall enough to shield his backyard from neighbours. Daniel looked around.

He walked along the patio, pushed at each window on the ground floor. Window cranks held them shut. He knew people in the city left balcony doors unlocked, thinking humans couldn't climb. He waited, pressed his fingers to his head, tried to stop the red cutting pain, then shinned up one of the posts to the balcony. It was slow and his head ached. He grabbed the vertical slats on the balcony, pulled himself over the railing. He was dizzy. Neighbouring windows reflected branches blowing in light breeze. He stopped and watched the reflecting windows for a moment, couldn't see anyone behind the glass, then tried the sliding the door; it shifted.

The door opened into a large bedroom with blinds partially drawn. The bedroom showed no signs of being used. He studied it. On either side of the double bed sat angular tables of dark wood. Miniature paintings in frames sat on the dressing table. Over the dressing table was an oblong mirror lit by a long fluorescent lamp concealed in a draped box. Daniel looked at himself in the mirror and thought about how, each morning, the vain Eddie Flannery walked into the empty bathroom, grinned at himself and straightened his bow tie in the same glass.

In the hallway, Daniel let his eyes adjust. One door concealed a linen closet, the other three opened into bedrooms. Daniel entered another bedroom and walked into the en suite. There was a mark of mascara on a towel, a pair of toothbrushes on the sink, a squeezed tube of toothpaste, an open bottle of green mouthwash, prescription creams and pills written out to Eddie Flannery, but nothing he recognised as Emma's. The frosted screen on the shower and the tiles were shiny clean.

On the bed lay two feather pillows with white pillowslips, side by side with depressions in each. Two white towelling robes lay on one corner of the bed. On the dressing table lay deodorant, a brush, combs, tissues, a box of tampons and talcum powder spilled along one edge.

In the corner sat a dirty clothes hamper. Daniel upended the hamper on the carpet and sorted through clothing. Mixed in with men's track pants, socks, dress shirts, and underwear Daniel found two sets of woman's briefs. He spread one pair out on the dressing top and sniffed them. Daniel pressed them to his face trying to find Emma.

The doors into the closet had cut-glass knobs and the closet wasn't entirely full of men's clothes. A woman's blue tailored suit, a pair of pumps on the carpet beneath the suit. Daniel touched the sleeve.

Next to the blue suit was a grey cape and hood. He pushed clothing along a rail and found a skirt. Under the skirt were running shoes. He thought of the woman running in the woods above Eddie's house, the woman he wanted to be Emma.

Daniel looked again at the grey cape and hood. Staring at them brought no lightning bolt, no creeping insight, only a slow realisation that carved into his brain. It cut into his red headache. Emma, he said.

Yes.

The voice shook him. He lurched around and saw Eddie backlit in the doorway, standing in his grey suit as if he'd just come from work. Eddie rested one hand on his hip.

Daniel looked up at him and said nothing.

You're in a bit of trouble, he said. There was no fear in Eddie's voice.

Daniel tried to gather his thoughts, but could only come out with, You're in some trouble too, Eddie. It felt lame and stupid.

Eddie shook his head like a disapproving parent. You can leave now, or I'll phone the police. Your call. He got the words out in slow, measured pieces.

Daniel watched him and touched the knife in his pocket, the headache pounding red behind his eyes.

Eddie stood in the doorway looking down at the upturned hamper, and the clothing scattered on the floor. He shook his head again and clicked his tongue. His eyes were steady and cruel. You've made quite a mess here, Daniel.

44

Nigel Plant castigates Daniel Bentham

David sat against the wall in Daniel's house, eyes down, trying to gauge whether Officer Nigel Plant knew him and linked him to the boy in the alley.

Daniel said, I want you to visit Eddie Flannery. Please. Search through his closets.

Nigel shook his head. You know I can't do that. In fact, you're lucky I don't charge you.

Please. Go see him.

This is the strangest thing. We learn about a break-in because the felon – well, alleged felon – phones us and tells us he just broke into a house. But the victim of the house-breaking doesn't phone us because he doesn't care. Now you're accusing him of something. What makes you think we'll find anything in that house?

I'll take that chance, said Daniel.

Nigel shook his head. Then you're loopier than I thought.

Eddie's arrogant, said Daniel. He'll probably invite you in.

Now that would be a mistake, wouldn't it? Eddie Flannery doesn't seem like a man who makes a lot of mistakes.

Daniel said, His vanity does.

So we interview his vanity?

Please, said Daniel.

Nigel held up the palm of his hand at Daniel. No.

Daniel persisted and David sat back with his head down, listening to his broken friend near tears.

Daniel pleaded, Just talk to him.

No. He looked over at David sitting with his arms folded.

Please think about it, said Daniel.

I don't think you're listening to me. On the strength of what you've said, I can't accuse Flannery of anything.

I understand that.

No, I don't think you do. And you need to understand this – Eddie could turn us away at the door and ask us to lay charges against you. Nigel shook his head again. Somebody's knocked a bolt loose in your head.

Yes, said Daniel, I understand.

Nigel watched him and the three went quiet until he said, Thanks, Daniel. He looked at David. We'll talk again sometime.

Nigel picked up his cap, looked at both men and said, Good day.

Nigel held off for a week, thinking about Daniel's bent frame of mind, turning it over in his head. Then he mentioned Daniel's request to Bill Scott, knowing that Bill would quash the idea. Bill didn't.

There's slavery in this town, he said. Women held captive as sex slaves right here. He pointed at the floor as if it was in their building. That's good enough reason to search Eddie's house. Get a written statement from Daniel Bentham. I'll take it to a sympathetic judge.

You sure you want to do this?

Bill said, Oh, I'm sure all right. We'll do it together.

45

Police in Eddie Flannery's house

Bill and Nigel stood on Eddie's step. Nigel handed Eddie a brown envelope.

Eddie was surprised at first, then he smiled. Sure, come in. Like some tea?

I would, said Nigel.

Nigel looked at the plush white carpet, oak writing desk in the corner, expensive three-piece leather lounge suite arranged around a giant Sony TV. Leather-bound volumes of *Finnegan's Wake, Ulysses, Dubliners, Playboy of the Western World, The Picture of Dorian Gray, Lady Windermere's Fan, The Ballad of Reading Gaol,* collections by Sean O'Faolain, Flann O'Brien in a rosewood bookcase. A Seamus Heaney translation of *Beowulf* lay open on the couch. Window curtains were bone-coloured and pricey. A brick feature wall held a gas fireplace that reflected in a mirror across the room.

Eddie led them into a bedroom and said, Look around, pull open the drawers.

Nigel thumbed a biography of Che Guevara on the bed stand. He pulled open the third wardrobe door and was taken aback. It was filled with skirts, scarves, dresses, Oroton handbags, and dozens of women's shoes.

Does someone else live here, Eddie?

There's a leprechaun in the attic.

You know what I mean.

Eddie smiled easily, walked over and stood next to Nigel. On the occasions when I invite them.

Nigel waved into the wardrobe. Emma Bentham leave her clothes here?

Emma Bentham? Oh, dear. These are for my guests. Sometimes my friends like to dress up, or partially dress up. That's all. Have a little fun. You should try it sometime. It's healthy.

Nigel pulled skirts, dresses, blouses, and coats along the rail and examined labels, looked inside handbags. The clothing was mostly small sizes like 8s.

Eddie said, You know, there's nothing like fashion to excite a dead party.

Why only small sizes? said Nigel.

Eddie sucked in air and clicked his tongue. Do I have to spell it out? I can afford to be discerning, so I am. Don't you prefer a certain size and shape?

Nigel looked away from Eddie into the wardrobe. Something about the clothes bothered him, but the bother wouldn't crystallise with Eddie standing so close. His breath smelt like peppermint chewing gum.

Bill explored upstairs.

So you have women come here, said Nigel.

No law against that, Nigel. So far. Eddie stepped closer.

Nigel squinted into a corner. I wonder how much power you might have over them.

Eddie leaned forward and forced a high, bird-like, cackle. Power? This little fella look like he's got power over anyone?

Nigel twisted his mouth as if his moustache itched. You've got a point there, Eddie. Nigel pulled out a black evening gown, hung it on the doorknob, and stood back tilting his head. Very nice, Eddie. Are we talking about normal-sized men, or little men?

Eddie smiled again. As I said, I'd have trouble convincing women to do anything.

I can relate to that, said Nigel. Women never do anything I ask them to do.

Eddie smiled. With the right outlook, you could change that. Unless, of course, you're in the closet. Eddie laughed at his little joke.

Nigel slid dresses and coats along the railing, then turned to face Eddie. I wonder if certain women do what little fellas tell them.

Eddie's face turned hard, as if locking Nigel into a wrestling hold. Then he grinned. Do you now?

Nigel grinned back. With all the little men in this world, it's a wonder us normal-sized fellas don't have a better chance. I was told once that men evolved to be bigger to protect their women from other men.

Nice theory, Nigel.

Bill turned and faced him. Look, we're hoping you could tell us a little more about Emma Bentham.

Eddie exhaled through his nose, his nostrils flared. Go ahead, superintendent. Hold my feet to the fire.

Just answer the question.

Nigel asked me about Emma before. Now, if you'll excuse me, I'm expected back at the office, clients to see. He held up his wrist, studied his watch.

Nigel looked around the room. I was starting to enjoy this.

Yeah, me too, said Eddie. But we're finished now.

Bill paused. Eddie pulled the door open, and waited.

Nigel said, Overall, Eddie, how do you think it went?

Today, you mean?

Yes.

Eddie said with a certain ease, Flattered. A police superintendent, a crack team of operatives searching my house. Can't wait to get back to the office and tell the girls.

Bill pointed at wires over the door. Good to see you've installed a home security system.

Well, you can't be too careful. Of course, if someone else did break in, I'm not sure who I'd call.

Bill stood with Nigel on the porch.

Nigel wrote in his open notebook, soaking up time, then he looked up. Sorry if this was unsettling.

Eddie leaned back and uttered a hen-like cackle. Oh dear. Do I look unsettled?

Bill smiled. Okay. Thanks, Eddie.

Eddie waved them off the step.

In the car, Bill said, What do you make of that?

Hard to tell. Could have been bravado, could have been winding us up.

Bill turned to him. Winding us up?

He set out to cause trouble, like he was trying to draw you in. I don't get it.

A few minutes earlier in Eddie's house, Nigel had watched Bill hide his anger. But now, riding in the car, he felt Bill's rage climb into his throat and nearly burst out.

Bill whispered through clenched teeth, The man hates women.

What?

He's an A-grade misogynist.

Nigel tapped the steering wheel with his finger, thinking as he drove. A lot of men hate women, sir, but women seem to forgive Eddie.

Bill's fists were tight. Yes, Eddie's different all right.

Nigel glanced at him and said, Be careful. He collects stories about people and he knows how to use them. He trips people up. If Eddie gets you to stumble, Eddie wins.

Bill's nostrils flared, his knuckles popped out, his white face growing red. Words came out in a low hiss. We'll see who wins.

I'm sorry to say this, sir, but I think he's winding you up so you'll make a mistake.

Bill stared ahead, looking blankly through the windscreen. He formed his lips into a tight line and said, I won't make a mistake. Nobody talks to me that way. Nobody.

46

Bill Scott meets Daniel Bentham

On the darkened brick porch, Bill Scott rapped on the wooden door; he leaned back with his hands at his sides.

The lock squeaked and Daniel's face peered out, straining in the light. He seemed troubled, his voice flat and mumbling. Yes?

Bill smiled. Acting Superintendent Bill Scott. I phoned this morning.

Daniel touched his head and dipped his chin a little. Oh yes, come in. I haven't been well. Daniel led him into the house and said, Can I get you anything?

Tea, if you've got some. Bill sat in a wicker chair.

Won't be long, Daniel's voice rang hollow from the kitchen.

The electric jug grumbled.

It's a difficult time for you, said Bill. I'm sorry. He nodded and knitted his brow. You know, we're doing everything we can.

Thanks.

Bill tapped a cigarette out of a packet and gestured to Daniel, Mind if I smoke?

I'll get a saucer.

Bill laid his cap on the glass table, lit the cigarette, and cleared his throat. He hollered to Daniel in the kitchen, You know, he brainwashes these women. No secret.

Daniel shouted back. Why would he do that? Daniel clattered dishes, pouring boiling water over tea bags.

Well, that's the mystery. Bill sat and looked around the room, waited and thought about tactics. He picked up a piece of wicker from the crumbling chair, rolled it in his fingers and looked at it.

Daniel came in, set the tray, cups, saucers and tea on the glass table. Bill thought about how domestic Daniel was, emasculated.

Daniel poured tea from a pot. Sugar or milk?

No, that's fine. Bill leaned forward. Look, Daniel, I think we understand each other.

Daniel held his cup with both hands and watched him.

We need to get something on this guy. He makes people unhappy, both men and women. You lost your wife. The guy makes a $100,000 a year out of other people's misery.

Daniel nodded.

Bill's out-blown cigarette smoke eddied against the window and gathered in a cloud on the ceiling.

What can you tell me about his behaviour towards you, and towards your wife?

Daniel hesitated. What do you mean?

Bill tipped ash in the saucer. What do I mean? Exactly what I said. You should know better than anybody. He wrecked your marriage, didn't he? Eddie wedges men against their wives.

Yes, well, maybe.

No maybe about it. The man's illegal.

Why don't you arrest him?

Bill smiled. Daniel, it's not that easy. He skirts the law, stays away from the psychologist-licensing agencies by calling himself a lifestyle coach. We're trying. God knows we're trying hard. That's why I'm here. We appreciated your help with the search warrant, but it turned up nothing. We need to show a clear breach of the law.

Daniel balled one fist and bounced it on the arm of the wicker chair. It's just that, um, I think a lot of it was my fault.

Bill squinted. Pardon? Your fault? How can it be your fault?

I know that's hard to understand, but that's the way I see it.

Bill shook his head, his face went scarlet. How can you say that? I mean, what is it with this guy? He causes women to leave their husbands, has sex with clients, and nobody raises a finger to stop him.

Daniel nodded and looked down. He saw the paradox and wanted to ease Bill's discomfort. He was unnerved that an acting superintendent was annoyed with him. Daniel avoided Bill's eyes and slumped in the chair with his hands around the cup.

Maybe, said Daniel, the wives are ready to leave. I don't know. Maybe Eddie can spot a woman who needs a change, a woman who needs someone to make her happy. Maybe he holds up a mirror and shows the woman something they didn't see before.

Bill looked down and shook his head in disbelief, rested back in the chair and tapped cigarette ash into the saucer. He looked up and watched Daniel, saw how frightened he was, and decided to comfort him, nod and respond, as he'd been trained to do. Look, Daniel. I see what you're saying. You're telling me that you feel uncomfortable about helping us.

Yes. I think so.

Bill leaned forward. I understand that. It must be a terrible time for you. He waited. He drew on his cigarette.

Vertical lines showed between Daniel's eyebrows. He looked up. Can I ask you something?

Sure. Ask away. Bill smiled and relaxed back and made the chair squeak.

Daniel hesitated and cleared his throat. I, uh, I wondered if you thought Eddie had anything to do with your own wife leaving.

Bill fiddled with a button on the sleeve of his uniform. What kind of question is that? I'm afraid that's none of your business.

Daniel looked down. Sorry. You're right, it's not my business.

Bill tapped his cap against his leg. I see what's happening here. Gossipy little town. Look, Daniel, I can only warn you. He paused. Don't believe everything you hear. There's two sides to every story.

Daniel nodded, looking down.

Bill leaned forward. Did Eddie tell you this?

Daniel sat back and folded his arms, No. No. I haven't talked to him about you.

They sat in awkward silence. The fridge hummed in the kitchen, a car rushed by in the street. A boobook called in the garden.

Bill stood and reached into his breast pocket. Well, thank you for your time. Here's my card. Phone me if you think you can help us.

Daniel nodded. I will.

I'll let myself out. He left Daniel sitting alone.

47

Amber's tip-off

Steps came down the hall. They stopped in front of his door and somebody knocked.

He turned in his seat. It's open.

She stepped in and smiled and David looked at her. She waited in the half-opened door. Thought maybe you wouldn't see me again.

And why did you think that? Light danced off her coppery hair. She came close and the desk lamp showed the spattering of pale freckles over the bridge of her nose, the white skin on her throat. How are you?

David looked at her and waited. What can I do for you?

It's about Sophie.

Again.

You had a bit of a win, I heard.

He paused. How do you know that?

Amber shrugged. We hear things.

He studied her, looking for signs of lying and left her standing in the doorway.

She paused, looked down, and said, It's about the draft letter.

Draft letter?

That Sophie found under your cup in the staff room.

Who gave you so much detail? They shouldn't have.

I'm here to give you some detail.

David watched her and realised she was going to implicate someone again, the same trick she'd used to tangle him in this mess in the first place. She would tell David how a group of students had set him up for the fun of it, or maybe to get back at Sophie.

It's just that, she looked down again, I'm not sure how to say this.

David waited. Just say it.

With her head bowed, she mumbled, Your technician.

His brow knitted. My technician?

Tommy Rose.

What about him?

Did you know he and Sophie were close?

He sat back and thought for a moment. What do you mean, close?

Amber looked at him and said, That's all I can say. Work it out for yourself.

Her voice warmed him a little. He sat back trying to form an image of this news. How do you know this?

We know.

He scrutinised her. That's cryptic. 'We know.'

I understand why you don't trust me. I'm sorry this happened, and I do feel responsible. But I'm telling you the truth, and I'm trying to help.

David sat back, staring.

She held his gaze and said, It might explain a few things.

Like what?

Like how the letter got into the staff room under your cup.

It's also a little too neat. Why does it feel like a trap?

Does Tommy Rose have keys to your room, and keys to the broom cupboard printer?

David said, I'm not going to answer that. But why would Tommy do such a thing?

Amber paused and watched him, Like I said. You work it out.

David sat back and stared out the window at students walking under trees.

Amber stood waiting, then broke the silence. David, I need to go.

He looked at her. Of course. He waved his hand. Go. He continued to stare out the window.

48

David meets Tommy Rose

In the morning, David stood in the hallway bent over his key. As the door opened, he caught a movement at the edge of his vision. Tommy the Tech came down the hallway in running shorts, saw David and skidded towards him, left a rubber mark on the floor, turned, and doubled back.

Hey, Tommy. Win last night?

Tommy grabbed the corner with his left hand, spun around and pulled back into David's view. Oh, yeah. Hi, David. Look, I didn't have time to set up that apparatus –

That's fine, Tommy. I want to see you about something else. Come here for a minute.

Tommy's eyes darted from side to side. I've got something to do, I –

David pointed to the floor. *Come here.*

Tommy rubbed his palms together, as if washing his hands. Okay. For a minute, I, uh, I can spare a minute.

Tommy's running shoes squeaked as he dodged David's eyes.

David ushered him through the door, pointed with an open hand, Have a seat.

David, I don't have –

Sit.

Tommy sat with his hands tucked between his bare knees and David watched him for a moment, then stepped closer, folded his arms, and stood over him. Tell me what's going on.

Tommy looked up, hunched and frightened. I – I don't know what you mean.

I said, What's going on?

Going on? I – I don't understand.

Yes, you do, Tommy. You understand perfectly well. Tell me what's going on.

You mean with the apparatus?

David pulled a chair in front of Tommy and sat knee-to-knee with him, level-eyed with Tommy. This is the part where you play dumb, a little confused, a little simple.

Is this about Sophie?

You know it is.

I want to stay out of it.

You're screwing Sophie, aren't you?

Twice his eyes slid sideways. What?

You're screwing Sophie.

No.

Look, Tommy, that was a simple lie. And I don't mind. But you are screwing Sophie.

Tommy's eyes widened, his head dropped. He started to dry-wash his hands again. Who told you that?

David looked away and chuckled. You can't hide a thing like that in a department like this, Tommy. It's written all over your face.

He loomed closer until Tommy looked up and said, Who told you?

Tommy, Tommy. It doesn't take a trained psychologist to see that you're screwing Sophie. Half the students know.

But I didn't –

Of course you didn't, Tommy, whatever you're going to say. But I've asked around. Half the students know you're screwing Sophie Moss, the other half are Jehovah's Witnesses. I asked a student just this morning. Sure enough, she knew. That's a little unprofessional, I know, but what the hell, I asked her anyway.

With hands on his bare knees ,Tommy looked out the window.

David watched him, and said, A few people were surprised that Sophie was a muscle feeler.

Tommy looked down, started to wash his hands again and said, You didn't talk to Sophie, did you?

David sat back. Sophie?

You'd better watch out –

David stood and walked to the window, stifling his rage. Tommy, all my life I've ignored pissy advice.

The lawyers think she has a good case.

That's third-hand, Tommy. Things distort in the retelling.

Third-hand?

The lawyers told Sophie, Sophie told you, and you just told me.

Another deep sigh, then, Don't tell anyone.

Your wife, you mean? Relax. Nobody cares.

Tommy glanced up. White anger blazed in David's face.

Tommy looked down again and said, Don't tell anyone.

David shook his head and sat down again, knee-to-knee with Tommy. He opened his hands, looked at his own fingers then stared into Tommy's face. Three-quarters of the married people in this building, academics and non-academics alike, have bonked someone in their spare time. You know that. So these people know what you're up to. David forced a gritty smile, let weeks of fear and anger spill out of him.

Tommy started to massage one thumb against the other. After a deep sigh, he said, I kno-know.

Tommy the Tech. Prince of Trickiness.

I-uh-kn – kn –

Oh, stop it, Tommy.

Tommy shook his head. What if the dean knows? Tommy's deep breathing was irregular. He looked back out the window.

What if he does? You started this mess with Sophie.

Tommy didn't look up. He scuffed the carpet.

Yes, Tommy, you did. You sent that student to me, then you put the draft letter under my coffee cup in the staff room. But why?

Tommy sighed. I don't know what you mean. Tommy stared at the door, swung out one knee as if he planned to escape when David wasn't looking.

You know full well, Tommy. Let me guess. You became Sophie's confidant, complained to her about me, and that sort of drew her close, didn't it? At the same time, you were complaining to me and a few students about Sophie.

Tommy slouched in the chair, like a bird dog, eyes shifting left and right, afraid to look at his disappointed owner. It struck David how petty all this was, how silly and time-wasting and small. If Emma was here, she would shake her head and say, 'Who cares?'

Say something, Tommy.

You don't understand.

Sure I do. Powerful mother figure like Sophie. Why not?

If she knows about this –

Meanwhile she's taking me to court and trying to get me fired, and you're fucking worried that she might discover your little games. She's bound to discover them sooner or later, Tommy.

I wouldn't know what to do.

Come on, Tommy. What's this? A suicide bid? Did you try this one as a nine-year-old?

It's just that, well – He sighed. I've got a lot to lose.

The dean will give you a fair hearing.

No.

Tell me. Do you do most of your bonking on Sophie's desk? Or down in your room? If you don't mind my saying so, it's a bit dingy. A bit greasy, with drills, and power sanders, and Perspex – though, come to think of it, an educated woman might find Perspex exciting. Can you see how Sophie might find a wooden table and four iron vices exciting?

I need to go.

What for?

He tried to look into David's face. What do you want from me?

Why did you do it?

He shifted in his chair. You don't understand.

You're right there. But why cause me this trouble?

You've got it wrong.

David leaned back and let out a deep chuckle. It poured over Tommy's bowed head. Of course, Tommy. But that doesn't tell me why you did this.

It's just that, well, it seemed like what she wanted to hear.

You told Sophie what she wanted to hear.

Yes. About you.

Oh, I get it now, it's my fault. Let me guess how it went. I have a reputation for being a hothead with the morons in this building, and she has a reputation for cruelty.

She believes in what she does.

You told me otherwise. She believes that she has to be a little cruel to be kind, to the Fatherland. Oh, incidentally, when you repeat this back to Sophie this afternoon, try to remember the word 'Fatherland', because it'll be far more offensive than 'Motherland'. 'Motherland' has a socialist flavour.

I have to go.

This turned nasty, didn't it? Got out of hand.

Yes. Out of hand. His expression was vapid. Yes.

So, tell me. When did you plan to tell Sophie the truth?

The truth?

David shifted his chair close, their knees pressed together. The truth, Tommy. What you've been doing.

She'll kill me.

Probably.

Tommy looked down with his thumbs against his forehead.

David said, Let's reconstruct.

Tommy didn't look up.

You took your master key, removed the draft letter from the broom cupboard printer, took my coffee cup from my office, and laid the draft letter under the coffee cup in the staff room.

Tommy was head-bent and silent, his breathing shallow.

Well?

No.

What do you mean, 'No'?

You left your cup in the staff room. You forgot it.

So you put the letter under my cup in the staff room.

Tommy sat quietly. His red eyes came up, trying to look steadily into David's, like he was taking a pledge of honesty. He looked back down. I'll tell her.

David shook his head. I don't believe you.

Tommy looked up and maintained a shaky gaze, Honest. I swear. I wouldn't lie about that.

Sure you would, Tommy.

Tommy wagged his head. You're right about some of it, but not all of it.

One more thing. You put those notes into my pigeonhole.

Quiet, head-bent, Tommy said nothing.

Tommy?

Emma. You wrecked Daniel's life. Daniel's my friend.

David jerked his head sideways. Get out of here.

Tommy stood without looking at David, waited, then spun around, jerked open the door and ran off.

49

Night-time in Cook

The kid walked through a narrow maze of lanes between houses, looking into windows, waiting for the dog as it waddled behind him. Fallen leaves stuck to the soles of his running shoes. He stopped in a small park with steel playing equipment surrounded by a cluster of eucalypt trees; bushes deadened his mumbling. Cap pinned to his belt, he whispered.

The kid cupped his hands and lit a cigarette, pulled a flat glass bottle from his pocket and sucked his mother's gin. It lightened his head.

The soot-coloured pit bull with grey hairs in its muzzle waddled stiffly at his side. He leaned down to the dog. We're gunna find this fucker.

The dog looked up and watched him, waited, and waddled ahead when the boy moved again.

Along the tree-lined bike path he stood and forced his hands into his pockets to keep warm.

No sound from the street.

He looked at the house, watched the windows, scanned backyards, and looked up and down the path. The park at the end of the path was deserted.

Gonna stab that fucker.

He circled to the side path, watching another yard. The house was dark. He checked each window, then walked on.

David lay in the dark thinking about Tommy. Then he ran the film of the boy's stabbing through his head over and over. At 2 a.m. he got up, tossed on some clothes, hooked the carabiner to his belt, attached the black baseball cap in case it rained. From the cupboard he pulled down the box of rolled oats and tipped them drumming into the plastic bucket.

Outside, the streets were cool and empty. A precious gleam of light, the smell of wet stone. In silver light he walked uphill with no torch, the bucket hooked on his arm. He ducked between wooden railings, passed through the iron gate looking for the mare. He rattled the oats, banged the side of the bucket with an open hand. Far away yellow lights dotted the city. He waved the other horses away and slipped the rope hackamore over the mare's ears and around her nose, talked with her for a while, then grabbed the base of her mane and swung up onto her back. They ran together in moonlight.

50

Freddy O'Rourke on the hill

There was fog that night. Streets were deep black as if freshly painted. Freddy drove to the CIT and left his ute in the parking lot behind a circle of street lamps. He untied his dog, let him jump out of the back of the ute and range through forest, sniffing dirt and lifting his leg against trees. Freddy patted his pants leg and called in a whisper, Paisley. The Rottweiler fell in behind him as he made his way up the rising path by torchlight.

He and the dog reached the hill over Dryandra Street and stood together in lacy moonlight, listening to the rustle of night things. Freddy shifted around trying to see the garage door and the upstairs windows through fire-blackened tea tree branches. The Rottweiler shook himself and lay down. Freddy sat in the dirt with Paisley and lit a cigarette, cupping his hands against the breeze. Over four nights Eddie had arrived at 10 p.m. in the four-wheel drive with tinted windows, opened the roller door from inside the vehicle and driven in. Freddy never saw the dark-haired woman again; he twisted around to see her step down from the passenger side before Eddie closed the roller door, but she never did. All four nights, Eddie had driven the car into the garage then closed the door and blocked Freddy's view.

Freddy spoke in a low voice, thinking about the woman in the house. This is a fine town, Paisley. Women are tall and lovely, they believe it, meet your eyes head on, expect a fella's gaze to wander down over their body. Don't mind a bit. Don't mind if a man's eyes drop down to a young maiden's cunt. Easy to get yer Johnson serviced in this town, Paisley. Not Derry. Fuckin Derry cracklin' with hatred, men spittin' on each other. Knee-cappers. Men pass each other in the street, hunted men, eyes down.

That's the difference. Men in Derry are hunted. You look at their women, you get a bullet.

Shit of a place. Fuckin' Catholics, fucking cartoon men. Fuckin Real IRA, real criminals is what they are. Fuckin' disgrace. I wrote SHAME over their slogans in Omagh. Pricks. Enniskillen. You should see it. Boarded-up windows, blackened walls, blew up the market quarter. This guy, Freddy pointed at Eddie's house with a stick, he hates the Prods, so he hates us and we hate him. Bomb on the curb near the fish shop, told people it would be over there, Freddy waved into the woods, gathered them in one place and BAM. Fuckin' criminals.

He watched the quiet street, blew smoke into the trees. Two possums grumbled in the top of a eucalypt, silhouetted against dark blue sky and stars.

This place has drawbacks, he said. At home you're chasing badgers down badger holes, runnin' deer through the forest, whimperin' otters in nettle beds at evening, ghost owls in belfries, marsh coot, hooded tits, bog martins, wild hogs in the swamp and woodpeckers in hollow oaks. I miss it.

A red four-wheel drive hissed down the street and turned into the driveway. Freddy stubbed his cigarette in the dirt and watched through binoculars. He fought branches for a better look. There was a pause and Freddy knew why. Eddie Flannery pressed the remote through the windscreen. Nothing happened. Now pointing it again through the windscreen, pressing the button hard. The door didn't move. Eddie pressed again, and again. Eddie switched off the motor and Freddy smiled.

Nothing happened for a full minute. Then Eddie stepped out of the four-wheel drive and stood beside the car; with the remote control at arm's length, he pressed the button. The door didn't lift. Eddie looked back over his shoulder and shrugged at someone in the vehicle. The woman stepped out from the passenger side.

Freddy watched through binoculars and said to Paisley, He's a queer one that Superintendent Bill. Got no faith in me. He shouldn't lose heart so easily. Beaten by windows of smoked glass when anyone can disable a roller door with a piece of wood. Freddy laughed.

Below him, Flannery said something to the woman. She pulled groceries from the back of the car and walked to the front door. He opened it with a key; she went in and Eddie looked up and down the street, followed her in and closed the door.

Freddy said to Paisley, Just the happy couple, aren't they? A police wife and a fuckin' midget.

Freddy watched lights flicker on through Eddie's house downstairs, then upstairs. The woman didn't show herself again. Freddy patted the Rottweiler and said, This is it, boy. We learned something tonight. Never bolt your door with a boiled carrot.

51

Freddy O'Rourke meets Bill Scott

At the bottom of Stockdill Drive on the Murrumbidgee River, two cars pulled up next to each other in the dark. Moonlight danced off the water.

Freddy lit a cigarette and said, Whad'ya got?

Did you see her?

I saw a red four-wheel drive turn into the driveway. The little creep stepped out from the one side, spoke to the woman who pulled groceries from the back. Couldn't hear what he said. They walked to the front door; he shoved the key into the lock and stepped inside. She followed and shut the door.

You think it's my wife?

Yup, from your description, it's your wife.

He's screwing them. All of them. Breathing heavily, Bill dragged a folded paper from his pocket, Freddy snapped on the dome light. Bill unfolded the paper and pointed with his finger. This is the downstairs sitting room. The stairs are here. Upstairs three bedrooms. Not sure where he sleeps. He pointed at two windows downstairs. All the doors are alarmed, this upstairs sliding door on the balcony is alarmed, but these two windows downstairs aren't. Bill tapped his finger. They have winders. Probably the best way in.

Where'd you get this?

I searched his house. Anyway. Memorise it, flush it down the toilet.

Freddy studied the map in the dim light. He didn't say anything.

Got that? Memorise it, flush it down the toilet.

Yeah, yeah. Stop fussing. He studied the map. Anyone else watching that house? Disgruntled husbands?

What are you talking about?

Fella sitting on the hill over the road. Got in my way.

Just check the house from the woods over the road for another week.

I tell you there's another fellow watching the house. I saw him. I was there trying to watch it myself.

This guy was doing the same?

He was. Don't know what he was after, but he arrived some nights and sat there.

Maybe I know him. Fool came back, broke into the house, but he won't do it again. Watch for him, be sure he doesn't see you.

The two were quiet in the car, swigging beer. Freddy tipped ash out the window.

Bill said, I'll meet you back here, see how you've progressed. And be careful. Eddie's suspicious. Don't let him spot you. Watch the house after dark, get a feel for his movements.

It's your party. Freddy clunked an empty bottle out the window. I need a leak. He stepped out of the ute and walked to the front.

Bill studied his outline in the blue night. He looked like a refrigerator with a head. Freddy leaned a sweaty hand on the bonnet and urinated on the bitumen. For a while, Freddy stood and watched the steam lifting up over the fender and drifting into tall grass over the river, then zipped his trousers, climbed back into the front seat and opened another bottle.

52

Amber's proposal

Alone in his office, David considered Amber's proposal.

I know a little about defamation, she'd said. We studied it as part of a unit. I feel responsible for your legal problems with Sophie.

Don't. And you already told me that.

He rested back in his chair.

She paused, her green eyes watching him. I'm sorry.

He shrugged. Don't be.

I can help you. Let me come along and take notes.

That would be inappropriate. And I've got bigger worries.

It's up to you. But you've got to start trusting someone.

David looked out the window and said, No, I don't.

She left and he sat watching her walk down the path. He doubted her sincerity and doubted she could help. He shivered when he thought about how much she knew, how stupid he'd been. She'd got him to talk, sneaking between gaps in his body armour. He'd talked to her about Daniel, and he regretted it afterwards, shook his head after she'd left and mumbled to himself, What were you thinking?

At home he fell into a troubled sleep.

In the morning, he was thinking of Amber. Something about the clean, matter-of-fact way she stood and held his gaze and spoke to him.

A bleak, grey morning, his mood desolate. He drank coffee laced with whisky, let it glow inside him. He tried to read the paper then stood up from the table, studied the yellow pages and phoned her.

Okay. I've got the name of a solicitor. Look, I've got a bigger problem.

If this guy's okay, I'll talk to him about Sophie, then get you to step out of the room while I talk to him about this other problem.

David went back to bed and wondered if he'd committed yet another blunder.

53

Lawyer

They waited in two massive black leather chairs set either side of a glass table on chromium tubal frame legs. *Time* and *Hello* magazines neatly stacked on the corners. David and Amber read without speaking until Martin Steadman, brisk and busy, dashed down the hallway in long strides on short legs.

He smiled, opened his hand and said, Hello, David. For a short man, he stood tall in a tailored, charcoal suit and neatly trimmed sandy hair. He was balding on top and did nothing to hide it. He reached across to Amber, Not sure we've met. Martin Steadman.

Amber stood and looked at him, as if to size him up, and said, Amber Griffin.

Martin said, Come on through, and turned and led them past three young secretaries rattling keyboards.

The secretaries didn't look up.

On Martin's desk lay a corpulent file with yesterday's letter on top:

LAROUSSE, COHEN, AND PINCH – BARRISTERS
DEFAMATION PROCEEDINGS AGAINST DAVID CHESS
Final Letter Before Court Proceedings Initiated

The open file, thought David, was to show us how carefully he'd briefed himself.

Sit down, sit down, he said. Can I get you anything? Tea? He looked at Amber.

Yes, tea would be fine.

White?

Black.

And you, David?

The same.

Martin punched a button on his desk and said, Julie, bring us two black teas, then turned to David. Now, can we talk in front of Amber? Amber knows the score?

Yes.

Well, David, I've been through all my notes, all that you told me over the phone, looked carefully at the documents, and spoke to the other side this morning – Robert Cohen – they're willing to settle for an apology, and an out-of-court recompense.

David squinted, What?

Sophie's angry, very angry. Well, you know how it works, the other side keeps them angry for as long as they can. Martin shook his head and glanced at Amber, then back at David. This Sophie must really hate you. How did things get so unpleasant?

David shrugged. We have some idea. A guy in the department, Tommy Rose, caused some of the problem. He told me as much.

Martin frowned, Yes, well, you told me that. I doubt if it helps us much.

But it's true.

Well, true or not, will this Tommy admit to it in court?

David sat thinking about Tommy and his schoolboy manner. In court he'd admit it, yes. He defamed Sophie more than I did.

But not in writing, you see. Not in writing. I mentioned your colleague Tommy this morning to the other side, as part of our defence. They didn't budge. They didn't seem worried. They claim that you caused Sophie so much suffering, a great deal of mental torment, for which she has a right to recompense. Lawyers can be wicked, David, wicked and merciless. Take my word for it, we'll need to prepare thoroughly for your defence, and with care.

Amber sat forward. Isn't that a tautology? I'm trying to imagine a lawyer preparing for a case thoroughly without care.

Martin sat back. Of course, of course. What I meant is, well, I told the other side David was carefully documenting any costs of stress-related illness, costs of any advice he sought, anything related to the case, and Sophie will have to pay these cost when she loses the case – we hope.

David's eyes narrowed. Why are you shying away from Tommy?

We can't rely on him. He might not admit to anything on the stand.

If I'm there, he'll admit to it. He took the letter from the print room and put it in the staffroom under my cup.

I hope you didn't threaten him.

Threaten him? He squirmed a little when I advised him to tell the truth. But I didn't threaten him.

Martin frowned. Because it won't help us at all if Tommy owns up because you bullied him, and you're sitting there glaring at him in court and the judge thinks, 'He's terrorised this poor little fellow.' Now that won't help us at all, will it? After all, David, Sophie's taking you to court because she claims you're a bully.

I didn't bully Sophie. I didn't bully Tommy. I don't have to bully him. He's screwing Sophie.

Amber said, I'm not so sure.

David leaned back and looked over at her. What?

I said I don't know.

But you told me –

I told you they were close.

But the implication was clear.

You forget that Sophie has a sixteen-year-old daughter in high school. People see Tommy with Sophie, but they've also seen Tommy with Sophie's daughter. Tommy hangs around the high school gate.

David shook his head, You didn't tell me that.

Could be either of them, mother or daughter. Or both.

Martin leaned forward, Forgive my scepticism here, but my job is to keep you out of trouble, son, so my job is to be cautious, extremely cautious. We have nothing in writing from this Tommy. We don't know if he's interested in Sophie or Sophie's daughter, and you're telling me that, in court, he'll say whatever you want him to say, he'll speak in your defence against Sophie. I don't think so. Martin looked over the top of his glasses. David, look, take it from me – the closer you get to the courts in this town, the more afraid of them you are. Bargain. Always bargain. Avoid court.

Amber leaned forward, Surely, if Tommy took David's draft memo, he's stolen David's property.

Well, uh, he looked askance at Amber, straightened his tie, Look, that may be true, but, like I said, we have no proof that Tommy took the document, and no guarantees that he'll admit to it in court. And it's university property, not David's.

Amber nodded and said, But certainly David's memo, even if he'd signed it, which he didn't, has to fall into the category of qualified privilege. David meant the document for the department head, not Tommy or Sophie or the staff. David meant it for his boss, and Sophie's boss. There's no evidence that David meant it for Sophie, or talked to anyone else about the memo. Where's the defamation?

Well, um, Martin cleared his throat, That, um, I was coming to that. I told the other side just this morning that we'd fight this case on qualified privilege. That made them sit up.

It *is* qualified privilege, said Amber. To express concern to your boss, to Sophie's boss, is qualified privilege. David didn't express any concerns about Sophie to her students. I was the student. I complained about Sophie. I'll go to court and say that.

David sat and listened.

Martin pulled at his tie and shook his head. Uh, now that would be unwise.

Amber opened her hands on the desk. So what's your plan? There's a good chance that David can back Sophie's lawyers down.

Well, uh, it's not that easy. And look – I'll do the backing down of Sophie's lawyers, not David.

Amber glanced at David, who sat back and watched. The police should talk with Tommy.

No, said Martin. He sat forward and raised a finger. No way.

Amber opened both hands. Why not?

That would complicate things.

He's suicidal, said David.

What? said Martin. You didn't tell me that.

David looked out the window at metal heating vents on the tarred roof. Drifting off, trying to focus, he said, Tommy told me in confidence.

Confidence? said Amber. Sure, after you scared the bejeezus out of him.

I don't want the police talking to Tommy, not in this town.

Amber leaned back in her chair. She looked at David.

Martin shook his head. Look, Amber, David's tangled up in this mess with Sophie, not with Tommy. We need to sort out one problem at a time.

Tommy is the same problem. It's all one problem, said Amber. I'll say that in court.

Martin raised and lowered his hand off the table, as if pumping up a tire, Slow down. Slow down. My advice to you, Amber, is to take care. You could be in breach of the law.

Amber shook her head, Come on, Martin.

Martin sat back. I wouldn't advise you to –

Amber raised the palm of her hand. That's the problem, Martin. You need to advise us about *what* to do. What to do, not how to do nothing. Take the fight to them.

Now look. I'll advise David what's best to do. He pointed. He's in this mess now because he didn't seek my advice earlier.

Amber nodded and watched him, then raised her wrist and glanced at the time. Okay. Martin, we have another appointment. Is there anything else you need?

Martin sat with his mouth open. Anything *I* need?

Yes, said Amber.

Now you look here. David's my client, not you.

Amber smiled. We've had a bad week, Martin. Sorry. But thank you, that's good news about qualified privilege.

She stood and waited.

Martin stood. He didn't enjoy clients looming over him. He paused,
extended his hand, Well, thanks for coming.

Amber grasped his hand. My pleasure.

Martin followed them out the door.

54

Amber judges Martin Steadman

Outside, Amber and David leaned against the Volvo.

He turned to face her. What the hell were you doing in there?

She watched him. You're angry.

Why did you say we needed to leave? We weren't done.

She looked down. How did you find Martin Steadman?

This afternoon, you mean?

No. Where did you find him?

Yellow Pages.

He's not brilliant.

No. Probably not.

You should have talked to me.

He looked over at her. I'm in this mess because I talked to you.

She folded her arms.

He pulled keys from his pocket.

Sorry, she said. I think I frightened him a little.

You sure did.

Amber shook her head. There all the same, aren't they?

They?

He 'earns', and I use the word loosely, $200 an hour. Today wouldn't have taken him fifteen minutes if he'd prepared better. He'll make chit-chat about the weather for $200 an hour if you let him.

She looked at David, wondering if he wanted to hear any more, then she said, Last year, as part of an assignment, we watched a case from the gallery, a domestic case from start to finish, about a will and a bequest. This retired fellow had lived on the New South Wales coast for ten years, living a comfortable life; he named his beneficiary, everything was in order, shipshape. On a notorious bend along the coast road, he ran his car through a guardrail. It killed him. The family was shocked. The main problem was that he'd been married for ten years to a shrew of a woman he didn't like. That notorious bend sorted his bad marriage.

A gust of wind caught her apricot hair; she held it down with one hand. David had never seen the freckling over the saddle of her nose in bright sunlight.

But his bequest wasn't settled that easily. He'd given everything to his two adult children. So the wife fought the children for two long years. It was worth sitting through just to watch them bend the truth, for us students an important lesson – lawyers are brilliant at finding problems, but no good at fixing them. They can locate difficulties in the most unlikely places, hidden in corners, behind fences. But they have no skill at fixing problems. They demand payment by the hour because they create problems that use up time. They never demand a lump sum payment for a problem they deliver you from because they wouldn't make any money. They work selflessly to liberate you from evil, then remind you, and ask you for two hundred dollars with each reminder.

Who won?

Who won the bequest?

Yes.

Nobody won. Bleak House.

David looked over the road at Martin Steadman's office, then unlocked the car door. Let's go. We can talk about Martin in the car.

They crept along Barry Drive in solid traffic. David noticed men staring hard at Amber from pedestrian crossings, from cars, missing green lights as they watched Amber smiling and laughing, moving her hands and talking about the law.

Alone, David pulled into his driveway and walked to the mailbox. The lid squeaked open. A business card lay in the bottom – 'Officer Nigel Plant AFP' in neat printing above a handwritten 'Hi, David. Visited today at 3 p.m. but you weren't home. Please contact me.'

David's stomach dropped. He started to shake, all of it coming back to him. He walked into the house and slumped in the chair.

That night he lay in the dark.

55

Amber and David walking

In the morning, David touched the letter box, as cold as stone to his fingertips. He fought nausea, too worried to pull open the flap. A handwritten note in the corner of the letter box, like a funnel web crawling into his sleeve.

He'd taught students about phobias in Psych 1 and shown examples on film. A woman so terrified of her letter box she couldn't walk near it let alone open it. She feared hopping frogs from a plague some years before when frogs had over-run the ground in her town, crawled into her house, plopping over linoleum into her kitchen. The phobia bit deeper when she found a frog sitting on a letter inside her letter box. She cried and reeled back. Then, as if mocking her, Australian Post printed species of green frogs on stamps. The chance of finding a letter addressed to her with a slimy frog on the stamp made her shake with fear, drove her back indoors. She cowered and wept. The video showed her trying to master the mail box, approaching it with a soft-voiced psychologist beside her, talking through each step, her eyebrows tight, elbows close to her body, whimpering, leaning away from the letter box. The psychologist's hand resting on her arm, coaxing her with soft words and steadiness, but the woman couldn't go near the letter box.

David's students hooted with laughter. They rolled around cackling.

David had watched the film a hundred times and today knew that terror in his chest, the absurdity of it, too frightened to lift a metal flap, talking to himself. Just do it.

He couldn't. Knowledge didn't free him. It counted for nothing.

He exhaled. A loud breath, he reached down again, drew back. He walked to the door, turned and walked back, faced the letter box. Shaking, he opened the metal flap and pulled out a brown envelope. Better than a card from Nigel.

Looking down on a sea of brown leaves, he placed the letter on top of the letter box and studied the leaves at his feet. He touched a finger to his lips, breathing deeply.

He picked up the brown envelope, thinking about the silly woman and her frogs, opened the letter and scanned its contents. Another summons from Sophie's lawyers, a notice hammered to his door.

He carried the letter inside and murmured, Her need for vengeance before she leaves this earth is more dangerous than her vainglory, hissing like a gander.

He sat in a chair by the window and listened to the evening grow quiet. In the cream-coloured room he mumbled, The beast is robbing me of sleep. He stared down at his backpack on the floor and thought about fleeing and he thought about the danger of over-analysis, constant monitoring of your own judgements and thoughts, a venom swimming in your skull. Blow out the lamp and sit with the good darkness around you.

He rested with his back against the backpack on the floor and dreamed of clear mornings with Emma, sitting well-fed and halfway through a novella, listening to orioles at daybreak before he and Emma stood from soft grass and left the woods.

Amber walked beside him, and sniffed whisky on his breath. The front of his shirt was crinkled as if he'd slept in it. Streets in Cook lay empty. David hunching his shoulders and trembling, eyes deep-set and staring. Amber led him onto an oval, kicking through leaves with her shoes brushing over cut grass. They stood with a gaudy red sun on their faces; it was quiet except for the shoosh of an occasional passing car.

After a time, he turned and smiled faintly. Thank you.

For what?

For coming. He looked down. I missed you.

They walked on.

She said, Do you want to talk?

David fidgeted with the top button on his shirt. He said, Maybe later. He gave her a glance. I need a small favour. His voice was hoarse. He undid his top button. Can you find me a better lawyer?

Better than Martin? That should be easy.

My first choice was a bad one. You were right. I might have bigger problems.

I'll ask around. Amber watched the side of his face and drifted next to him. Is that all?

He walked as if alone, gave an empty stare in her direction and said, No, it's fine. I'm fine. His lifeless tone seemed to loom nearby and slow their pace, drag at his feet like river weed.

Amber said nothing as they drifted, but she understood the lilt in his throat and the defeat in the curve of his back. As they walked, his moods seemed to blow in from all directions.

Near the far edge of the oval he slowed, and sat down against the wide base of a manna gum. She rested her shoulder against the tree looking down on him, then sat next to him on the ground with her knees up. After a time, David felt a chill and stood; Amber stood next to him and waited. He turned his face into light breeze drifting over grass and through trees on the oval. Blue light fell through peppermint gums; a rippling sheet of starlings came over them travelling to a roost.

She felt low sun on her neck as they walked. She watched David's hand swing back and forth. Leaves on manna gums hung down like sharp knives.

Halfway across the oval, he stopped as if he'd decided it was pointless, meandering with no destination. It's a form of terrorism, you know. Fat brown letters. They understand the potency of a letter. A hammer to the head and they know it. So they hammer me.

Words leaned over them, pressing down as they trudged over the oval. Amber worried that she would fumble slight words meant to console him, David wrestled with a secret logic that only he understood. He could do some good for others if he escaped punishment over the boy.

They walked.

I need to tell you something.

Amber listened but he walked and said nothing, as if deciding.

There was a sort of raw grieving in his throat, a melancholy in the tilt of his head. Amber's hands were cold. She pushed them deep into her pockets.

He dipped his face a little as they walked. Why can't I control this fear? Yesterday I wrote on a piece of paper, 'Hang the traitor inside your head.' Stared at the phrase, but it did no good. Nothing does any good.

Amber said, I'm sorry. She pulled a hand from her pocket and looped her arm through his. Not many of us are good at it.

I wonder sometimes if you laugh at my naiveté.

Amber shook her head. You did the right thing. Sophie believes students need to be remade in her own image. It's the pinnacle of narcissism.

I'm learning about the law, he said. Sophie's energy is boundless. I've plunged my fist into a tar baby. His lips were compressed and pale. The board stood by my decision to alter the rules of appeal then the university washed its hands of the defamation case that came with it. They say it's between me and Sophie.

They could smell wet grass and for a time couldn't think of much to say. Blue dusk fell around them. They left the oval and walked empty streets.

Close to home, he spoke to the ground. I suppose I should clean the flat. The place is a mess. The state of the flat can't help.

She smiled. No. It can't.

56

Clean-up

Amber started with cups and glasses stained with grease and wine and milk, cracked dishes in the sink crusted with old food. Bits of soggy cornflakes plugged the kitchen drain hole. David was embarrassed. Lost in his own flat, he followed her around like a puppy. He dried dishes that she handed to him, pulled the vacuum cleaner from the closet when she asked for it. Then he left her, picked up a broom and moved through rooms to brush cobwebs from the ceiling and out of corners.

Amber vacuumed. Her thick orange hair swished forward and covered her face.

Why are you doing this? said David.

To protest against everything Sophie stands for. I'll tell her I did this. She stopped, turned her head and frowned. Someone needs to tell you, and it might as well be me.

Tell me what? David leaned against the wall and folded his arms. His blackness had lifted some.

Amber said, Nobody will stay around a helpless man very long.

David dwelt on this for a moment. Panic had overtaken him when Emma disappeared. He knew Emma held secrets from him, a condition of their staying lovers. Love was meaningless without silences. They'd learned the habit of repose. But Emma's silences had frightened him, even more than her words did. Amidst rage and blackness, their time had glided to a rest. He'd panicked, felt sorry for himself, drifted into deep melancholy, moped around and stayed in bed, slept in his office. The moping fed melancholy, and the melancholy detached him from Emma. He's lost the person he loved.

Amber handed him the vacuum cleaner. I'm leaving now. The rest is up to you.

57

Nigel Plant visits the Kellys

Nigel locked the car and mounted the step. Curtains were drawn and he knocked three times but heard nothing from inside. Then the latch rattled and the door opened just enough to show the pasty freckled face of Shannon Kelly.

What do you want now? His voice sharp, his eyes cold blue in the morning light.

Not at school today?

What does it look like?

You all right?

I said, what do you want?

Nigel leaned forward. Can I please come in?

From a back room, Who is it, Shanny?

Staring, he said in a loud voice, Cops again.

The bed springs screeched and the shuffling of bare feet to the sitting room.

Shannon slumped in the kitchen doorway, knees under his chin forming a triangle blocking their way.

She squinted through the door. Yes?

Hello, Mrs Kelly, said Nigel.

Mandy said, You found him then.

Not yet, Mrs Kelly.

Glancing back at Shannon in the doorway, fear in her eyes. Then what do you want?

Can I please come in?

A twitch under her right eye. Okay, come in.

She unhooked the safety latch and the smell of dirt and shit and the smelly dog hit Nigel. He tried to breathe through his mouth.

Mandy shut the door.

Thank you, said Nigel.

Mandy walked to the same wooden chair she'd sat in last time, and slumped with her hands twisted in her lap. Shannon wedged in the doorway. Nigel sat on the brown sofa under the Jimi Hendrix poster. The soot-coloured pit bull terrier waddled into the room and banged its tail against Nigel's leg.

Mandy said, Well, what is it?

We'd like your help with other leads.

Redness crept into Shannon's face. He started kicking at the doorway and the pit bull waddled over and licked his face.

Mandy looked at her hands folded in her lap. You're nowhere then. She massaged her thumb.

Nigel said, I'm sorry, but we need to consider drugs. We need to know if Rodney had other friends, or family, people who might know this man.

Mandy shook her head. We've been through this.

With his hand resting on the dog's back, Shannon looked up from the kitchen doorway and said, Pay attention, Nigel. She said 'No.'

The dog wandered over and tried to lick Nigel's hand.

Mandy said, We can't take any more. Just find him. We can't do your job for you.

We understand how difficult this is, Mrs Kelly. Rodney was carrying a knife. There must be people he was afraid of.

She sighed again. Of course he carried a knife. They all carry knives. She hunched forward with her hands folded in her lap and started to rock back and forth.

Mrs Kelly, if you don't mind, I'd like to ask Shannon some questions.

Mandy looked down at her son in the doorway. So ask, then leave.

Nigel looked at Shannon. Do your friends carry knives?

If they feel like it.

Mandy interlocked thin fingers in her lap. She turned her face towards Shannon.

Nigel opened his hands. We'd be grateful for names of your friends. We don't know if we're looking for a man, a boy. Names would help.

Mandy turned to Shannon still slouched in the doorway, then back to Nigel. That's enough. Leave us alone.

Shannon stared at Nigel. Awkward time passed, he seemed not to blink. In the quiet, Nigel heard a car rush by.

Shannon?

He said nothing.

Nigel said, Names of your friends would help.

Through tight lips, the boy said, So?

Mandy seemed to fire scarlet, her teeth held tight. She stood and faced Nigel. Look, we don't know.

Nigel said, I'm sorry, I didn't mean to upset you. Can I –

Mandy glared. Look, that's it. No more.

Shannon stood up in the doorway, walked to the sofa and stood over Nigel. She said 'No more.'

Mandy rubbed her chin with the back of her hand. Nigel waited. The same dog barking somewhere in the neighbourhood.

Shannon walked back and sat down and started kicking the wall with the toe of his shoe.

Mandy shook her head slowly. We can't help you.

Nigel noticed the likeness in their faces; Mandy would have been Shannon at the same age. Shannon slammed his head back against the kitchen door. He turned and stared as if the power of hatred in his open blue eyes would drive away the police. Fucking moron.

Shanny. Mandy's voice was faint. She stood from her wooden chair. You don't use that sort of language here.

The boy seemed to boil with indecision.

Nigel thought, If I wasn't here, he'd defy her. But Shannon stood from his slump in the doorway, turned and walked into the dark part of the house.

Mandy's white face blank with quandary against the dirty cream wall, her red hands knotted like brambles in her lap.

58

David in the night

David stirred sometime in the night. He'd been dreaming about a restaurant in Dickson they used to visit, how the windows glowed yellow when Emma walked to the front door and wrapped her long fingers around the door handle, the curve of her neck, the way she leaned in against the heavy glass door, eyes shining as if she'd just remembered something important.

Emma searched the room and found David's table, gave a slow smile of recognition, came over and stood at an angle with her hand on one hip. I hope we haven't been careless.

David told her about some triumph at work, the details were garbled in his dream, something about a staff meeting where he fought off seven academics to win a concession for students, critical powers over courses they'd paid for, a victory.

In the dream, Emma shook her head, rose scent coming off her skin, and she laughed at him. Come on, darling. It's me you're talking to. Your lover. The woman who knows you better than anyone. She paused again and said, Why tell me this story?

But it's important.

She laughed again. Important? You want me to pat you on the head and clap, like you're a dog walking on its hind legs.

In the dream, David sat back and watched her, studied her hands resting on the table. He looked up and tried to watch her eyes, concentrate on the blue in them. He said, What do I need to understand?

The strong afternoon light cast a white glow over Emma's head.

He squinted and searched her face and said again, What do I need to understand?

She smiled and he woke and knew the dream meant she was dead. His hands were cold.

David switched on the bedside lamp and opened a novel about posing and clean shots and squandered chances in the Rift Valley. The author quoting from memory what his dead friend had written: In the dark night of the soul, it is always 3 o'clock in the morning.

He tried to finish the chapter but couldn't. He slid in a bookmark, and waited in the dark, eyes open. He thought about Emma's first night in his bed. In the kitchen, David had slid his hand onto her shoulder. It was heated and tight from their long, fast walk. He leaned down and kissed her naked arm. She stood close. David touched her cheek with the backs of three fingers, bent over and kissed her mouth. They held each other and she gusted warm breath in his ear. He knew the scent coming off her, and the scent lifted memories. He slipped his hand inside white cotton onto her skin.

They climbed the stairs. Dusk lay around them, steel blue. He undressed her as she stood in front of him; she stepped out of her underwear with her hand resting on his shoulder. He lifted Emma onto his bed then stood and undressed as she lay and watched with one hand behind her head. He climbed in beside her.

David slid his hand down her back. She rested her cheek against his shoulder. An open hand slid down her belly. She brushed her lips against his ear. David pushed her long hair from their faces. Emma whispered.

They were hot and she kicked off the blanket. In charcoal light, she wrapped her legs around him and dozed with her hand on his leg.

With his head on the pillow, he watched her deep breathing, the way she stretched out on the bed and slept, rolled onto her side and tucked her face into his body, curled round him. The consolation of her cool hand in the dark.

59

David visits Eddie Flannery

Daniel crying over the telephone, smacking himself in the head, giving little one-word answers to David's questions. David pushed him to talk and Daniel said he's visited Eddie Flannery at his office. Flannery had laughed at him and said Emma was gone.

David sat in his office for an hour, drinking and trying to settle his fury. He paced to the wall and back again, lay on the floor with his head on a pillow, stood and paced for another half hour, drank from the bottle until his head floated, eyes watering. He dropped the bottle into the drawer and decided to visit Eddie. He would size him up, listen and nod to Eddie's platitudes and lies, Eddie's fake healing words. Reassure him. Get his measure, find him another time, maybe in a week, outside Eddie's house, watch him from a dark corner of the yard as he fumbled with his key trying to open the back door, and hammer the little man into the ground.

The door fell open and Eddie said, David, it's been a long time – welcome.

He gave an easy laugh, but didn't offer his hand and David wondered if it was clammy.

How you been? in a deep Irish brogue.

David stepped past him into his office and eyed the space above Eddie's desk. Southern Cross School of Hypnotherapy, the Life Skills Institute, the University of the New Age.

The room smelt of Dettol.

There was no obvious fear in Eddie. He stood close to David, stretching and arching his back with his hands on his hips, pleased to see him, or so it seemed. David studied him. Eddie trusted his own abilities, brandishing certitude; he must play this game every day in his office, thought David. Toy with people.

He kept his reddish hair cropped and neat, probably visited the barber once a week. His grey Saville Row suit didn't hide his narrow shoulders. A bright yellow bow tie set him off like a roman candle.

He looked straight at David with china-blue eyes and didn't flinch or blink, as if competing in a stare-down that David could never win. He seemed to say, 'Well now, my friend, let's pause for a moment and look at where I am compared to where you are. Who's moved along then? Who's master today?'

Find a chair, David. Can I interest you in some tea or coffee?

He nodded. Tea. Black, please.

Eddie turned and stood over his desk, telephoned his receptionist and said, No interruptions for fifteen minutes, please, then looked out the window. Nice day out there.

Yes. Warmed a little.

Eddie laughed. I never know summer from winter stuck in this hermetically sealed room.

David studied his broad smile, as warm as a toasted bun, the healer scattering charm and compassion. Eddie walked back and sat behind his desk, rubbed his thumb against his forefinger, almost imperceptibly, and David wondered if Eddie stayed behind the hardwood desk because he wasn't that fearless. David turned his head slightly. You don't make house calls then.

Oh no, heavens no. Booked solid every day. Why do you ask?

Just interested in what a lifestyle counsellor does, that's all.

Eddie chuckled. Straight to the point. I like that. But you're a psychologist, you know what we do.

David smiled, Actually, no. We're pretty theoretical up there, and the work of a psychologist differs from the work of a lifestyle counsellor.

Coach, David. I'm a lifestyle coach. And yes, of course it differs. He grinned. I think you're laughing at me a little.

Didn't mean to offend.

He leaned back and laughed again. Relax, David. You could never offend me. But look around. He raised his hand and waved it around the office. We help a lot of people in this room, depression cases mostly, and phobias. Mostly women. Men are different. When they find themselves low, they go out and kick a football around, or sail or play squash. You know how it goes.

Or kick the significant other.

Yes, that too. Of course. The bulk of my work is protecting women from men. Cruel types. But look, you're not here doing a project on lifestyle coaches.

David leaned forward. No, I'm not. I understand you know Daniel Bentham.

Daniel? Yes, he's a client. You know I can't say any more than that.

Well, I'm not so sure about that. Psychologists and doctors are bound by a code. I don't know about lifestyle coaches.

The rules are exactly the same. Otherwise business would crumble.

We certainly don't want your business to crumble, Eddie. But how well do you know him?

He came in five or six times, maybe seven, along with his wife, in those early days when all of us thought there was something to rescue. You know, those early days of hope. That phase when a couple tries to resurrect a dead marriage.

You saw Daniel yesterday, and, watching you now, I can see how you handled him.

Handled him?

Sat back and read that he's feeling some guilt, blaming himself for the failed marriage.

Yes, well, he was starting to feel some guilt over his attacks on Emma, and I tried to help him. But, well, you know how men are these days, spiritually undernourished, too obstinate to seek real help. They seldom rise to the task of transformation, travel to the heart of their pain until those last few moments of red torment. Before they crash. Daniel stopped meeting his appointments – that is, until yesterday. Eddie shook his head. Sad, sad business. A victim of his own melancholy.

David leaned forward again. Have you spoken to Emma?

His face didn't change. I haven't seen Emma in months. Nobody knows where she is.

Daniel wants Emma back.

He shook his head a little. That's not really your concern.

Tomorrow, if she's not back home, I'll tell the police about you. You're screwing your clients and that needs to be made public.

Eddie smiled. Ah, the hero. Problem is, the hero's a pretender, a perverted university lecturer carrying a grudge. He wants me to give out information about his mistress so he can find her. Otherwise, he'll report me. See how absurd it looks?

I'll just have to risk that.

And you're in trouble already.

Meaning?

Meaning Sophie Moss and her Jew lawyer.

David paused and tried to collect his thoughts. He said, Daniel wants Emma back home. He's suffering because of you.

Look, you want Emma back in Daniel's house so you can access her. That's understandable, she's a beautiful woman. It's also reprehensible. Maybe somebody needs to publicise the perverted little triangle you've manoeuvred this poor couple into, maybe a strong feminist at the university, a woman who thinks that you stick up for rapists.

He was more skilful at defending himself than David remembered.

David paused and said, Just tell us where she is.

Eddie shook his head. You mean tell *you*.

You're evasive, Eddie.

Eddie rolled his head back and laughed. Come now. I haven't seen her in months. No idea where she is.

Daniel thinks she's dead. I do too.

Then call the police. Eddie was looking out the window, then held up his wrist and consulted his watch. Sorry, I've got people to see.

David watched him for a moment. Eddie's expression was blank.

Thanks for your time. You understand what I'll do next.

Eddie smiled. Sure. I understand. You came to my office and threatened me, and you failed.

David watched him again and Eddie continued to grin.

He said, Good day. Thanks for coming. Eddie held both hands open, Look, nobody wants to see Daniel suffer. It must be a nightmare for the poor man. I want to help him as much as you do. As Eddie smiled, his dimples showed. Well, David, you come back if there's anything I can do. Anything. Understand?

Oh, I understand.

And David, remember two things. First, what goes around comes around.

David waited.

And second, in this office I hear a lot of stories. Women come to me and talk.

Your point?

My point is that you have a lot to worry about. You have a past.

David stared and Eddie broke into another crooked smile.

You're here because you feel guilty about something. I'm not sure what it is. You've changed since the supercilious arrogant lectures I was forced to sit through. Something's hit a switch. Sooner or later, I'll find out what that is. Eddie stood and said, We'll talk again. Soon. He walked to the door and held it open.

David passed the receptionist.

She looked up and smiled, Thanks, David. Have a nice day.

Eddie said, And, David…

David turned and faced him.

Tell Daniel to stay away from my house. He'll get hurt.

David left.

60

Hospital

Daniel Bentham thought he heard giggling. He tried to force one eye open. He rolled his head, opened the eye a slit, felt one ear filled with dirt, his right eye jammed into the ground was full of leaves. He could see the hazy form of a bicycle leaning against a white tree.

Giggling again, a whisper – Is he awake?

Daniel felt prodding with a stick. The stick forced his head to roll. Two boys, maybe twelve or thirteen, loomed over him. One stood and the other crouched and prodded him again. Daniel's lips were fat and pasted together.

The boy crouching over him noticed his eyes flutter.

Daniel squinted, tried to roll forward and say, Help me. But the words didn't come.

The boys wrenched their bikes away from the tree, leapt on and raced down the track. As they disappeared, Daniel heard one yell, Fuckin' told you.

When they'd gone, he heard the drone of traffic. He knew where he was but not when.

He rolled over and lay flat on his back, twigs pressed into the back of his head. A stringy bark waved over him. Daniel wrapped his hand around the base of the tree, pushed against the ground, rose up the trunk, lurched forward, and stood wavering and waiting for the nausea to lessen. He stumbled from tree to tree with the sun at his back.

A middle-aged police officer with a rusty moustache stood inside the white curtain. He looked down and said, Well, that's broken the monotony, hasn't it? Not much good for the inner ear, though.

Daniel didn't respond, didn't like the police making jokes.

In the cubicle next to him, a ten-year-old boy wailed about his broken leg, screamed at the young doctor who looked like a schoolgirl in a white coat, Don't fuckin' touch it again, you slut. Don't touch me.

The police officer said, Don't know if you remember me. Nigel Plant.

A squat, middle-aged nurse split the curtain pushing a steel cart laden with rattling bottles, bandages, and instruments. She stopped next to Daniel's bed, leaned over him, peering at the side of his head. Lucky you were stretcher distance from the hospital, she said. She leant down, shook her head slowly and touched his hair, It's very dirty, my dear, very dirty. You must have lain in the mud for quite a while.

He mumbled, Most of the night.

I'll try to deaden it. You tell me if this hurts. She leaned over Daniel, spilled clear antiseptic onto gauze, breathed on him whistling through her nose as she picked at the wound with tweezers. The doctor will be here soon.

She swabbed his scalp, lifted out debris with tweezers, flat pieces of bark, tiny round twigs, then she tipped a vial upside down, pushed a needle into it, and parted the hair from the bloody dent in his head. She slid the needle under his scalp and Daniel winced.

How's that?

I can still feel it.

What hit you?

I don't know.

Nigel shook his head and said, We haven't found anything out there. You get a look at the person?

Daniel watched the nurse wince, as if she knew the needle would sting him.

She wasn't listening to Nigel. Won't be long now, she said.

Daniel flinched and gripped the sheet around his hips. I can still feel that.

I'll shoot in some more. The nurse loaded the needle with another dose, and moved it towards the injury.

The curtain slashed open and a little white-haired man shuffled in. Good morning.

Oh, good, said the nurse, Dr Goodrick's here.

He leaned in close and peered through bifocals. What do we have here? With a shaky hand he pulled away blood-matted hair and squinted. Round, hmmm. Deep. What's happening Trudy? The doctor had the snuffles.

From behind him, the nurse said, We need to deaden it a little more. I've tried to clean it, but it's full of dirt. He can feel the tweezers.

Dr Goodrick slipped into pale rubber gloves and leaned against the stainless steel bed. The nurse slid the full needle into the doctor's faltering hand, and he tried to focus, placing the side of his thumb and forefinger in a half circle against Daniel's scalp, squirting anaesthetic around the wound. Then he blinked, aimed the needle at the wound between his thumb and forefinger. As Nigel and the nurse watched, he trembled close to Daniel's scalp, slipped, pricked his own thumb through the rubber glove, and continued into Daniel's head, all in one move. Daniel saw the nurse stiffen, and Nigel's eyes widen.

Damn, said the doctor. Damn, damn, damn. Same trick I pulled last week.

What? said Daniel.

Only a needle-stick. Nothing to worry about, er, Mr –

Bentham, said Nigel. Daniel Bentham.

Let's finish up. He continued to clean the wound, then asked the nurse for a needle and thread. You know, he squinted, it's round.

Round? said Nigel.

Yes. Have a look, officer.

Nigel leaned in and wrinkled his nose.

What do you think it looks like, officer?

Ten-cent piece.

Like a hammer, said the doctor. Seen it before, in domestics. Not living with a hot-tempered friend, are you, Mr, ah –

Bentham.

As the doctor worked, the nurse said, He claims a woman named Emma did it.

A woman? said the doctor, Well, now that's fashionable, isn't it, a woman. And a strong one too. She didn't like you very much, son. Might lower your IQ a few points.

Doctor, said Daniel. That needle-stick.

Oh, don't worry about that. Happens all the time. Damn nuisance. I'm sure it'll be fine.

The doctor reached a curved needle and thread past the line of Daniel's vision.

Doctor, did the needle go into me first, then into you second, or into you first, then into me second?

Doctor Goodrick wagged his head. Well, I didn't quite follow your question, son, but last week it was the other way around, dirty fellow he was too – oh, that's probably the wrong thing to say. He pulled a stitch through. Look, we'll follow procedure. Test for Hep B, and C and HIV this week, and test you again in a month, then six months from now.

Six months.

Have to be sure. He leaned close. You know, look at the edge of this hole, Trudy. It really looks like a hammer to me.

Daniel blinked. Doctor, you said this happened before?

Mr Bentham, we're as careful as we can be. But sometimes it's rushed in here, we can be a little tired. Don't worry, you'll be fine.

Daniel watched the doctor study the wound. As he leaned closer, Daniel noticed he had missed a square of white whiskers on his cheek. What else beside tests?

Well, no sex of course, without a condom.

Nigel's radio beeped. He leaned down and said, Yes. Okay, right away. He looked at him. Sorry we didn't have a chance to talk again, Daniel. Accident on Belconnen Way. I'll be back in an hour. You're in good hands. He smirked.

Daniel winced. I'll be here.

Or in the basement, said Nigel.

Oh no, said the doctor. He squinted and sewed the wound with his mouth open. The basement's the morgue. Your friend here'll probably go to Ward Six, upstairs.

Nigel said, Might not be the right time to ask, Daniel, but what were you doing out there at two in the morning?

Hard to explain.

So how come we found your car out there?

Daniel winced as the doctor pulled through a long stitch. I thought I saw someone. A woman.

The doctor looked up at Nigel, Ask him another time, officer, please. Another place.

Sure, said Nigel.

Daniel reached up and tried to touch the back of his stinging head.

Uh, uh, hands off, said the doctor. Please.

Sorry.

Reminds me a little of my dad, said Nigel. Always said the Americans were the best bosses, he wouldn't work for anyone else. Said they were meant to be bosses. Back in those days that meant Hertz Rent-A-Car, the Tidbinbilla tracking station, or the Coca-Cola bottling plant in Queanbeyan. Dad chose the bottling plant but he said it was only a matter of time before you could pick any job you wanted, anywhere in the world and be working for the Americans. Boy, was he wrong about that. Anyway, the point of my story: on the assembly line at the Coca-Cola bottling plant, he gained factory-wide fame for perfecting the standing nap. He'd catch twenty winks for half an hour and still go through the motions, never miss a bottle. What do you think about that, doctor?

The doctor dipped his head and glared over the top of his bifocals. Officer, I'm not quite sure what your point is.

Nigel smiled. Yeah, I can see that. He pulled the curtain aside.

As Nigel left, the boy next door started screaming again.

61

Heroine

On the front step, Bill took his wife Carolyn aside, stabbed his finger into her chest and said, Think, woman. Think. You're making a serious mistake.

Vengeance clouded each working day, demons chased him, burning his eyelids, burying him in smoky nightmares. Ghosts shouted in the room, grinning from corners, robbing his aptitude for a job he'd done easily for seven years. Dreams of killing Eddie Flannery made him sweat. He wrestled in the night on twisted sheets and decided to break Carolyn first, make her fold. He directed his solicitor to write threatening letters. He upped the number of telephone calls and increased their ferocity. Standing on the porch of her parents' home in Ainslie, he watched Carolyn shudder and bow her head and acquiesce. She rubbed her chest and made promises.

Bill returned to his office and breathed easily. She's defeated.

The next day Carolyn recanted as if Bill had never stood on the porch and shouted and stabbed his finger into her chest, as if he'd never paid solicitors thousands of dollars to write chilling letters.

He turned up in Ainslie again, demanding to see his daughters, stood in uniform with his partner Lieutenant Gail Sheeny, resting his thumb on the butt of his pistol. Carolyn waited and shivered as he spoke. Head down, she agreed to his demands.

A day later, she changed her mind again. She wouldn't bow.

He exploded. He knew it was the lifestyle coach giving Carolyn the muscle to stand against him.

On a Tuesday afternoon, Bill and Lieutenant Gail Sheeny knocked once again on the door in Ainslie and stood back. No response. He knocked again, stepped off the porch, left shoe prints in black soil in the flower bed and tried to peer through the window.

A young blonde woman opened the door. Bill said, Excuse me, I need to see Carolyn Scott.

She's in the bath.

Bill squinted, Excuse me, but you are…?

The woman said, That's none of your concern. What exactly do you want?

Now just a minute here, stabbing a finger at her face. Who do you think you're talking to?

The woman's face was impassive. What do you want?

He leaned towards her and said, You could end up downtown.

Tell me what you want.

To get a message to Carolyn Scott, and I want to see my children. Who are you?

The woman stood and faced him. I'll give her the message. She folded her arms and watched him, a tense stand-off on the steps.

Bill glanced at his partner then back at the woman. You could be breaking the law.

I don't think so.

Bill watched her, looked again at Gail and pointed at the woman's face. Expect us back.

The woman said nothing, only stared.

He turned, and Lieutenant Sheedy followed him to the car.

Inside the house, Carolyn huddled in a back room with her parents; her black hair tangled, her piercing blue eyes wide. She stood and walked into the sitting room and said, Thank you.

The woman smiled and said, I see what you mean.

Carolyn glanced at her parents and shook her head. He's coming back sooner or later. He'll come back and get his own way.

I see why you think that. Let's go for a drive. He won't be back in a hurry. She glanced at Carolyn's parents. You don't mind, do you, if Carolyn and I go for a drive? You'll be okay?

Carolyn's parents nodded. We'll be fine.

Carolyn slumped in the corner and said, I'm a mess. Every day I want to shriek. I never want to see him again. I can't take any more.

The woman put her hand to Carolyn's face, then on Carolyn's shoulder and said, It's fine. Come on.

Down the cement path they climbed into the car.

62

Walking on Black Mountain

Carolyn said nothing in the car. They reached Black Mountain and parked opposite Wangara Street, stepped out and walked to the gate. In the car park, an orange Holden utility pulled up and unloaded a dog that ran to them. Carolyn squatted and patted the Rottweiler while the man studied the 'No Dogs' sign at the gate. Carolyn murmured to the dog and stroked him and the man walked up and glanced down but didn't smile.

She's lovely, said Carolyn.

He was red-bearded with red stubble on his head and a red face. He didn't speak as he bent over, slipped through the gate, and called his dog to follow. The dog jerked away from Carolyn and ran to him.

The women walked and didn't speak. Sun pressed between trees in long tawny grass. Breeze sifting through hanging leaves and salmon-coloured trunks along the path. Carolyn followed the woman down the narrow trail. Glimpses of the man running his dog flashed through forest above them.

Carolyn walked with her head down, kicking lazily at shadows. Her soles scuffed on a plank bridge over a creek and they came to a fire trail in a quiet part of the woodland.

The trail intersected a road big enough for Carolyn to fall in beside the woman, who said, Feeling better?

He still frightens me.

Don't let him.

I've never seen that happen before.

What?

You backed him down, made him leave.

He was bluffing.

He's hungry for vengeance against anyone who crosses him. Five years ago, there was rumour of a rape charge. The woman claimed he followed her home after writing a traffic ticket, came into her house and told her he'd forget the ticket if she took off her clothes. She refused, and, according to this woman, he raped her. The woman reported him, but the commissioner said she was a vindictive liar who'd been ticketed and was now bent on revenge. Bill's friend Lieutenant Gail Sheeny, the same one who was there today, claimed she'd been with him on the night of the alleged rape. She lied. The rape allegation went no further because Gail lied for him. She lies about me. She stood by him when he went for acting superintendent and she stands by him on my parent's front step.

They walked in shadows and sun, both wrapped in thought.

Carolyn drifted to the edge of the path, rubbed her chest below her throat. How could I be so stupid? Thinking I could change him, change his moods and bad days.

Is he from Canberra?

His father was an army administrator, moved the family around Australia, to England, America, rose up the ranks, obsessed with making good. His mother was a strange woman. With all the house moves, she grew despondent, angry, pissed off that her husband worked long hours and ignored her. Sometimes he stayed away for weeks. She drank in the afternoons and tied herself to Bill, her twelve-year-old boy confidant, her best friend. Bill received her confessions. You can imagine how she received me.

With some resentment.

A few years earlier she'd taken a lover, 'Gorgeous George' the schoolchildren called him. He was a Lothario who preyed on married women in military housing in Campbell Park. Bill's mother took Bill along as if George was a family friend, a favourite uncle. George was polite, told Bill stories. At George's house they talked and played cricket in the backyard. George patted him on the head when he hit the ball over the fence, said he was a natural, gave him sweets and comic books. 'See you in a little while, kid,' George would say, then go into the house with Bill's mother while Bill waited in the backyard and bounced the ball against the fence. Sometimes he waited in the car until she and George finished.

Bill's father learned about the affair from a fellow officer. His mother spent the day crying and nervous, she drank vodka in the mornings, accused her husband of snooping, and accused her son Bill of ratting on her, betrayal, called him a little snitch.

Bill knew there'd be a showdown between his father and Gorgeous George, a settling of scores. Bill thought his father would shoot him, maybe knock him down and finish him with an army sword. Restore the family honour. But that didn't happen. His father regarded the affair as an administrative task he could solve with good management. He wrote a letter outlining his concerns, asked George to telephone him, which George did. He organised a meeting between his wife, George and himself. They drank coffee, ate biscuits from a bowl and talked. Bill's father had them work through a list of solutions on paper he'd laid out on the table. The affair stopped.

End of problem.

Not quite. Bill's mother was desolate. She felt betrayed and started drinking again.

As the two women talked, the man with the Rottweiler was standing on a hill above, watching them. He looked like a slab of redwood. He walked down the hill, approached them and walked past, the dog panting and dripping.

A tepid wind scuttled leaves over the path, rippling Carolyn's print dress. Their shoes crunched dead leaves and sun blinked through the canopy.

So that's Bill. I put up with his silences for days at a time. A man who carries a gun to settle scores. People don't understand that. I'm taking a man to court who carries a gun that he says he'll use on me.

They bumped arms.

The woman laid her hand on Carolyn's shoulder. Call me if he tries anything.

I will.

Ahead they saw the gate and the car.

Carolyn said, You have the hint of an English accent.

Cherry Hinton in Cambridgeshire. I came out when I was eighteen.

With your family?

No.

Your parents still live there?

My mother died when I was seven. I lived with an aunt and uncle.

And your father?

I didn't see much of him.

As they neared the car, Carolyn waited and watched the side of her face. It was patterned from overhead leaves.

The woman stared ahead and said, It's a common story. The burden of being female.

At the gate they slid between posts and magpies were carolling in the trees.

63

Final plans

In the dark, Freddy O'Rourke edged his ute next to Bill's car on the track overlooking the Murrumbidgee River. Moonlight sifted through she-oaks and sparkled on the water. Freddy killed the motor, got out, leaned against the ute and lit a cigarette. Bill handed him a stubby.

They got back into the cab of Freddy's ute, blew smoke through the down-cranked window, slugged down beers looking out at the stars.

Bill said, Wadda you got?

Went by the house a few times, had a squiz. Went to the ridge like you told me, cold as a friggin' patch of bog berries up there. He's a queer one, that Eddie.

Why?

Hasn't had a priest to dinner yet.

See anyone on the ridge?

One guy. He won't come back.

Eddie?

No. Eddie doesn't like the outdoors. Eddie drives into the garage and uses an inside door to the house. It's hard to see who comes in and out with him.

My wife stays with him. I'm sure.

Maybe she does. What do you want me to do about it?

Disable her. But disable Eddie first. You're bigger than the two of them put together. Knock Eddie, then knock her. She'll be in bed with him. Smack him hard, hold her down while you smack him. Beat the eyes out of his head. Then finish her.

Happy to.

And wear a ski mask.

Yeah well, rubber mask maybe. He wiped his hand over the stubble on his head.

They swigged beer, Freddy tipped ash out the window and Bill said, Watch them for another week. And be careful, he's suspicious.

Yes, boss. Freddy sat quietly for a moment, then said, Can I ask something?

Go ahead.

His cigarette winked in the dark.

I like to run my dog on Black Mountain, chase 'roos there. I saw this blonde woman with your missus.

Bill stopped smoking and looked at Freddy. He waited, then said, Bullshit. You've been following my wife.

Freddy shook his head. No, look. I was just helping you out.

You don't need to follow my wife. That's not what I asked you to do. Stay away from my children.

Just doing some homework.

Bill swigged his beer and sucked on his cigarette. Anyway, your point?

My point is this. What about your ex-wife and the new girlfriend?

Bill paused and looked into the dark. She's not my ex. Not yet.

What's she doing?

Taking me to court, charging me with abuse.

With this new girlfriend?

I don't know anything about a new girlfriend. You worry about Eddie and my wife, not the girlfriend.

Why not catch your wife at her parents' place. Fix her there.

You're afraid of Eddie Flannery.

Freddy chuckled. Hardly. Look. Your missus is the one giving you grief, not Eddie Flannery.

My kids are in Ainslie.

Look. Catch her in the dark when she arrives at the parents' house. Hand over her mouth, stop her from yelling, needle-full big enough to leave her with some heavy remorse. Leave her troubled and sore. You tell a tame officer, they arrest her for drug use, you get your kids back. Simple.

Just like that.

Just like that.

You mean, do my wife instead of doing Eddie?

It's important to be tactical in life. Your problem is planning. Why be indirect? I'm not talkin' about some fuckin' act of atonement. What good does it do to hit two people?

Don't go near Ainslie. Understand? If she gets hit, the police come straight down on me. I'll wake up with six officers standing on my doorstep. So don't. Do not. Get it? Stop Eddie first, and that'll stop Carolyn. That will fix my problem. She'll lose her nerve. There'll be no court case. That little prick keeps her upright with his hard-on. She'll fall over when he stops giving her the big rally, or can't get a hard-on any more because his brain is mush. There's a dozen men out there who want Eddie disabled, some bad, Keith McGuire, Tad Bennet, some of them not so bad. You'll be the silent hero. We throw suspicion onto them instead.

Freddy shrugged in the dark. It's your party.

Bill handed him ten hundred-dollar bills that were folded in his shirt pocket. This is a start.

Freddy fumbled the money in the dark. Can I take a friend?

No. Go on your own.

Stop frettin'. This is a friend I can trust, a lookout.

No. People talk.

Well, we won't be having a game of cards on the hillside in the dark. Can't play a game of cards with a pair of paws.

Up to you. Just do your homework. And one other thing.

What? Freddy watched the tip of Bill's cigarette glow orange in the dark.

You flushed that map down the toilet, right?

It's done. Stop frettin'.

You know which windows to try?

I know which windows to try.

Good. Bill set his beer on the dash and reached into his pocket. He pulled out four pieces of white-painted wicker. Am I giving you too much at once?

Freddy snorted and blew smoke into the car. Come on.

Bill handed him the sticks. Leave these on the carpet.

Freddy rolled the wicker twigs between his fingers. What are they?

Freddy studied them and Bill flared a match and lit a cigarette.

What do they look like?

Freddy held them close to his face. The match went out and Freddy held them against the windscreen, trying to use moonlight. How the fuck should I know? I can't see in the dark. Look like pieces from a hanging basket, painted white. What the fuck are they?

From a loser who sits around in crumbling wicker chairs. Just do it. Scatter them on the stairs.

Freddy pushed them into his shirt pocket. It's your party.

They finished two beers, tossed the bottles out the window.

Bill said, I'm off.

Freddy listened to crackling gravel as Bill left, shifting gears on the way up Stockdill Drive. He got out and stood next to the orange ute, smoking and dumping butts on the ground. He gazed at the stars and talked to his dog. We got a few more nights out there, Paisley. Two or three more nights.

A wet easterly blew in from the coast. It smelled like the sea and reminded him of Ireland. He listened to Bill's motor whine as it pulled up Stockdill Drive then he climbed back in the ute and left.

He drank alone at the Pot Belly Inn until 2 a.m.

64

Daniel Bentham with Eddie Flannery

Daniel's eyes were shadowed with stress. Something in the room smelled like lavender. He looked around and saw a vase of fresh-cut flowers on a side table.

Eddie walked in, handed him a cup of tea and said, Thank you for coming.

Daniel fumbled with his keys, looked at his watch and said, I thought about it all day.

How's your head? There was some warmth in Eddie's voice.

Daniel lifted his eyes just enough for a grateful smile. Better. Daniel said, It's just that, well, I had this visit from Bill Scott.

Eddie nodded. I expected that.

It was frightening, you know, a policeman leaning on me.

I expected that too. Was he alone?

Daniel nodded.

In uniform?

He nodded again.

Eddie smiled.

Daniel's tone was serious. He doesn't like you much.

Eddie leaned back. No, he doesn't.

There's a look in his eyes. You know. He wants to hurt you.

I know.

Bring you to ground.

Eddie eyed him steadily and said, I can take care of myself.

Daniel grimaced, as if suffering another headache. This is different. He's dangerous. This look in his eyes. You're messing with a powerful man.

Eddie watched him. Still, I'm surprised to see you here.

Daniel looked at the floor. I'm not sure why I came.

Eddie watched him, Daniel folding his hands in his lap, getting up the nerve to say, You should stop seeing Superintendent Scott's wife. He seemed relieved to get it out.

Eddie smiled. You can't help yourself, can you?

He looked up. Meaning what?

You don't hate very easily.

Daniel shifted in his chair. I guess not.

A serious failing.

I've got quite a few.

And maybe, you were thinking, 'If I go see Eddie, tell him about Bill Scott, he'll find Emma and send her home to me.'

Daniel fidgeted and looked at the floor. I don't know. Maybe that was part of it.

Eddie smiled again. Tell me something. Your father, when people cheated him, always forgave them, didn't he? No matter what people did to your father, he always wanted to be friends.

Daniel thought for a moment. Yes, he was like that.

Eddie shook his head a little. You can't imagine how foreign that is to me.

Daniel was silent.

And your mother got angry with him, didn't she? Wanted him to stand up to people.

That's pretty much it.

Eddie leaned back in his chair. You know, for whatever reason, when I was about nine or ten, we sneaked into a shopping centre, a sort of outdoor plaza in Belfast. Two of us. We got near a crowd of people, tossed in a couple of bombs and ran. Both bombs fizzled, a bit of a joke really, didn't hurt anyone. Some fire and smoke, nothing more. We built them in the back shed, Rory and I did.

We were caught and placed in a lock-up, clean floors, well-lit rooms, police guards, but the people in town knew, like they could see us through the walls. When the police interviewed us, we puffed up like wildcat kittens and spat in their faces, acted like hard men with no remorse. We folded our little arms across our chests even though the shame was acute. We were disgraced because we got caught, not because we'd done anything wrong. My father taught me to hate – the rich, the police, the Prods, the Queen, jailers, most everybody. Each morning on the way to school, I walked past frescos painted on brick walls, phrases about struggle and victory, honour and sacrifice, but especially phrases about payback. Ferocious payback.

My mother, you see, never went in for the honour and sacrifice claptrap, she was too grown-up. When the police caught us, I was too afraid to face her. Too many Catholic men preached sacrifice. They were patriots working in secret to bring down the British empire, warbling treacly songs about freedom, and cheating on their wives at the same time with young girls. They didn't make any sacrifices at home. They ignored their sons and daughters. No honour or sacrifice for their children. My father was a vain, preoccupied little man, angry with a lot of things, especially angry because middle-age had ambushed him. The dirty injustice of it. He never grew up. Always struggling to prove that he wasn't a timid man, when really he was a timid man. Weak. He showed no respect for Mother, but he feared her. She could stop him with a glance, stand up to him like a rock. She kicked him out of the house, and raised six kids on her own. At first I resented her for doing it, but later I was glad she booted him out. What else could she do? She was the only grown-up in the house. What Belfast mother needs another adolescent in the house? She had to boot him out.

The police saw a lot of bad behaviour in Belfast. It was inevitable, they said, 'What do expect from papists? Disciples of the anti-Christ.' The curse of their birthright. On the day we tossed the bomb, my friend Rory was the brave one. The police said, 'You tried to hurt those people.' We laughed in their faces, hardened against the enemy like miniatures of our dads.

He paused and looked at Daniel. That's what you need to watch out for. Your father's manner of swearing, talking and growling that gets caught in your throat. You never quite remove that sound of your father.

Daniel didn't look up.

Hard-wired by my ancestors to howl for vengeance. The police ready to stand on my throat, like they stood on my father's throat and his father's throat before him. Settling scores. Arranging payback. Shackled to corpses. The police are more afraid of me than I am of them.

Daniel sat quietly.

Stand in front of the glass in the bathroom tonight, Daniel, and look at your father in the glass. There he sits, forgiving people. Mine stares back advising me to hit back. 'Better to avenge than to indulge in mourning,' he'd say.

Daniel sat quietly. He looked at a silver picture frame on the shelf, a photo of a woman of indeterminable age with bright steady eyes.

Eddie saw him looking and said, Ghosts in picture frames.

Daniel said, Is that your mother?

Eddie seemed distracted. We come to women for courage, a moral force to rule us.

Daniel tried to think about this, knitted his brow.

Eddie said, After I left, she was killed. I went through a bad time, nights feeling the heat she left in her passing. The university's full of simpletons. Children. They don't understand evil. Too stupid to grasp how wickedness and hatred can breed good deeds, it's better to be feared than loved. To be a winner, you don't fight fair, you fight well. Emma taught us that there are only two types of men – those who perpetuate evil upon women, those who sit back and let it happen. That's why these wife-beaters are winning. Mongrel lawyers get them off. The abused need more defenders with mongrel badness in them. Your friend David has a little mongrel in him, but he never puts it to good use.

They waited in the room listening to the rattle of typing through the door. Daniel continued to look down, his face creased by some memory, or the pain of trying to think of something to say.

Eddie said, We've started posting the names and home addresses of bastard lawyers who win bail for wife-beaters, or drag women through the courts until they're bankrupt. The most powerful force against evil comes from hard-line haters, not saints.

They were quiet.

Finally Eddie said, You want Emma to come home, don't you?

Daniel nodded and said, Yes. Worry crowded back into his face and Eddie knew he wouldn't say any more.

When Daniel looked up, Eddie was staring at the framed photograph. His eyes were damp.

Eddie reached over the desk and shook Daniel's hand. Thank you for coming. He walked across the room, and held open the door.

65

Restaurant

He waited but she didn't come.

It was hot in the city when David parked and sat in the car and thought for a moment before walking into the café. He sat, hushing the talk inside his head, stilling the terror in his hands. Alone at a table in the corner with nothing in front of him. The waiter came and bothered him; David shook his head.

Ten minutes later, the waiter came over and bothered him again. Are you certain you wouldn't like something to drink, sir?

With the back of his hand, David shooed him away, No.

The windows glowed yellow.

The phone call from Emma had caught him off guard. Where are you? he said.

It doesn't matter. I can meet you tomorrow.

Finally she walked to the front of the café, her long fingers wrapped round the door handle. David saw the curve of her face, the way she leaned her shoulder against the heavy glass door, and all planning failed him. A moth fluttered inside him, his forehead turned damp. One hand trembled; he buried it deep in his lap.

Backlit in the doorway, she hooded her eyes and strained to see into the dark restaurant. David raised his free hand like a child in school. Emma hunted until she found him, let the door swing shut and strolled between tables and stood next to him. She smiled and David reached out and took her hand.

Thank you for coming, he said.

Your hands are cold. I hope we haven't done something stupid.

No, said David. I don't think so.

Looking down at him, she said, You sounded hurt on the phone, a little sad and broken. Well done.

It's just that, well, your call came as a surprise.

She sat and looked around the room, then at him. In her blue eyes there was no urgency to talk, but she said casually, How are you?

Not too bad.

Good. You look a little tired. Sophie keep you awake last night?

No. He looked down for a moment. Things I can't forget keep me awake at night. A cricket kept me awake last night. And you?

Emma continued to look around the room. I'm fine.

A blur of donkey-like guffaws from a group of businessmen behind them, laughing at the punchline delivered by the fattest of the group. David waited until they stopped. The smell of Emma's skin distracted him.

She laughed, It's reassuring, isn't it? Gloomy economic forecasts never sap the city fat cats of their faith.

No, David said.

So, tell me, what have you been doing?

David shrugged. Where do I start?

Start with Sophie.

Apparently you already know about Sophie.

Emma shook her head. So petty. How did it get so out of hand?

A long story.

That's why academic battles are so vicious. The stakes are so low.

Yes, maybe.

How is work otherwise?

Not much fun.

She gazed at him. It hasn't been fun for a while now. You need a change, sneak up on your gloom and dispatch it.

David looked down again. It felt like a poorly written one-act play, a young couple stuck in a bedsitter in the city; they communicate badly, drag their past baggage into the room.

That sounds like advice Eddie would give.

She dropped her head a little and laughed. Now that you mention it,

Eddie did give me that advice, about a month ago when he told me that it was better to throw hand grenades than to catch them.

Sometimes, in the past, after they'd made love, or after she was so critical of Daniel, David felt anger in his throat. He would grow to dislike Emma, feel in his bones that she looked down on any man who fell in love with her. As if male affection was failure and neediness. He would see her as a selfish and a dangerous liar who Daniel had blundered into and fumbled against like a moth. The feelings passed when David fell into rhythm with her and understood which remarks and looks and proclamations came from Emma's heart, and which came from the barricade raised for her protection. Body armour.

He said, Did Nigel Plant speak to Eddie again?

She smiled again, Nigel's a cynical fellow, isn't he, very dry and a little mistrustful.

He's meant to be mistrustful, that's his job. Maybe his cynical remarks serve up some protection, like yours do.

She smiled. Yes, maybe. She looked around the room, then back at him. It's been a hard time for us, darling.

Yes.

When she said 'darling', he shivered a little. Any time she said darling in the past, or shook her head a little and let her hair tumble, or met his eyes, or touched his hand, he wanted to leap forward and obey.

She looked out the window and back at him. We thought we were suffering in some kind of dark of exile. She sipped her drink. In hindsight, it was a little over-dramatic, wasn't it? Against the bigger picture it was B-grade. It didn't amount to a hill of beans.

David watched her hands, No. I suppose not.

There was an awkward silence. David didn't know what to say, and Emma didn't feel the need to say anything.

Where do we go from here? he said.

She smiled. To spring rolls and noodles.

They finished eating.

She was silent and stared out the window then dragged her eyes from the street and said, He seems like your main tormenter now.

Who?

Eddie. Now that you've got me here, why make small talk? Talk about Eddie.

David tried to hold her gaze, stammered a little, and said, Why do you say that?

Emma shook her head as if correcting a fibbing child. Come on, darling, it's me you're talking to, remember?

He looked into the street where Emma was looking and waited and watched the side of her face. Why Eddie?

Isn't that obvious?

No, it's not obvious at all. He's a fraud. Everybody sees through him but you. Brother Eddie scattering charm and healing over the city.

Well, a man who's good with women, really good, is never completely trusted by other men.

He's a liar.

She smiled. Well, you might say that, but let's look at your question more deeply, tease it out from the bitter rift between you and Eddie.

Rift?

The rift going back to Eddie's university days.

I failed him in a course.

Yes, well, I know that. But he's done well in spite of university, or lack of university, don't you agree?

Is that why you stay with him?

Eddie's exactly what he claims to be, a businessman out to survive in a difficult city, a man who helps pure-hearted, downtrodden women, a man who chases men instead of being chased by them, throws bombs for other men to catch. There's something wholesome in that, don't you think?

That's not Eddie.

He's fearless. He helps women who the police won't help, women who're beaten up by the police. I've never felt more useful. I'm doing something real. I stay with Eddie because my own kind failed me so badly.

Your own kind?

Intellectual, dreamy, petty, literate, useless airheads. Fossilised in dusty rooms. Talkers.

But we – Daniel and I – never understood.

Her voice darkened. Exactly. You never understood. You don't understand now.

Understand what?

What it was like living with Daniel.

For whatever reason, the mention of Daniel's name weighed on him like a mountain. David sighed and rested back in his chair and let a wave of sadness wash over him. Daniel was shackled by his own goodness, he said. He's kind. He tried to keep peace, give you an anchor. He did everything he could to make you happy.

There was hostility in Emma's voice, her eyes narrowed and her throat hardened, Look. I'm not telling you what's right or wrong, I'm telling you what is.

And I'm trying to find some moral sense in all this.

Colour rose in her cheeks. How can you be so stupid? How can someone who stands miles away from moral problems in a university find any moral sense anywhere? I left the marriage to find a new life.

But why be so angry with Daniel? And why did Eddie hit Daniel?

She leaned forward in her chair, shaking her head, looking across the table at him. You don't know anything. That had nothing to do with Eddie, and nothing to do with me. I'm sorry about what happened to Daniel. It's terrible, and I want him to mend. But you don't understand much about Eddie, or me, and neither does your delightful friend Nigel. She smiled. Eddie has fun with Nigel, and he has fun with you, and with Bill Scott. He toys with all of you and we laugh about it afterwards. Bullies amuse him. But he didn't attack Daniel.

The remark angered David. Rest assured, Daniel and Nigel will bring Eddie to ground, it's only a matter of time. He suddenly realised how stupid the remark was.

She tipped her head back and laughed, as if laughing at the ceiling,

Bring Eddie to ground? She laughed again. Bring Eddie to ground for what?

For ambushing Daniel in the woods, for what he did to you.

As Emma laughed, she scratched the side of her face with her little finger and shook her head. Come on now. You don't really believe that.

David leaned forward. I do. And who caused me so much trouble at work?

Emma shook her head, as if in disgust. Pure Sophie. Telling me you're the victim of an evil mastermind won't help your case. Feeling sorry for yourself won't help your case either. You pursue fierce women like Sophie Moss, you pay the price. Simple. And Daniel's a child. He's always whining about this or that, frightened of one thing or another. He and his new chum David. What a pair.

Why did you leave?

She looked down for a moment. I just told you. Eddie thought it was best to make a break. I was angry at you. I needed to be away and think. Eddie was setting up a network of safe houses for women because DVOs don't apply between states. A DVO in Sydney doesn't count if she's in Canberra. It was dangerous, I helped.

That doesn't make sense.

Too bad.

Eddie told us he didn't know where you were.

Of course he did. I told him to say that.

He uses women.

What?

Daniel saw clothing in his house.

Where?

In the room where you sleep with him.

You need to understand something. Women need a place to stay, and they need clothing when they arrive, or when they go to a safe house, when the beast they left behind starts chasing them. It could be anyone's clothes. Look, Eddie has faults, I'm not blind. But Eddie's the price we pay.

She looked out the window again. Like I said, I needed a clean break, and I didn't want to be linked to universities any more. You're a boy crying in the dark. Clueless and stumbling in the fog.

Apparently. David leaned back and folded his arms. As much as we try, as much as Daniel and I try to work you out, try to understand where you're coming from…

Then give up.

But you…

Yes, darling, 'I did this, you did that, Eddie did something else and Daniel did nothing.' So what? Wake up. Until you do, you'll never make sense of me, and we'll never be able to talk. You're incapable of making sense of complicated people, even though you're supposedly trained to.

David waited, his face red and heated. Explain then. I'm listening.

You work it out.

David looked at Emma, her hands resting on the table. He tried to watch her eyes, did his best to concentrate on the blue in them. She was backlit from strong afternoon sun, windows cast a yellow glow over her head and shoulders. David searched her face.

The police hit Daniel.

David's first reaction was natural. The police? Of course she would say that. Emma was trying to protect Eddie, creating a story, trying to hide Eddie's crimes, that was her nature, and David drifted with this notion for a time. He remembered the iron bonds between lovers, and Eddie was her lover. Blind sacrifice, faith and denial.

Emma said, This legend about Eddie you've contrived with Nigel has no legs, nowhere to go, it's a fiction, one of your delusions.

They were quiet. Emma had calmed a little.

She looked out the window at people passing in the street and said, Anyway, you were going to pour out your heart, and I poured mine out instead.

Looking into her face, David hunted for some warmth, some glimmerings of human kindness, something of the old Emma he used to caress in the forest. A drop of perspiration ran down her throat between her breasts. With her napkin, she reached up and dabbed it; there was determination in her face that David hadn't seen before. She had changed.

I have to go, she said.

David could only nod. Thank you for coming. He raised his hand to signal the waiter.

She smiled and said, You know, it takes very little to make me happy.

David reached across the table and laid his hand over hers. She was warm.

When the waiter came, she slid her other hand on top of his and said, There's so little time left.

David held her hand on the table and said, I understand. But he didn't understand and regretted the lie.

She stood from the table and slowly pulled her hand away. I love you, she said, and walked across the restaurant into the street.

David sat for a time and considered how badly he and Daniel had failed Emma. He asked for another coffee, but the machine was shut down for the day.

Plates clinked and silverware chimed as waiters cleaned the empty restaurant.

66

Daniel Bentham and David walking

He decided not to tell him.

David arrived and let himself in the front door. Daniel sitting alone at home, unravelling in his setbacks, meditating in shadows, condemned to a dark house with no Emma.

The house smelled of stale beer and they sank into chairs in the back bedroom. Daniel had bluish shadows under his eyes and their talk came around to Daniel's needle-stick injury at the hospital.

Have the tests come back? You don't mind if I ask?

Daniel shrugged. I don't mind. What does it matter anyway?

It matters.

I don't think so.

They drank and Daniel said, Let's get out of this place.

Where to?

Anywhere. Let's walk.

They finished another bottle and dumped empties into the sink.

Hands deep in their pockets, they walked south towards the commercial heart of the city where roads turned in on themselves. A light wind brushing manna gums on the border. They sucked in metallic cold air. Like a broken man robbed of spirit, a man who'd been away for a long time, Daniel needed a friend to unburden to. David listened and Daniel spoke only of Emma.

Under a tangle of telephone wires, then under an open sky with a clear vision of winter's first blood moon, they turned east through woodland shadowed by animals and wings beating in the trees. Strips of torn bark rattled as they scuffed over a plank-wood bridge onto Mount Ainslie.

Daniel spoke to Emma as if communicating with an angel, forgetting that David was there. When you come back, he said, It'll be different.

After all this time, thought David, when the rest of us know she'll never come back, he mutters about reconciliation. A man buried in one woman's embrace, a man with childish hopes in adolescent denial.

Daniel spoke in murmured apologies. We won't stay at our house at first, he said. Too many bad memories. Mostly my fault. We'll move out and buy a new house in O'Connor. He turned to David. So she can walk to the office.

David knew that a man once abandoned is never quite the same. Maybe, he said.

This sort of thing is important, you see, because of her devotion to students and work. She won't stay with Eddie for long, I know that. She'll need a place to stay. And she probably won't stay with you. Daniel glanced over. Sorry, that was stupid.

No. You're probably right. She won't stay with me.

To make things easier, I'll keep a room all made up. A room for each of us. He moved his hands as he spoke.

Yes, said David. That would make things easier.

The night wind muffled Daniel's voice. Trees stood pale as old bone. In dim light, the path wound uphill. They came out on the lip of a ridge with the moon over them. David stood and looked out over a thousand points of light, surveying the past two months for betrayals and cruelty. He found plenty. Some people had caved in to various forms of heartlessness, but Daniel never had. Daniel had carried this fog inside his head, never quite certain that he hadn't caused Emma's unhappiness. Emma had lived with Daniel for six years, a good man, a simple man, honest and kind and giving, and came away seeing all men as cloven-hoofed beasts. All men except Eddie.

Daniel talked about Bill Scott, who'd smoked up his house with lit cigarettes, leaned on him with questions and demands, trying to recruit him against Eddie, then snarled when Daniel asked about Bill's wife.

Daniel described how Eddie scoffed at warnings about Bill, even consoled Daniel about Emma. You know Eddie's mother was killed?

No. I'm sorry to hear that.

Eddie told me he was sorry about Emma.

David paused and said, As people do when they have the upper hand.

No, said Daniel. You don't understand. He's not as bad as some people think.

David smiled but it wasn't a happy smile. I hope you're right, Daniel. I hope he's not as bad as some people think.

The wind fell and they turned and walked towards home. A gust of wind came up and hit them in the back like a shout in the dark.

67

Freddy O'Rourke prepared

At 2 a.m. he left the orange ute in the CIT car park. The night was chilly. He lifted a hammer from the back of the ute and walked through forest, watching Paisley range ahead of him, lifting his leg on trees. Wet leaves stuck to the soles of his boots.

Freddy stumbled over a limb and stopped in a cluster of bleached eucalypt trees that deadened his mumbling to Paisley. These trees have faces of malign intent, he said.

He looked around in the shadows and set down the hammer, cupped his hands and lit a cigarette, thought about how it looked winking in the empty forest loaded with darkness. Like a firefly, he said. He pulled a plastic bottle from his pocket and squirted whisky into his mouth, let it roll around behind his teeth and burn his tongue. We'll have a jar at the Pot Belly when this is over.

He wiped his mouth with the back of his hand and tucked the bottle into his pocket, leaned one hand against a tree with the cigarette between his fingers and emptied his bladder.

Paisley watched him and waited, ran ahead when Freddy zipped his trousers.

Freddy picked up the hammer and launched forward, breaking dead sticks under him. Roosting cockatoos burst out of a tree-top squawking. They circled in the night making a racket. Freddy said, Wait, boy, and they waited until the tight group of cockatoos finished circling and settled back in the tree. He walked on.

On the hill overlooking Dryandra Street, he forced his hands into his pockets to keep warm. He found a low scoop of land and stretched out.

Come on, boy, try it. Lie down. Warm in here, like a pocket under an upturned boat.

The street was empty. He squirmed on the ground, reached under his hip and pulled at twigs and pieces of tea-tree. Like fuckin' sleeping on blackberry clippings.

He lay for another ten minutes then stood, brushed his pants, and looked at the house. He pulled out binoculars from his pack, watched the dark house, scanned the woods behind him and looked up and down the street. Deserted.

Gonna clamp the mouth of that scheming little prick.

Freddy rubbed his hand over the top of his head and pulled out a rubber Halloween mask from the pocket of his pants that were torn and greasy. It was an ugly, wrinkled troll mask with a wart on the end of its giant rubber nose.

This is the night, boy. Ready for a fight. Tonight's the night. You know, when I was a young boy, they put me in a home just because I hanged a cat in the woods by my school. Said it was a sign of things to come. What the fuck would they know? Cat deserved it. You hate cats like I do, don't you?

Eucalypts around him creaked like masts on a galleon. He pulled out binoculars again, watched the dark house and scanned the woods, battled branches for a better view. The street still deserted.

After ten minutes, he knew the time was right and tied Paisley to a tree. You keep a lookout. Give me a bark if someone comes. I'll be listening.

The Rottweiler shook himself and lay down. Freddy walked down the hill swinging the hammer by its short handle and crossed the street. He circled to the side gate, passed through the backyard and stood at the back door. The house was dark.

He noted from memory the doors and windows that Bill had sketched on the map; wired to alarm. He checked each window on the ground floor, studied them in the dark and moved to the side windows that Bill said were clear. He checked each window on the ground floor, quietly pulled and pushed at them.

68

Inside the house

Cranks held the windows shut. Freddy unloaded a rubber suction foot from his pack, stuck the glass cutter against the window, cut out a circle, going slowly so the scratching and scraping didn't wake anyone. He lifted the circle of glass from the window and laid it on the patio. He reached in through the hole and cranked slowly until the window opened wide enough for him to unhook it and swing it open. He crawled into the laundry head first, got one leg in then the other, dragging the iron hammer behind him.

The door from the laundry opened to a hallway lit dimly by street lamps on the road. Freddy crept; he was patient. The hallway had two angular tables, one at each end, and he could see in the dim light miniature frames set next to each each. Freddy wondered if they held black and white photographs of Eddie's dead Catholic ancestors.

Halfway along the hall, he caught his dark reflection in a rectangular mirror; it startled him, the rubber troll Halloween mask with crooked nose and wart on the end. He passed by the glass. The only noise was the hum of a refrigerator in the kitchen, and a dog barking maybe two blocks away, not Paisley. He hoped it didn't set off Paisley.

He could see in the dim light shiny lettering on the spines of books in the bookcase, and a piano in the corner on white carpet.

He bumped the toe of his boot against the carpeted stair, climbing a step at a time on the balls of his feet. Part way up, he stopped, reached into his pocket and sprinkled the white pieces of wicker over the carpet. In case you forget later, he thought. Keep Bill happy. Use your head, keep thinking.

At the top of the stairs, Freddy stood in the hallway. Doors were shut except for one at the end. The white bathroom illuminated the hall from a dim green bulb, some kind of electrical appliance. A skylight in the ceiling caught the white glow of the moon and from dim yellow lamps in the street. He walked to the first bedroom door and pushed slowly, taking his time, pushing with his finger. He didn't hear the bottom of the door brushing carpet, he knew he was pushing just right. Damn good job, he thought.

The bedroom appeared empty; Freddy switched on his pocket lamp. On each side of the wide bed were angular tables in dark wood, with miniature paintings on the dressing table, like the ones in the hallway. He slowly lifted the bedclothes a centimetre at a time and found the bed empty. He looked around the room. Over the dressing table was an oblong mirror and he was startled again by the troll mask, and his black clothing filling the room. He rubbed the rubber mask, it was starting to itch. He looked in corners of the bedroom with his pocket light, quiet, careful. Nobody. Satisfied with his work, he crept back into the hallway.

One step at a time, patient, thinking about how pleased Bill would be. Not a bit of trouble, Bill. No more honeyed words from this little prick.

He stood outside the second bedroom, the map in his head. He pushed slowly, no brushing sound on the carpet, pushed a little more, shifted the door. He saw rumpled bed covers, two lumps under the sheets, alive and lifting then falling as they slept. The blonde head lay closest to him, breathing heavily. She gave a little twitch in her sleep. He could see someone on the other side. Eddie.

He waited, let his eyes adjust with no pocket lamp. He watched the woman's head on the pillow, crept forward with the hammer, ready to hold down her face and reach across the bed and splatter Eddie's skull.

69

Freddy O'Rourke attacks

Freddy watched the blonde head, the calm face in white moonlight. She sniffed a little. He remembered how she'd looked in the woods on Black Mountain walking with Bill's missus, lithe and long-legged. He watched Emma and thought about her small breasts and high bottom under the sheets. He felt pressure in his pants, his cock rising and he continued to watch her, wondering how long he could stand and study her before she woke. He imagined her smooth belly under the blanket and wondered if she was naked, curled there, feeling safe. He wanted to fuck her, and he knew then that he would. He would reach across to hammer Eddie, hold down the woman and hit Eddie again, then hold her in the bed and fuck her.

He studied Eddie on the other side of the bed, head and body covered by a blanket, breathing against the wall.

Freddy moved closer, looking down on the blonde head, the hammer cocked over his shoulder. Pop his eyes out the front of his head, he thought.

Her eyelids fluttered.

Freddy lowered the hammer to his side and watched her again, reached down and shifted his cock to the left inside his pants, uncomfortable now and hard. He could hear his own breath whistling through his nose. The rubber mask made him sweat, he reached up and scratched and stood watching.

He pressed the woman's face into the bed.

No. Her scream echoed off the walls. She threw up an arm, the hammer glancing off her hand. Sitting up, she beat at Freddy's face and arms.

The other body rolled off the other side of the bed, lodged against the wall and screaming like a woman.

Emma on her feet, struggling with Freddy, scratching, biting his hand, grabbing his shirt, smacking his face, grabbing his arm.

The body next to the wall in a T-shirt, dark hair, white legs. Freddy pushed Emma away, but she hung on. Freddy brushed her off, pulled her by the hair, leaned over the bed and crashed the hammer into the dark head next to the wall.

A scream, crawling on the floor, seeping blood, neck of the T-shirt, Emma standing attacked Freddy.

He brought down the hammer slamming into the head on the floor, the body escaping on its knees, Freddy confused, slammed it again, Emma's hand stopped him.

A groan from the body on the floor, Emma wiped her eyes with her wrist, punched and kicked him, her T-shirt soaked in blood, gripping his fist, grabbing the hammer with both hands, kicking, Freddy yapping in sharp cat-like yelps, Let go, you fucking whore, muffled by the rubber mask.

Click at the doorway, a light flickered on. Pieces of teeth on the floor. Clumps of blue-black hair on the bed, a fingernail. Someone hit Freddy with a baseball bat. A sharp blast of nausea.

The dark-haired woman on her knees crawling out the door.

Freddy hits Emma with his fist, swings at the man with the bat, Emma punching his face.

Freddy pushing her away, holds her with one hand and Eddie Flannery hits him again with the bat. Freddy brings the hammer down on Emma's face, glances off her arm, tries to shake her off, slams the hammer into Emma again, the hammer across Emma's forehead. She weakens, limp, turning him loose.

Eddie Flannery slams the bat into the side of the rubber troll mask, the taste of copper coins in Freddy's mouth, Emma down. Freddy shakes his head at the little man with the bat in the doorway.

Little Eddie swings again BANG, the giant Freddy O'Rourke going down now, slipping in coppery-smelling blood, he falls over, puts his big freckled hand on the carpet, tries to stand but the little man slams him in the back while he's down. Freddy stands, blocks the bat with his hammer.

Bleeding dark-haired woman is gone, half-naked, crawling down the hallway crying.

Freddy swings the hammer, Eddie blocks the iron head with the bat and Freddy swings again, knocks Eddie down.

Bleeding, Emma crawls into the hall. Carolyn at the top of the stairs, tumbling down the carpeted edges, crying and bleeding on the ground floor.

Carolyn crawls to the front door, whimpering on her knees, struggles with the lock, stands fighting it. Nothing. She fights the deadlock, kicks the door, dripping blood on the white carpet, hits the lock with her fist, twists it. Nothing. She hits it again, twists with both hands – clunk – it opens. She staggers outside.

Emma struggles down steps holding the railing. Lying on the carpet, breathing heavily she stands, falls again, stands and rocks forward through the open door. On the path, lying in the dirt, one hand on the ground trying to stand, wavering on her knees she falls.

Outside, long red splashes in the driveway under street lamps. Carolyn tottering down the street crying.

Upstairs, Freddy bangs the little man in the mouth, trying to kill him. Again, BANG. Eddie slumps, Freddy clubs him to the floor, women crying outside, Paisley barking on the hillside.

Fuck, screams Freddy. Stay down, you little fucker! Hits him again. Freddy screaming and cursing.

Eddie stays down.

Freddy rushes into the hallway, biting smell of urine and coppery blood on the carpet, patches of damp black. He jumps down the stairs, two at a time, following the crying women out the door. Cut and bleeding, running with the hammer gripped halfway along its stubby shaft.

In the yard, Freddy moves his head from side to side, runs toward the woman as she staggers down the road crying and Freddy knows he'll catch her and shut her up. Emma steps out from the corner of the house in a bloody yellow T-shirt, naked legs under. Freddy hits her in the face with the hammer. She folds as if her body had no bones.

He stands back, looks down the street, runs out of the yard, chasing the crying woman. Stops, listening with an ear cocked to the street, runs with his head bobbing. Rectangle windows glow yellow, lights flicker on.

Fuck, he mumbles.

Paisley barking, other dogs barking now, families awake, houses lit up and Freddy running.

Blood trail leads down the road, shiny black splashes and drips; he follows the cold bitumen, running down hill with bushes in front yards in houses on the left, forest on the right, a fence separating the road from woodland. Doors slamming inside houses, more lights popping on.

He follows the bloody drips under street lamps to a gap in the fence between two posts. He slides in sideways, hammer banging against the post.

You cunt, he mumbles, looking down at a wet patch in the dirt.

He lopes into brushy woodland with the hammer banging against his leg.

In a pool of moonlight, he stops and listens, shadows waving above him, one hand on a tree, resting and listening. Paisley barking on the hill, people outside mumbling in backyards.

Standing in the open space between trees, rocking and waving his head from side to side, listening to parts of the woodland. He lopes forward towards a shady glade. He knows where she's hiding. He'll find her and beat her into the dirt, then run. The brassy taste of blood on his tongue. He swills it around his mouth and spits into the grass. Fucker made me bite my lip.

Standing and listening, watching the hill for shadows in the moonlight. Paisley barking, he touches his finger to his lip. Fucker won't do it again.

Footsteps snapping dead sticks. He looks around and moves closer to the cracking, stops and listens; he glimpses a moving shadow.

A voice behind him mumbles, Hey.

70

Nigel Plant on night duty

Nigel ran cold water over his face and ripped off a paper towel. He rubbed his face dry and left tiny brown shreds of paper in his whiskers. He tossed the wadded paper in the waste basket and went back and sat in front of the computer. He continued to scroll down the list of utes looking for names he recognised. It was 3 a.m. and he had another hour on the night desk.

That afternoon, he'd visited the injured student in hospital. Progress was slow. The boy remembered little, or didn't want to, but on days he seemed to trust Nigel he told him about a big Irishman driving an orange ute with a dog in the front seat.

An Irishman. The coincidence seemed too great and Nigel hunted all vehicles licensed to Eddie Flannery over the past ten years but came up with nothing. He believed in this link to Eddie Flannery and drug dealers, but the troubling thing was the student's claim that he saw the man selling drugs to a policeman.

The boy said, I thought maybe it was a fake uniform. You know. Why would a policeman buy drugs in uniform?

Maybe it wasn't a policeman. But Nigel was thinking, Maybe it was a policeman. Just arrogant. Or maybe he knew the power of the uniform.

Nigel said, I won't be able to answer that until we determine if he was a real policeman, then find him.

Then you think it was a real policeman.

Like I said. I don't know. An officer in uniform could argue that he was on the job getting the dope on some dope dealers.

The student was silent.

Nigel said, Could you identify this policeman?

From what? In person, you mean?

In person, or from a photo.

The student knitted his brow and thought for a moment. No. Not for sure. But I could identify the Irishman.

Nigel tapped O' into the search engine. The number of names startled him, but he worked methodically down the list looking for orange utilities of any make.

He heard the telephone ring at the duty desk.

An officer picked up the receiver. Yes. Yes. Can I have your name, please? Address? Okay. Someone will be there inside five minutes.

She walked around the cubicle and laid the paper on Nigel's desk. Some kind of disturbance on Dryandra Street. Probably a domestic. Woman running down the street with a man chasing her.

Where on Dryandra Street?

She gave him the street number.

Eddie Flannery's house.

71

Nigel Plant at the crime scene

The house lay quiet. Nigel clicked on the lamp in the sitting room and looked at the oak writing desk in the corner, the piano, and lounge suite in front of the TV. Nigel caught himself reflected in the hall mirror, stepped around an open copy of *Beowulf* on the floor. He could smell the sharp tang of blood and urine splashed in patches on the white carpet.

He climbed the stairs. On the second floor, moving past darkened bedrooms where moonlight poured out through doorways, he stepped around more wet patches and Officer Lisa Charles watched him from the bottom of the steps.

Eddie lay with a baseball bat resting in his open palm, his jaw bent, front teeth broken and smeared with blood. White carpet around him glistened scarlet. Blood splattered over the bed, onto walls, and into the hall. Furniture was pushed over.

Nigel squatted next to him and said, An ambulance is coming.

Eddie whispered through clenched teeth, Outside.

We know. Emma Bentham. We found her.

Slowly he shook his head and whispered, Car…

Nigel turned an car towards him. What?

Eddie lifted his hand off the floor, trying to open two fingers.

Two people attacked you?

Painfully he shook his head.

Two people outside?

Eddie winced and gave a single nod.

There's another person outside with Emma?

Eddie nodded, almost imperceptibly.

Someone will come up and stay with you. I'll look outside.

A slight nod.

Nigel went downstairs and sent an officer to stay with Eddie. He asked three officers to follow him.

Outside, light from neighbouring houses lit shrubbery and fences, made narrow glints along telephone lines. Babies in houses were crying, young children chattering like crickets, adults muttering. They passed Emma curled on the ground in a bloody T-shirt, an officer kneeling beside her. Lisa Charles hammered in steel pickets to shield her from view, and taped the crime scene as a barrier to stickybeaks.

Nigel hunted the yard, shining the torch beam under bushes, in corners, over the patio, and told the others to do the same. They spoke over the fence to neighbours in the night, checked the garage.

One officer shouted, There's blood in the driveway.

The air was sharp and clean. Two uniformed men and three women waved torch beams over red-black smears on the bitumen, faces down like hounds following scraps of blood. Nigel shone his torch up and down Dryandra Street into front yards, then turned and followed red-black drips on the road leading downhill. He could see how the person had veered between two wooden fence posts that divided the road from woody bottom land sloping up to a ridge. A rubber Halloween mask lay on the ground.

They squeezed between posts and crunched over a stony path flanked by stringy barks, brittle gums, and deep green native cherries. Bats flickered overhead on paper wings as the officers climbed uphill in a snaking line.

Knotted cords of blood strung over grass into bushes.

'Head wound,' thought Nigel. He turned to the others. This isn't good. I want you to spread out over the hill.

Their pace slowed as Nigel ran his torch over the forest floor looking for splashes of blood on a tussock, a leaf or broken limb. He searched for shiny black dampness on bare rocky soil, for pieces of dried mud kicked out of a standing ant nest. He stopped and Officer Sara Gleen stopped behind him and waited.

He cupped his hands and shouted into the trees, Hello.

They stood and listened.

They walked further into the reserve, up from a stony gully. The ground was littered with branches and a few animal bones. A kangaroo bounded in long arcs through the beam of Nigel's torch, coming from uphill where someone must have spooked it. In tall grass, it looked like a fleeing man.

Nigel led the officers in broad circles over the bushy hillside, scouting the ground, hiking uphill then down, trying to link the long spaces between splatters of blood. They crossed a gap cut in the forest for an old telegraph line, looking for patterns of how the woman fled and the killer followed. They climbed into a broad saddle between charcoal-black columns of trees.

He saw a plastic bottle on the forest floor with dampness leaking out of its neck. He knelt and studied it, then sniffed at the neck. Whisky. Leave it here. Mark it for later.

Wind from the east cooled their backs and made the leaves chatter. The wind had dampness in it, the breath of a storm. Nigel glanced over his shoulder at an escarpment of black cloud silvered by moonlight. Heavy rain, he thought, will sluice away any sign of blood.

Keep moving, he said.

The saddle was tangled in tea-tree. He knelt beside a puddle of blood cupped in a dead leaf. By torchlight he studied the ruby colour in the tawny leaf saucer, then stood and walked uphill. The officers followed him, spread in a line over the saddle. He tried to imagine where she lay, where she sought refuge.

Drips speckling the outside of a tight bundle of tea-tree caught in his torchlight. With elbows in front of him, Nigel crouched and ripped his way through, and two officers followed. Thorns cut at their arms and faces and Nigel batted at sticks and branches with his sleeve. He searched the ground and broken tea-tree in front of him and saw where the person had dived into the thicket.

The white circle of torchlight fell on flattened grass where the person had curled and bled. He could see where she crawled on her belly deeper into the middle of the thicket. Nigel crawled forward on his elbows, pushing at sticks in his way. A thorn ripped open his left cheek.

The woman lay on her side, curled and half-naked. She pressed her back against the base of a tree that was poking up through the tangle. Her eyes were shut. Nigel pushed through on his belly and touched her. She was shivering. He pulled off his jacket and wrapped her in it, tucked her elbows in and grasped her cold hands to warm them. He brushed hair off her face and held two fingers to her throat.

It's okay, love, he said. Don't worry.

She didn't respond.

Nigel turned and shouted, Radio another ambulance. He leaned in close, You'll be out of here soon. He stroked her hand.

Sara Gleen stumbled downhill into the circle of light, panting and wide-eyed. She looked around and shouted, Where is he?

They pointed into the thicket and said, He found someone.

She panted and tried to catch her breath, looking into the thicket where Nigel's dim light was shielded by leaves. So did I. She breathed heavily, bent over with hands on her knees, then she stood up and said, I found a dog up there.

A dog?

A dog. On the ridge. Tied to a tree.

72

Daniel Bentham in the morning

Daniel lay in twilight between sleep and waking. Emma spoke to him in the room, her voice echoing softly.

He got up, stood by the window and judged the day. Pale sunlight cut between trees, the yard was freshly washed with rain. A slender mountain gum stood shining and white next to the fence and songbirds were carolling.

Daniel walked down the hall and stood with his hand on the door of Emma's room. Her yellow T-shirt lay on the pillow but the bed was empty.

He climbed downstairs into warm morning light and looked into the kitchen. On the bench was a stained white cup that he must have used in the night for camomile tea, but he couldn't remember. A carton of milk standing next to the cup had warmed overnight and he poured it down the sink.

The neighbour's cat was stretching in the morning sun. Daniel wandered into the sitting room.

73

Gail Sheeny investigates

At 7 a.m. Bill Scott's eyes were empty and black and a little contemptuous. Smoke drifted gently across his desk and eddied around Gail Sheeny.

He pointed with his cigarette. I'm more than a little compromised. You head up the investigation.

Cleaners moved through the building, and Bill and Gail spoke over the roar of a vacuum cleaner in the hallway.

A man knocked on the door, opened it with a vacuum cleaner harnessed to his back and the nozzle gripped in his free hand. Okay to do your office?

Bill shook his head. No. The cleaner shut the door and Bill said, Well?

A rail of smoke rose from his cigarette. Gail watched him sit back in his leather chair and knew he was waiting for a show of solidarity.

She nodded and chewed her lip. At day's end, you need to understand, there's protocol to follow. Two men will assist me with our enquires, and you know who they are.

Tiny beads of sweat showed on his upper lip. He reached absently for his cigarette and tapped it on the edge of a saucer. Of course. I understand that. But one of those men is guilty, the other is innocent. Simple. And Peter Jones and Freddy Breem will sign affidavits. Drinking with me at 2 a.m. last night.

Gail scraped a fingernail on the edge of her coffee cup, looking at Bill and thinking about loyalty, betrayal and enemies. Young officers Peter Jones and Freddy Breem were little boys, needy, loyal and deeply dishonest, as tethered to Bill Scott as tame puppies.

You know, she paused and thought for a moment, you've got a big problem.

I've got a few big problems. Which one concerns you?

She continued squeaking her thumbnail on the handle of her cup until he looked at it. She stopped and said, Carolyn said the killer was chasing her, not Emma Bentham. He went over the top of Emma to get at Carolyn with a hammer on the other side of the bed, and Emma stopped him.

Bill pursed his lips and expelled smoke. His tone was dry and annoyed. Come on. Nobody knew what was happening. It was dark and chaotic in a house in that middle of the night.

Gail eyed him, and stayed quiet for a time. Okay, Bill. Dark and chaotic.

Officers reconstructed the scene over the road from Eddie's house. Police fanned out through woods, turning over stones, looking through leaf litter, photographing green plants and blood spatter. They believed that the man attacked Eddie and Emma, then chased Carolyn into the woods and searched the woods until sirens wailed down Macarthur Avenue, or maybe waking neighbours spooked him. He found himself disoriented in the dark and couldn't find his dog.

Gail expected no cooperation from Carolyn Scott because Carolyn had faced Gail on the porch in Ainslie, standing next to Bill Scott with Carolyn's parents huddled in the back room. But Carolyn spoke in a weak voice from her hospital bed and strengthened Bill's claim to innocence. The man who attacked them, she said, wasn't Bill. One man attacked them in the house, not two. But she had a vague memory of two men in the forest – one chasing her, the other fighting the Irishman before the big man could reach her in the tangle of brush. There was shouting and scuffling, the Irishman swearing. She didn't know if she had dreamed this second person coming out of the dark, knowing she was going to die, or if the man was true.

Gail said, We found the rubber mask near the gate. If this man fought him, the Irishman may be an accomplice.

Gail visited Eddie Flannery two doors along in the same ward, and Eddie agreed with Carolyn. There was only one man in the house, and it was not Bill Scott. This man was bigger, broader, with red hair on his knuckles, a gorilla with freckles on his arms. Find a big, mean Ulsterman.

Gail left the hospital and interviewed seven men who boiled inside with grievances against Eddie Flannery, after their women ran away. None matched the big Ulsterman with red fists. All seven had alibis.

The police learned that Emma Bentham and David Chess had been lovers. They explored this but scoffed at the idea of David attacking the house. They interviewed David once and decided he was not one to murder. He was of no consequence.

One said, It's fashionable these days for an academic to find a girlfriend with psychiatric problems. He changed lovers as often as most people changed their socks, and David had no reason to murder Carolyn Scott or Emma Bentham. A womaniser and failed academic, yes, but not a person of interest.

Gail visited Eddie Flannery again and Eddie spat angry words from his bed, What's wrong with you people? The killer was chasing Carolyn, not Emma. He rested back on the pillow. Emma and Carolyn shared a bed, I slept in the next room. The killer targeted Carolyn. Daniel had nothing to do with this. You people don't listen – I said Bill Scott wasn't the villain with the hammer. I didn't say Bill Scott wasn't the villain. He *is* the villain, as sure as I'm lying here. Bill rented a giant Irishman to break my head.

Gail let him rave and curse at the police. She knew Eddie was sick to his empty core with hatred for authority. She dismissed his raving. When he'd shouted himself dry, she said, Why do you keep insisting that Acting Superintendent Scott is involved in this?

I know his style.

His style?

The man who broke into my house was a Prod. Bill's little joke.

Little joke?

Irish on Irish. The lad was built like a haystack, and he cursed like a

Presbyterian. And Jaysus, there was a fierce smell of drink comin' off him, as they say. You tell him I said that when you catch him, if you catch him. He'll understand. No wonder he botched it.

Gail thanked him and left.

74

Wicker sticks

Daniel spent days staring out the window. Police visited him and Daniel offered no alibi for the night except David Chess. He said they left Daniel's house at 11 p.m. and walked. He didn't seem to care if police believed him or not.

Gail Sheeny met with Nigel Plant and said, I think this David Chess is lying. Call it misplaced guilt over sleeping with Daniel Bentham's wife. I don't think Daniel was with him. Daniel drove the killer to Eddie's house around 2 a.m. on the night and David Chess is protecting him now. How well do you know this Daniel?

Pretty well, said Nigel. I visited him a few times.

Gail paused and thought. Does he trust you?

I think so. Why?

Is he a tough guy? Angry?

Nigel snorted. Hardly.

Any risk that he'll run?

Nigel shook his head. No.

Go see him. Lay out the case we have against him. See what he says, but don't bring him in just yet. Keep it informal, and go alone. See him as a friend. Let him open up.

I can do that.

Nigel visited Daniel Bentham. David arrived soon after and sat back listening.

After condolences about his wife, Nigel pulled out of his pocket a sealed plastic bag labelled 'Evidence #2' containing a white painted wicker stick. We found these on Eddie Flannery's staircase. Left the other pieces back at the lab. Look, Daniel, I don't want to cause you any more grief, but I know where they came from and so do you. He pointed to the crumbling chairs. I'll take pieces from your chairs back to the lab and we both know what they'll find. Don't we?

Daniel's hands were shaking; he sat quietly looking at the arm of the wicker chair he sat in.

Nigel waited, glanced at David, and back at Daniel. There's going to be a match, isn't there?

Daniel nodded, sitting with his hands together as if being scolded. Probably.

So how did they get there?

What?

How did those pieces of wicker stick end up on the carpet inside Eddie's house? Like they were stuck to somebody's clothing.

Daniel looked at the fragment, sighed, and shook his head. I told you. Bill Scott came here one night and tried to turn me against Eddie.

Yeah, I know. You said that but Acting Superintendent Scott denies it.

He's lying. I told you before. He came to my house.

Nigel wagged his head and said, Look, sorry, Daniel. But I didn't see Bill Scott come to your house. He pointed to the floor. You *told* me he came to your house. Nobody in your neighbourhood saw his car parked outside.

David leaned forward. The house smelled like cigarettes the next day. Daniel doesn't smoke.

Nigel looked at David. You'll say that in court?

Yes, if it helps.

Nigel eyed him steadily. It won't help much. There was a look of contempt on his face as he studied David. You've managed to stay on the fringes of this mess, haven't you?

David looked away.

Well, engage a little more constructively, Dr Chess. So far, you've only made things worse.

David sat back and folded his arms.

Nigel held up the plastic bag. Daniel, can you propose any other story for these wicker sticks?

Daniel shook his head.

What do you know about that circular glass cutter we found on the back porch under Eddie's window?

Daniel shook his head again. I didn't know such things existed.

Nigel stroked his red moustache. You're a lab technician and you didn't know such things existed? Look, you need to see this from the other side, from the police perspective. The police know Daniel Bentham is lying and he needs a story about the wicker sticks on Eddie's steps. The killer visits Daniel's house more than once to plan the murder before Daniel and the killer drive off together in the dark night and try to kill Eddie Flannery and Emma. The killer's a smoker, there's cigarette butts on the hill overlooking Eddie's house, a pile stubbed into the dirt next to the tethered dog, and Daniel admitted to the police that he'd watched Eddie's house from that same hill. The *same* hill, Daniel, the hill where the killer sat and watched Eddie's house. Daniel gets hit with a hammer, probably hit by Eddie Flannery, a week earlier. Eddie belted him in the woods to keep him from peeping into windows. Following me? Daniel knew that Eddie Flannery belted him.

Daniel didn't respond.

So you organised payback.

Daniel head down looking at the floor, says, No.

Nigel threw up his hands as if defeated. Look, cops are simple people. Concrete. Coincidences like this are just too big for your average cop to grapple with. Too many flukes. It holds together as long as the story's not too demanding. Motive's there because the husband's suffering and angry about his wife hiding out in Eddie's house, angry that Eddie belted him in the woods to keep him from peeping into windows. Nigel sat back and watched him. What do you say, Daniel? That's a story that works. Help me out here.

Daniel sat with his head down and David sat forward again. Emma told me the police hit Daniel.

Nigel glared. Oh good, Dr Chess. The police hit Daniel. That'll fly, for sure. Why would the police hit Daniel? Eddie wasn't exactly a police groupie, was he? He'd cook up stories to blame things on the police for sport. There was a running battle between Eddie and the police. So the police hit Daniel for peeping into windows. Give me something better.

David shook his head. You know I don't.

Nigel threw up his hands again. Come on, David, you're an intelligent man. You know that story's bunkum.

David sat back and folded his arms again.

Nigel waited, then looked at Daniel. Think it over and ring me if you come up with anything better. He stood and left.

They sat quietly for a time and David said, Phone me if he comes again. I'll help you get through this.

Amber Griffin phoned and said, I'm sorry this has happened. You all right?

I'm fine, but I need your advice.

Can I come and see you?

Yes. But I need the name of a good criminal lawyer, the best in town.

For you, or for Daniel?

So far just for Daniel, but maybe for me.

I'll see what I can do.

You know, it's strange.

What's that?

He was quiet.

She waited and said. What do you mean?

I wasn't afraid.

Today you mean?

He paused. No.

She waited, and said, I understand.

He was quiet and she said, Take care.

75

Nigel Plant on the case

They barred Daniel from Emma's room unless police were present. They allowed him to sit for half-hour vigils with an officer in the room, for her safety, and to record anything Daniel said to Emma, or Emma said to him if she woke. But she was unresponsive.

Amber found a lawyer for Daniel. Seb Lake, short and boyish, wore fine Italian clothes and two days' growth of manicured black stubble. He drove a vintage black Fiat X19, had a quick-fire temper and expertly moderated this temper in front of a judge. He could suppress it or unleash it at will.

Nigel Plant made a fourth visit to Daniel's house, and Seb Lake stood in grey slacks and a black turtleneck between Daniel and the police, shook his finger and berated Nigel for amateurish blunders, flawed logic, unprofessional conduct, and numerous failures in legal protocol. His eyes flashed with indignity.

Seb Lake told Daniel not to answer any questions. Don't say a thing.

Daniel sat quietly on a chair. Nigel watched him, tried to ignore Lake's tactics, and Daniel grew uneasy. The look on his face told officers trained in reading criminal intent that Daniel was guilty. A criminal, spooked and hiding behind a corrupt, baby-faced lawyer.

Four officers, including Nigel and Gail Sheeny, met for an hour and brainstormed ideas on a whiteboard, a plan to hammer Daniel to a cross.

Eddie didn't help. The police remained his principal enemy.

You lads are inept, he said. How can you be so stupid and bungling to think Daniel had anything to do with this? Bill Scott hired a Belfast thug in some twisted kind of payback. Eddie turned his palm upwards on the bed sheet. Why can't you blockheads see that?

Eddie gave a vague description of the killer and Nigel visited the police sketch artist and said, Draw me a giant man with red hair sprouting from his knuckles and freckles on his arms, wielding a short-handled hammer. Draw it to scale.

The sketch artist dummied up a faceless ape with broad shoulders and reddish hair. Eddie and Carolyn were unable to say whether he wore a beard or moustache, they couldn't help with the colour of his eyes or tattoos or the state of his teeth.

His breath was fouled by alcohol and cigarettes, said Eddie.

Nigel watched over the sketch artist's shoulder and guided her. When she finished, he tapped on the paper. Pencil in a black Rottweiler next to him.

She sketched in the dog and Nigel said, That's good.

Low-ceilinged chambers filled with rows of indigents on bar stools. Smoky dives with beer spilled on the floor, and urinals you could smell out on the footpath. Patrons and bar owners shook their heads when Nigel showed them the sketch. Two nights of questioning and holding up the sketch in front of hundreds of faces generated no leads.

Nigel drove back to his office and scrutinised the case, tried to determine what he was doing wrong. Maybe, he thought, I should drive to Sydney or Melbourne and troll through bars there.

Exhausted, he slept for an hour with his feet on the desk and decided, No, I won't drive to Sydney. The killer's local, and even if he's not local, too bad, locally I'm going to search. Stuffed if I'm driving all the way to Sydney.

He revisited the same pubs in a second sweep.

On a Wednesday night at 12.30 a.m., he pulled up to the kerb outside the Pot Belly Tavern. He showed the sketch to a drunk sitting alone. The drunk stared at the drawing, pushed it to arm's length from his bleary eyes trying to focus. He slapped at his shirt pocket looking for glasses and Nigel reached in and pulled out his own glasses for the drunk to use.

The drunk pressed Nigel's glasses to his face with the heel of his hand and stared. Yeah, I know him.

You sure?

Fuckin' lunatic.

He comes in here?

Sometimes he comes here, sometimes to the Boardroom down the street. Bit of a loner.

That's original. Psychopath who's a troubled loner.

What?

Look, Nigel rubbed his eye with his fist, what's his name?

Freddy.

Nigel scribbled in his notebook and said without looking up, Freddy what?

Don't know.

Nigel held his moustached upper lip tight to his teeth. He kept writing in his notebook. Well, what *do* you know about him?

Now look, don't get snotty with me. I'm trying to help you out here.

You know where he lives?

No idea. But he drives an orange Holden ute and ties the dog in the back. Loves the dog, and tries to bring him in here sometimes. They don't let him. The dog slobbers on the seats of the ute while he sits in here and drinks.

Nigel left the Potbelly and drove back to his office, noted the time – 1 a.m. He fired up the database, pulled up utility registrations from the ACT and regional New South Wales at the point where he'd left the search after talking to the student in hospital. He narrowed the search to Holden utilities and saw there were still too many. He decided to limit himself on this run to surnames beginning with O' – O'Brien, O'Callaghan, O'Connell, O'Connor, O'Donnell, O'Donoghue, O'Dowd, O'Farrell, O'Keefe, O'Leary, O'Malley, O'Neil, O'Regan, O'Reilly.

At 3 a.m. he was angry and needed sleep; he decided to quit. His brain told him 'No more' and he obeyed his head.

He brought up one last name – Freddy O'Rourke, and his rego details – an orange Holden utility. The photo showed a mean lowlife with cropped red hair and a red beard, a hundred and ninety-three centimetres tall, it said, ninety-nine kilograms. Freddy was a casual labourer, with three charges against him for sexual assault, seven for peeping in windows, seven for common assault, and two for petty theft.

Nigel studied the face for another ten minutes, got to know him and fell asleep.

76

Narrabundah

They drove east out of the CBD along Canberra Avenue, over Kings Avenue Bridge and then south to a dead-end street in Narrabundah. They parked in front of a run-down cottage with peeling paint and a scabby front lawn. Car parts lay scattered over the cement front porch, an engine block, tie rods attached to a steering assembly and a bent orange fender.

With two officers, Nigel left the police van, walked into the backyard and stood over the empty wooden doghouse. He leaned down and picked up the loose chain curled in the dirt, and knelt and looked inside, then stood and spoke to the others.

They walked over dog's droppings in the dirt backyard, stepped over an uncoiled garden hose and mounted the back porch. Nigel knocked on the back door.

A big man answered, with short-cropped hair and a red beard. He wore a dirty grey T-shirt and green army underpants, looking through the wire screen door with a lit cigarette between his fingers. Whad ya want?

Freddy O'Rourke?

I said, Whad ya want?

Nigel held up a photograph of the Rottweiler. Found a dog tied to a tree up on Bruce Ridge the other night. Wondered if it belonged to you.

Freddy looked at Nigel and chuckled as smoke rolled out of his nostrils.

Nigel waited and studied him. Didn't catch your answer.

Oh sure. Three kind-hearted police officers come to my house to return my lost dog. Now that's service.

Nigel held up the photograph against the screen. Is this your dog?

Freddy stared at the photograph with a blank face, then mused for a while at Nigel and stared back at the photograph through the wire. He looked at Nigel's chest and said, That's a fine badge you've got there, officer. Always wanted me one of those.

Mind if we come in?

He laughed out more smoke. Yeah, I do mind.

Then you'll need to come downtown with us. Come on. Get some clothes on.

Freddy tapped cigarette ash on the floor; smoke curled out of his nostrils. He shrugged and opened the door. Ah what the fuck. Come in.

Nigel and a female officer entered Freddy's house. The house smelt of dog food, cooking grease, beer and cigarettes. The ashtray on the scarred wood coffee table was full of butts. There was a weight-lifting bench in the kitchen.

Nigel handed the photograph to Freddy. You didn't say if this was your dog.

Freddy sat on a chair with his legs apart, sucked on a cigarette and blew smoke over Nigel and the female officer. He peered at the photograph and shook his head. Sorry, that's not him. Had one like him, but he ran away.

Mind if we ask your neighbours?

He squinted. Now you're a queer bloody man asking me questions like that.

Then you don't mind if we ask your neighbours.

Freddy tilted his head and shut one eye. You don't strike me as an honest broker, Mr Copper.

I'm an honest broker about asking your neighbours.

He shrugged. Fuckin' go ahead, ask the neighbours if you want. They're not fuckin' stupid.

Nigel smiled. Mind if we sit down?

Go ahead. He pointed with the cigarette.

Nigel pushed some clothing out of the way on the sofa to make a space for himself. He looked through the kitchen door at an old shank of bone on the floor in the corner, the knuckle shining white.

The other officer removed a newspaper from the foam rubber cushion on a chair and sat down.

Nigel looked at red scratches on the backs of Freddy's hands. What kind of work do you do, Freddy?

He shrugged. Work on and off for various people.

Doing what?

Freddy sat on the chair in his green underpants, knees spread. Waves of stale whisky and cigarettes came across the room on his breath. Writing a book on sin, I am. And the wages attached to it.

Sounds interesting.

Oh, yes. Very interesting. Should be a best-seller.

I'm still not clear about the kind of work you do, Freddy.

Yeah, it worries me too. Worries me a lot. I pray to God every day for a simple vocation. The dignity of a calling.

From the scratches on your hands, it looks like you do some pretty rough work.

Freddy saw him staring at the red cuts. A thick braid of smoke rose above him and he waited. So what's your problem?

It looks like you've been in a fight.

Freddy tightened his fists and glanced at his white knuckles. Oh, that. Rough job on the ute, that's all. They're a bastard to work on.

Nigel knew the opposite was true. Mechanics loved working on Holdens; Holden utes were roomy under the bonnet. He said, Just now I was talking to a friend of yours.

Freddy nodded. Oh? Who was that now?

You can talk to him soon. He's sitting out in the van, but this friend told me you got those scratches in a fight.

Did he now? Bring 'im in. Always look forward to seeing a friend.

He doesn't want to come in just yet. But tell me, where were you last Wednesday night, about 2 a.m.?

Freddy grinned, playing his fingers over his bare knee like a keyboard. He leaned back and watched them.

Nigel waited. I can see what's happening here. Any questions about last Wednesday night are going to be like stones clattering on a tin roof, aren't they?

Freddy pursed his lips and nodded. You know, Mr Copper, I try to be helpful. I really do. I'm answering your questions as best I can. I like treating a grilling from the police with the seriousness it deserves. Always been a good citizen.

A mob of boys were playing cricket over the road, cursing and yelling insults at each other. Nigel looked out the window at a small woman with a narrow fox face peering over the fence at the police van in Freddy's yard. Nobody spoke. In the kitchen, a refrigerator motor kicked on.

Nigel watched Freddy and Freddy watched Nigel. The air inside the room was dead still and Nigel expected Freddy to suddenly stand up and prowl around the room, get abusive, toss them out or maybe walk to the kitchen for a glass of water. Show some nerves. But he didn't. Freddy sat with a meaningless grin on his face, coughed occasionally and puffed on his cigarette. Nigel waited and watched and saw that he'd never crack Freddy. The man was armoured.

Nigel put his hands on his knees. Well, Freddy. That's all we need for now.

Freddy looked open-eyed at Nigel and turned and looked at the other officer. That's it?

For now.

He shrugged. Okay. It's your party.

They stood to leave and Freddy led them out to the back screen door and opened it. The Rottweiler bounded up the steps, straining at the lead, yanked the officer up the steps, banging its tail against the door as it jumped on Freddy, barking and licking him. Freddy reached down and patted him.

Nigel watched and said, Happy dog.

Yeah, I'm good with animals.

Freddy, I'm no dog psychologist but he seems to know you. And this place is full of dog hairs. We can test the dog hairs in the doghouse, in the ute, all over the yard, on your shirt, the hairs on your head. We can test the dog hairs on your pillow, probably on your toothbrush against the hairs from your happy friend here. We can test the cigarette butts in that ashtray, he pointed at the scarred wooden table, against the butts we found on top of Bruce Ridge. We can test the dog turds in your backyard against the ones your friend here left on the hill.

Freddy patted the dog and shook his head. That's a pretty big job, officer.

Not really. We can manage.

Freddy grabbed the dog's muzzle affectionately and smiled. Do what you like.

Come on, Freddy. Let's drive into town.

He smiled. It's your party. I'd better get some trousers over these spindly white legs.

77

Freddy runs

On the porch, Freddy dumped his cigarette and crushed it on concrete like a cockroach under his bare foot.

Nigel eyed the wooden building in the backyard. That a shed, or a garage?

I work on the ute in there.

Mind if I look around?

You're gonna do it anyway. Just don't light any matches.

Why not?

Spilled a little petrol in there, and a lot of sump oil. It's soaked into the dirt floor. Whole place'll go up.

Nigel nodded slowly. Okay, Freddy. I won't light any matches.

Freddy shrugged. Let me get my shoes. He stepped back into the kitchen.

The officers came inside and waited.

A crash, the back door swinging, Nigel ran through the house and saw Freddy dash across the backyard, clear the back fence, running hard. The Rottweiler barking, trying to follow him but held by the officer.

Nigel yelled, Come on. Nigel ran to the fence, vaulted over.

Angry dogs were barking up and down the alley in back yards. Freddy gliding and bobbing through laneways glanced back over his shoulder at Nigel running after him.

Freddy wiped his nose with the back of his hand, running down the middle of the laneway, onto a front lawn, around the side of a house to a fence, grabbed the top board, pulled himself over, flipped into the backyard. Sprinting across the lawn to another high fence, pulled himself up, threw one leg over. A deep growl, vicious snarling, the dog slammed into the side of the fence snapping at his dangling foot. He pulled up his leg, dropped back into another backyard and ran.

Freddy peered around the yard, scurried low, running into shadows at the back of the house. On his belly, he edged under a concrete step, pushed aside tools and rubbish, curled and waited and watched Nigel run past in the laneway. In the space under the step, he lay with his face in the dirt, then jumped out and ran the other way, around the corner of the house, stumbled to the grass, down on all fours, up and to a fence; he jumped over.

Standing in the laneway, swivelling his head, Nigel scanned the yard, couldn't see Freddy, dogs barking. He drew his pistol and looked under a bush. A dog snarled from next door, slammed against the fence. Nigel waited for the demented dog to stop. He listened and watched.

78

The shed

Carolyn Scott studied the drawing of Freddy and the Rottweiler.

Do you know him? said Nigel.

She nodded. We saw him.

We?

Emma.

Emma Bentham?

On Black Mountain. She paused, her face papery white. A few weeks ago. Running his dog. She lay back on the pillow.

I'm sorry that I have to ask you this. I know it hurts to talk, but do you think he was shadowing you?

She looked at the photo for a moment, then nodded.

Look, I'm sorry. We've lost him. But we'll double the guard on your room. I promise you, we'll find him.

Nigel left the search to a dozen officers and drove back to Narrabundah. He searched Freddy's yard, turned over the cottage and impounded Freddy's ute. Inside the ute, it smelled like dog and cigarettes. Beer bottles clinked on the floor. He found dog hairs everywhere, but no hammer. Cigarette butts in Freddy's ashtray matched the brand they found on the hill above Eddie's house. Freddy, if they found him, would say the cigarettes belonged to an unnamed friend. Standard lie. DNA would test the lie.

He drove to Daniel's house and searched through garbage for cigarette butts that matched those from the hill and the butts strewn around Freddy's house. He found none.

They knew Freddy was their man, and they knew that Daniel had hired him. A duo, the cuckold and the lump of redwood who killed and raped women for kicks.

Police searched for a link, a hammer, a wad of money, shared tools, a neighbour, a walker who saw Daniel and Freddy together.

Nigel searched the back shed again, the attic, the ute, and accessed Freddy 's bank accounts. He found nothing, and Freddy hadn't used them since he ran off.

Another team grilled Daniel. He broke down crying, close to admitting guilt. Seb Lake the boy-lawyer tried to protect and gag him, but Daniel was driven to help anyone who persecuted him. He ignored Lake's instructions and answered all their questions. The police knew he felt remorse over something. Brimming with guilt. They would apply more pressure and crack the fragile little man. Another day and he was theirs; he'd confess to paying Freddy O'Rourke.

Nigel visited Eddie in hospital. Eddie shook his head slowly as if his brain still hurt. He raised his finger off the bed and said through clenched teeth, You girl scouts. It's pointless interviewing a man like Freddy O'Rourke, even if you do find him. You won't get anything out of him.

Why do you say that?

He could have dumped the hammer in the lake or buried it. Don't bother looking for the hammer. Look for new money in his house. Shiny bills. Look for messages written on the wall in pencil over the telephone, or numbers scratched into a wooden table. He'll be close to illiterate, he won't have much use for books. Look inside his books. Look for notes pencilled in the margins. Look for photographs. He'll store things in unlikely places.

Nigel visited Freddy's house a third time. Wearing latex gloves, he pulled out notebooks, opened drawers, checked under the telephone, turned the house upside down, shook things, shook the telephone book, checked each page, checked the walls, the table for imprints from a pencil or pen, old receipts, photographs, TV guides.

He walked outside to hunt through the shed. The dirt floor soaked in oil smelt like a latrine. He must piss in here too, too lazy to go to the house.

He examined ute tracks in hard mud. He dug around with a spade, searched corners, tapped joists and timbers listening for hollow pockets.

After half an hour, eyes now adjusted to the dim light, he noticed high up on the wall a tiny red corner, at the junction of the back wall and the ceiling. He climbed onto a wooden sawhorse. Lodged behind a support beam, he found a greasy repair manual for the orange Holden utility.

Nigel shook his head. How did I miss this?

He opened the manual and fanned through pages, looking at Freddy's oily thumbprints. He turned the manual upside down and fanned the pages again. A bookmark fell out, a folded sheet of paper. Nigel picked it up from the dirt floor and unfolded it, but the drawing meant nothing to him.

He walked into sunlight, squinted and stared at the creased sheet of paper. He turned it around, upside down, angled it to the light until he saw it was a map, a diagram of someone's house.

Nigel studied the map in bright sunlight. A floor plan, with scribbling against two windows on the bottom floor – 'Alarmed' and 'Not alarmed'.

Nigel squinted, blood thumping in his ears. Tap tap tap, with his finger on the map.

He smiled.

79

Eddie Flannery asks for David

Standing naked in the kitchen, David rubbed his eye. The phone call felt like a summons. Eddie wanted him at the hospital.

Why didn't Eddie pick up the telephone himself?

The nurse didn't respond.

The rotten tang of urine, ammonia cleaner and faeces caught in the back of his throat. David recognised the nurse who arrived each night in a freshly laundered uniform to begin her night shift. She squeaked down the hall on rubber-soled shoes, lifted the silver watch pinned over her left breast, consulted the time and passed him with a frown, as if David had no right sitting where Daniel should be, with Emma.

Eddie was propped up on pillows. Doctors had wired his jaw shut to knit bone fragments, broken teeth, torn gums and prepare him for dentistry. They ordered him to stop talking. He'd been talking too much and talk delayed his healing.

David said, Thanks for calling.

Eddie was impassive.

I heard Bill Scott isn't involved in the investigation any more. He's helping them with their enquiries.

Eddie seemed uninterested. He looked out the window and David suddenly saw himself from above, standing and waiting for Eddie the self-anointed prince holding bedside court.

David said, You called me.

Eddie looked up, then out the window again. Did you ever see your mother beaten? The braces holding his jaws together stiffened his speech. He slurred a little.

David shook his head. No.

Then he was a decent man.

David said, When I was six, my father shot through. Left a note for my mother saying 'Thank you'. Said he was grateful.

Eddie considered this and mumbled, Grateful. He pulled a fat blackened hand from under the blanket, leaned across and dragged a tissue from a box on the bedside table, touched the corner of his mouth where it leaked. Holding the tissue in place, he said, I need your help.

David said, I'm listening.

He dabbed the corner of his mouth again. Whose problem is it?

What do you mean?

When Sophie's steamed up, she looks like a beast out of mythology. And that's not a bad thing. I enjoy it. But does it do any good?

David said, You're asking the wrong person.

Eddie touched his mouth again, winced and closed one eye. She holds to this fiction that males are a form of corrupted female. She doesn't understand pure evil and that makes her useless.

David watched him.

Bad-ass men are more frightened of Emma than they are of Sophie. Why do you think that is? Eddie opened his eyes.

David said nothing and Eddie said, You didn't answer my question.

It's rhetorical.

Emma saw two groups of men in this world – those bent on wrecking women's lives, and those too cowardly to stop them. No third category. Eddie's blue eyes roamed over David's face, waiting. I want to thank you.

For what?

You were there Wednesday night.

When David looked down, Eddie said, It mystifies me why you don't tell the police.

David looked away.

You have to understand something. Bill Scott can have both of us killed. There's a double guard on the ward now, but no guard at your house. And Freddy's loose. If you got that rubber mask off his face, identified him, Bill will happily supply your name and address to Freddy O'Rourke.

David shrugged.

It's worse. You shamed him. Payback is on the cards. You made him look the fool.

David said, Other things might kill me first.

Eddie touched the tissue to his mouth. I need your help.

You already said that. For what?

Two frightened women.

David watched Eddie rest back on the pillow, in pain again. He tried to picture the two women, maybe huddled in a back room or hiding out with friends. You were seeing them?

Eddie shook his head. No. Emma. It was an illusion. I was the front man, the public face, Emma did the planning and work.

Neither of them spoke for a time. David said, You're in love with her, aren't you?

Eddie hesitated, then nodded. But never lovers. She loves someone else.

Is that why you do this?

Eddie looked exasperated. Understand something. I left the bones of my mother in County Antrim. The dead live with us. They have claims on us. Women are killed in this town. Because of lawyers. A lawyer got Ivan Milat off so he could kill again, said that two lesbians he raped really wanted it, said they were being treated by therapists to reverse their lesbianism. Milat was the good guy, helping them out. That defence got him off. If a doctor botches surgery, a train driver derails a train or a ship captain runs aground, he can be jailed. A lawyer's not held to account for the people he kills. Men won't change if there's an excuse available and lawyers dream up excuses. They blame the victim. Bastards: 'Why didn't she just leave?'

David followed Eddie's gaze out the window. Down in the parking lot under smoky lamps a man with three children loaded a dark-haired woman out of a wheelchair into a car. David guessed she'd been crippled in a car accident and they were taking her home to recover. Or maybe not. Passing clouds hid the sun and the man in the parking lot put his hand on the car roof and seemed to worry about rain. David's eyes drifted back to the room and Eddie staring up at him.

David said, You can't stomach losing to one of your enemies, can you?

Eddie shrugged. You're naïve, David. You're a child waiting around for pure intentions. Grow up. I'm feared, not loved.

Emma inspired love.

Eddie hesitated. That's Emma.

What do you want from me?

Protect these two women. And help us publicise the names of the two lawyers who freed their husbands, freed these woman-beaters. Or, of course, you could go back and lead a workshop at the university. Call it 'Whose Fault Are Men?' to make it topical.

You didn't protect her. He felt a heavy stone on his chest.

Eddie lay back on the white pillow and closed his eyes. Then go back to the university and waste more time deciding whose fault I am.

David watched the family down in the parking lot finish loading the woman into the car, slam doors and drive off.

Eddie looked tired and touched his jaw. He mumbled with eyes closed, Will you help?

David watched Eddie trying to conjure up some wicked story about loyalty and betrayal and injustice he could use to manipulate the argument.

Eddie raised his voice and slurred, There's a pig dog in all of us. You know that. Just bigger in some men.

Why me?

Eddie shrugged. Who else is there? I get the measure of a man after I've fought him.

David looked at Eddie, face bandaged, jaw wired, forehead discoloured with purple lumps and red cuts, lying on a pillow calling the shots. I'll talk to my friend and tell you in the morning.

Eddie nodded and tried to smile.

David said, You know who she is, don't you?

Eddie closed his eyes and nodded. Amber's an adult. She can make her own decisions.

David waited, listening to a nurse rattle down the hallway with a tray full of bed pans and medicine. Thank you for calling, he said. You did the right thing.

Eddie nodded, almost imperceptibly.

David left.

Two doors along, he passed Carolyn Scott, head bandaged, eyes blackened and shut. Tears glazed her purple cheeks.

He passed the policewoman at Emma's door and sat beside Emma for an hour. A nurse came and checked equipment, read her chart, looked into Emma's face. He thought about the warmth in Emma's smile, the way she used to stretch out in bed until her warm toes touched his. Her warm breath in his ear. It came to him as an overwhelming sadness and he bowed his head and started to weep.

Trees outside were lit yellow by hospital windows. Grey streaks of rain hit the glass.

He left Emma and sat near the telephone as nurses and visitors passed. He thought about phoning Amber, she would be home sleeping now, and he thought about returning to Emma.

Nigel Plant came down the hall.

David nodded.

I hear Emma's no better.

The same, he said.

Nigel was quiet for a time maybe out of respect, then he said, David, we need to talk.

David nodded, I know.

Nigel watched him for a moment, Friday?

Yes. Friday.

I'll be at your house at four.

Nigel left and David watched him walk down the hall. David sat with his head in his hands watching rain spatter the windows.

80

Daniel Bentham in Cook

Daniel Bentham drove to Cook. He parked on the kerb outside David's house, knocked on the door and stood waiting on the step. Nobody came and there was no thumping or rustling from inside. He listened to the tick of the cooling motor on the curb. He looked at his feet, then looked up and down the street, watching corellas feeding in a tree.

He stepped off the porch and peered into David's window. He murmured, Nobody home.

He left and parked in Booth Crescent and followed the stony path up the spine of Mount Painter. As sun moved off his face and the blue sky deepened, he looked down on cyclists heading for home. A tawny-coloured hare broke from long grass in a twisting uphill run.

He stood under the steel pinnacle and looked out over the city. Orange street lamps were snapping on and snaking along roadways to the south. A black curtain of rain fell on the mountains. Puffs of cherry cloud drifted past.

In grassland below, he saw a bright-haired young woman standing next to a man. David. Two figures walking close to each other, the young woman talking and moving her hands. Light danced off her copper-coloured hair. The couple stood in a coral wash of light, and David faced her and seemed to listen.

Daniel thought, I can talk to him now.

The couple bent and climbed between wires in the fence and ambled towards David's house.

Daniel watched them and said to himself, No. Not today.

The police knocked on Bill Scott's office door.

He said from his desk, Come in.

Two officers stood in the doorway and one said, Bill, we need to talk.

Fine. He waved them in. Sit down, talk.

The officer looked down for a moment, then looked up and said, We need to talk downstairs.

Bill looked at one officer, then the other. What's this about?

I'm afraid we can't say.

We'll talk here.

No, sir. Afraid not.

Bill stood and straightened his cuffs and brushed his uniform. He walked around the desk, grabbed his cap from a hook on the wall, and shut the door behind them.

Nigel stood waiting on the stairs. He nodded and said, Bill.

When Nigel entered the room and handed Bill the map of Eddie's house, Bill understood the gravity of the moment. He faked confusion and shrugged. What's this?

We were hoping you could tell us.

He looked at the paper again. Looks like some kind of house plan.

Yes, said Nigel. That's what I thought. But then I recognised your handwriting in the margins. He pointed to 'Alarmed' and 'Not alarmed'

Bill looked at the words. He frowned. You'll have trouble proving that's my handwriting from three words.

Nigel nodded. Yes, probably.

Bill looked around. Where's Gail?

She asked me to handle this.

He paused and looked at Nigel. I see.

They were quiet for a moment and Bill said, I'll need to see my lawyer.

Of course. And please don't try to contact Freddy O'Rourke.

Bill said, Fine. I don't know anyone named Freddy O'Rourke.

81

Fearing Freddy O'Rourke

On Wednesday, Carolyn Scott and Eddie Flannery were released from hospital. Carolyn and her girls stayed with Carolyn's parents in Ainslie. Freddy was loose and the police said he'd probably fled the ACT for safer ground in New South Wales or maybe Victoria. But Nigel told them he would organise a prowl car to regularly check both addresses.

Expect them to occasionally shine a search light in your gardens and walkways, he said. Keep doors locked, alarms switched on, never answer the door or go out at night, and phone the police if you see or hear anything suspicious.

David took unpaid leave and divided his time between sitting at Emma's bedside, talking to her, though she never responded, and patrolling the roads and woodlands at night outside Eddie's or Daniel's house. He stood for hours and watched for moving shadows in the woods and gardens, listening for barking dogs or snapped twigs or footfalls, and sniffing the air for Freddy's rancid scent.

Amber waited nights at David's house. At 1 a.m. on Thursday, she heard the neighbour's dog, crying and barking in the front yard. He growled and made a racket for some five minutes and Amber knew Freddy was standing outside watching. Amber tried to gauge the prowler's location in the yard. He seemed to be moving to the side of the house, under the bedroom window.

Downstairs she grabbed the phone and walked around and checked the windows and locks; she switched on the mobile phone ready to call David and waited, but the battery was dead.

When the dog settled, she thought Freddy was gone. Amber took off her clothes, put on a long T-shirt and climbed into bed. It warmed her and she let her body go limp, but she couldn't sleep.

A crash from outside. Amber leapt from bed, covered herself with a robe and listened. Another bang from the porch.

She opened the bedroom door and rushed downstairs, breathing deeply. She padded into the kitchen and stood listening. It was still and the dog was quiet. Freddy had killed the dog to silence him, she thought, or maybe the neighbours had taken him inside.

She peered out the kitchen window into the backyard, then switched on the porch light, waiting for Freddy's face to loom out of the night. Crippled by stories of Freddy's evil, she crouched on the floor and waited, heart thumping in her ears.

She climbed back upstairs and looked through the back window. In the porch light, a possum sat on the railing. Amber shone a torch through the window into the backyard and tried to look past the animal for Freddy in the corner of the yard, skulking behind a wall. The possum raised itself, balanced on its hind legs and brushed its nose with one paw.

Amber's deep, fast breathing made her light-headed and a little sick. The circle of her torch beam raced around the backyard, to the path, the neighbours' back wall. Nothing. She switched off the torch and waited.

That morning, Amber told David about the noise and David said, You can't stay here any more.

But please, she said. I recharged the battery. I can phone you or the police if there's trouble.

No. That's final. Stay with your parents until this is over.

At the hospital, David dozed slouching in the chair next to Emma's bed. In visions, Emma slept cradled in his arms. David shielded her from black dreams, a dark curtain billowing in the room, a girl left unattended. She was a woman and a ghost.

When he woke, the blinds in the hospital room were up, the walls and sheets brittle white in the morning sun. A nurse checked Emma's charts and pulse and a police officer sat chewing a toothpick in the hall watching each patient being wheeled by.

David said goodbye to Emma and left.

Wind blew in the night. A voice made Daniel turn over in his sleep. He propped himself up on one elbow and stared out the window. The dark stared back.

He touched Emma's yellow T-shirt lying on the bed next to him.

He waited in the dark, then rose and snapped on the light. He climbed upstairs to a window looking out over the path leading to the back door. He heard a belled cat near the fence. The neighbour's Burmese sneaking along the fence in dark cat shadows. A shimmering white mountain gum in the corner of the yard.

Daniel pulled out matches and a box of candles, lit a candle and placed it on the windowsill in a white saucer, watching the candle flame and flickering likeness of the candle in the window.

He let the candle burn halfway down, then leaned back watching the path leading through the back gate.

He watched the night.

In bed, Daniel heard a floorboard creak. He knew Freddy was in the house somewhere, moving downstairs, in the sitting room.

A cracking stick outside. Daniel listened. Another stick cracking in the yard.

He peered outside, then switched on the porch light. The yard was empty.

Daniel phoned the police.

The police arrived and shone torches around the yard, walked up and down laneways, in the street, and found nothing.

Daniel was rattled and sat in the kitchen.

Police left and told him to phone if there were any more noises.

The wind fell. On wet grass, David looked for bunched horses, saw their dark forms near the eucalypt grove and rattled oats in the bucket. The grey mare came to him. David shooed the others away. With her nose in the bucket he slipped a hackamore over her ears and around her nose and tossed the empty bucket on the ground.

At 2 a.m., a patrol car saw a big man cross Bindubi Street running east. The police skidded to the verge, radioed another car to intercept him at Caswell Drive while they gave chase through woodland on foot.

The fugitive turned and fell into a stumbling run through wet forest, his coat flapping. He ran from the edge of light.

Behind him, an officer shouted, *Stop. Now.*

The man vaulted the fence, darted between trees, running and bobbing through shade and light.

Glimpses of the moon brightened stalks of white trees and sooty-coloured bushes around him. Pelting leaves and twigs burned his face and hands. Freddy lost the police and raced onto a muddy track, slipped, reached down into the ooze, staggered, slipped onto his side, banging his head against a rock.

Freddy ran and the moon spread his shadow crawling over logs and uneven ground. He shouldered through branches towards the centre of the woodland, burst down a slope towards a low gully, looking ahead, left and right, dodging between trunks. He stood in the middle of the forest, listening for the police crashing behind him. Nothing. He waited. It was quiet and velvet black. Then a broken stick, a brush of cloth against woody branches.

Rubbing sweat from his chin, Freddy charged down a gully running east towards Caswell Drive and Black Mountain, through pools of still water splashing over his soaked trousers.

Caswell Drive was empty of cars. Panting, both legs tight and aching, Freddy stood in a damp wind with his hands on his knees. The wind cooled his dripping face and stopped him from hearing cracking sticks or fabric brushing leaves behind him. He stood and planned for a moment, loped forward, tired now, prepared to cross the open space.

From nowhere, a female officer tackled him. He stood, tossed her off like a rag doll and ran again but two more officers caught him and the three held him down and cuffed him at the side of the road.

David lay curled with his back against a fence post, eyes shut, blood strung over long grass. Six horses stood in a half-circle circle with their heads down, nostrils dilated, snorting and taking scent. One rolled the empty bucket with its nose.

Nigel turned to the others and said, Search the corrals, the car park for tyre prints, footprints, weapons, and check both ends of Booth Crescent.

Seven uniformed officers studied smears on the grass, the adjoining path, the road and the fence line.

They took David to intensive care and allowed no visitors; he was critical.

Eddie cursed and swore, muttering obscenities between clenched teeth. The idiot, he said. I warned him. He wouldn't listen. Why don't people listen?

Nigel waited and let him rant. He couldn't tell if Eddie was angry or hurt.

On the bottom floor of the police station, Bill Scott passed Freddy O'Rourke, his fists hanging like cracked bricks, flanked by two officers. Bill looked straight ahead, ignoring Freddy and Freddy scowled and ignored Bill. The performance told Nigel quite a lot.

The police had said that Freddy left the city. After his capture, they searched Black Mountain and found a camp in an isolated gully where he'd fashioned a shelter from native cherry branches and canvas. There was a ring of stones where he boiled meals in an abandoned two-litre can. Around the camp lay wrappings from packaged food he'd apparently stolen from local shops and houses. They also found a knife.

They interviewed Freddy O'Rourke about various acts of violence in the city over the past six months. They knew he was responsible for the attack at Eddie's house, probably for attacking David Chess, and attacking

Daniel in the forest and the student on Black Mountain. Freddy was stony and silent but Nigel noticed an almost imperceptible difference when they questioned him about David's stabbing. He frowned at the mention of David's name and shook his head. His demeanour changed.

<h1 style="text-align:center">82</h1>

<h2 style="text-align:center">Arrest</h2>

The marked car crunched over gravel into the driveway. Nigel killed the ignition and locked the car. He and Lisa Charles mounted the step. The curtains were drawn and Nigel knocked three times and heard rustling inside. The latch clattered and Mandy peered out.

What do you want? Her voice frightened, her eyes cold.

Can we talk?

With a faint moustache of perspiration on her upper lip, she said, I suppose. Come in.

Shannon slumped in the doorway between the kitchen and sitting room with his knees under his chin.

Mandy sat down and said, What is it?

Mrs Kelly, we need to ask if you've ever seen this knife. Nigel held up a clear plastic bag with a bloody butcher's knife in it.

Mandy grabbed at her throat, then sat back, locking her thin fingers deep in her lap. She turned her head a little, away from Shannon.

Redness crept into Shannon's face.

Mandy sighed and continued to look away. The dog wandered over and started licking Shannon's face.

Barely parting her lips Mandy said, Please. Don't take my last one.

I'm sorry, said Lisa. We understand how difficult this is.

Mandy glared. No, you don't. Leave us.

Lisa turned to Shannon slouched in the kitchen doorway. Mrs Kelly, if you don't mind, I'd like to ask Shannon a few questions.

From the doorway, Shannon glared. He didn't blink.

Mandy said. Ask your questions.

Shannon looked at his mother, eyes full of hate.

Lisa said, Shannon, a neighbour told us he saw you and your pit bull up at the horse corrals. You know a man was stabbed up there two nights ago.

Shannon put his arm around the dog and looked at the floor.

Mandy said, Who?

David Chess, a lecturer.

In the quiet, Lisa heard a car rush by and children laughing in the street. She looked at Shannon. We understand that you knew about him.

Through tight lips, he said, So?

Lisa waited, saw the boy was shutting down. Okay, Shannon. We can talk down at my office.

Mandy looked back across the room at Shannon on the floor, his feet jammed in the doorway, kicking at the skirting.

Mandy shook her head. No. He stays with me. Her voice was flat.

Shannon sat with his arm around the dog.

Lisa leaned towards him. Shannon?

Mandy glared. That's enough. No more.

Can I –

Shannon stood, walked over and sat on the floor next to his mother's chair.

She said, Leave us alone.

Nigel pushed an open hand towards him. Okay, son. Settle down.

Mandy said, looking at the floor, Sophie Moss said this lecturer pinned a hat to his belt when he went to the shops. She told the police too.

Nigel was calm. He turned to Shannon. We'll go now.

They stood and led Shannon to the car, loaded him into the back, and reversed into the street.

Mandy stood on the porch and watched the car leave.

83

Emma

Sophie was unrepentant. Hoop earrings bobbled as she jabbed an accusing finger at Nigel. *You knew*, she bellowed. Tommy said he carried a knife. I did the right thing and told you and you did nothing. *I told you.* And Mandy had a right to know.

But she's lost her other son, said Nigel.

Yes, well, I know. But don't you worry. Some judge will let him off.

Nigel understood now. Coming up against Sophie's black malice, David had to lose. Hard core animus wrapped in a blanket of hate. Many would say the city needed Sophie, a strong woman, powerful and true to her beliefs, a modern warrior, a champion of the downtrodden. Some thought otherwise.

There was no wakening from Emma. Daniel Bentham and Eddie Flannery came and stayed each day and Eddie would talk and Daniel would listen, then Eddie would go home and Daniel would stay with Emma as long as he could.

On Thursday morning, a nurse stepped into Emma's room and knocked on the open door. Can I come in?

Sure, said Daniel.

The nurse said, How are you?

I've been better. Has David changed?

No, said the nurse.

Daniel choked, struggling to speak. He stood and made a circuit of the room, then sat.

The nurse put her arm around him, pulled him close and said, I'm sorry. But don't give up hope. He's still with us.

Daniel leaned into her and wept.

She said, You were friends.

Yes.

She held him and waited for him to settle.

A single tear ran down Emma's cheek and wet the pillow.

Eddie came to the hospital and talked about David for a time, his goodness and purity of soul, a brother in the fight. Then he talked about Emma and this warmed Daniel at first and Daniel listened but eventually tired of Eddie's talking. He needed to be alone. Daniel hadn't eaten since breakfast, he was light-brained with hunger. He left the hospital and walked home in the rain.

Alone in the night, Daniel was haunted by Emma. He drove to the top of Black Mountain, looked out over the town and thought about the last few crowded months. Evil had kidnapped the city. Sudden gusts of cruelty in the houses and streets. A handful of men had caused mayhem. Self-deluded narcissists settling scores.

He walked to a rocky pinnacle where he'd stood with Emma. Coloured lights swam in the lake. Far to the south, bright points of light glittered like diamonds on black cloth. He remembered how Emma once said that freedom from tyranny was the last and greatest of human dreams. She'd come to this city of promise, white buildings, a beacon of hope, a refuge. But looking for sanctuary she'd found only orphans.

Eddie and Daniel met late in the day at the hospital and didn't speak. It had all been said. They stood quietly at Emma's door. Eddie left and returned with two paper cups of coffee, and they pulled up chairs either side of Emma's bed. When the door opened and they looked up expecting a nurse, Carolyn Scott shuffled in, leaning hard with each step on a silver metal cane. She waited in gold afternoon light, her black hair tied back, her blue eyes clear.

Daniel stood from his chair and said with an open hand, Take mine.

Carolyn smiled and said, Thank you, eyes shut as she eased herself
slowly and painfully into the chair, resting the metal cane against the
bedhead. There was murmuring outside, and rattling bottles on carts and
beds on squeaking rubber wheels, tapping footsteps, ringing telephones
and the music of people laughing.

Carolyn reached over and touched Emma's face. She folded Emma's
fingers into hers.

At midnight, Daniel thanked Carolyn for coming. I should go, he said.

Then Eddie said, I'm spent. I need time away from the hospital.

Carolyn looked up and smiled, and said, We'll be fine.

The men left.

She pulled her chair close to the bed and watched the rise and fall of
Emma's breathing through the night. She was there when Emma stirred
in the morning.